Take Me HOME

Silversmith
PUBLISHING

Across Time & Space series

The Eternity Stone
Mountain of Glass
Desert of Fire
Desert of Ice
The Hidden Door
Whiter than Snow
City of Light

Fairytale Memoirs series

The Mostly Forgotten Memoirs of Rose Red
Viola Sends her Regrets
Gifted: a Fairytale Memoirs novella

Standalone novels

Breaking the Glass Slipper
Unshakeable
Tyger: an out-of-this-world tale
Take Me Home

For information on new and upcoming books,
go to **mmarinanbooks.com**

TAKE ME HOME

A sci-fi survivalist
adventure novel

by M. Marinan

First published in New Zealand in 2021 by Silversmith Publishing

A catalogue record for this book is available from the National Library of New Zealand

Hardcover version ISBN 978-1-99-001414-7
Trade paperback ISBN 978-1-99-001413-0
E-book ISBN 978-1-99-001415-4

For Kate, for freely reading
a sort-of sci-fi novel.

With extra thanks to Anne-Marie,
for the usual reasons.

Contents

PART 1:
The Wilds

Chapter 1

Demi

"This is the worst thing that's ever happened to me," I say, my throat choked with horror and emotion. "The. Absolute. Worst."

I'm crouched against one end of my tiny two-person tent. At the other end is my sleeping bag: shiny, red, and currently harbouring a mutant escapee from some barren hellscape. I can't see it, not anymore, but I know it's there.

I shudder.

"Demi?" I hear Tara's voice through the fabric wall. "Aren't you up yet?" A moment later my coworker's head sticks through the unzipped entrance. Her short, bleached hair is tousled, but her eyes are bright behind her glasses. Unlike me, she's clearly been up for a while. "We need to pack up the tent, or the others will leave without us."

That would be bad. I'm here on this 'fun', team-building camping trip so I can show my boss that my awesomeness extends beyond a computer screen and a headset – same as most of the other dozen people here. So being the last one ready (yet again) isn't ideal. But I can't overcome my current challenge, so I just point mutely at my sleeping bag.

"It's not another spider, is it?" Tara asks, sounding unimpressed. "Because I said yesterday that I wouldn't get rid

3

of another one for you."

"It's not a spider." I pause. "It's an eight-legged hairy abomination the size of my palm."

And it's in my bed. *In my BED.*

Tara sighs heavily. "How old are you, Demi? Twenty-six, twenty-seven? Get rid of your own hairy abomination, alright?" She glanced emphatically over her shoulder to where a fair-haired guy with glasses is rolling up his tent, studiously not looking in our direction. "Or shall I call Connor over to help you out?"

I'm twenty-eight, actually. But she's said the magic words to get me moving, since I'd rather be bitten by the bloody thing than have my ex remove it for me. (Yes, we still work at the same office, and yes, it's awkward.) "Wait!" I blurt out. "I can…get rid of it…myself?"

I sound uncertain even to my own ears, but Tara seems to accept my words at face value. She shrugs, then gives me a friendly nod. "Go on, then. I'll grab a coffee while I wait, then we can put the tent down together."

I give her a thumbs-up along with a grin that feels more like a pained grimace.

Tara moves away from the tent, and my smile falls away as I stare at my hidden nemesis. I've worked with these guys for a year now, and I dated Connor for most of that time. I think I've put on a pretty good act in the office, pretending that nothing fazes me. Even our recent breakup was handled in a mature, sensible fashion, at least on the surface. But if I don't deal with this thing myself, I'm going to be teased about it until I leave my job – and I've been hoping that Connor will go so I can stay.

Grumbling under my breath, I shuffle my way backwards out of the tent. I'm already wearing jeans and a hooded sweatshirt over my thermals, having well underestimated how cold it can get up here in the mountains even in the summer, and I shove my fluffy-socked feet into my sturdy boots. My blisters pang at the contact, and I take a moment to silently curse the boots I bought especially for this trip. Not only are they ugly – hardly comparing to my usual sneakers or low heels – but they're as tough as an old saddle. After two days of walking, my feet feel like they're more blister than skin.

I grab the end of my sleeping bag and drag it slowly out of the tent, as carefully as I'd move around a ticking bomb or a poisonous snake. I drag it right through the emptying campsite, full of a dozen others all industriously taking down tents or not-so-industriously sitting in fold-out chairs, sipping at what smells like hot chocolate.

"You alright?" Connor calls across to me. Of course he's already finished his tent, and he's the sort of guy who'll offer to help his ex-girlfriend, and mean it too. Jerk. "You need a hand rolling up your sleeping bag?"

I fake-smile at him too. *No, Connor, I do not need your help for anything. Anything at all.* "I'm fine," I reply casually. I don't mention that it's a spider, because then he'll insist on helping. Out of everyone here, he knows that I'm a city girl, and I don't like things that crawl.

I focus on finding somewhere safe to dispose of it where it won't run into someone else's baggage. It seems like there are folded tents and packs everywhere, so I find myself moving further and further away from everyone else, until finally I'm well away from the campsite and back at the well-worn path we'll be continuing on today.

It's early in the morning, in spite of certain people's peppiness, and the path is right up against the edge of a low, boulder-filled ravine. Beyond the ravine is another stretch of rock, then the ground falls away entirely, revealing a fantastic view of this mountainous region, lightly covered by a veil of mist.

At this time of the morning it feels fresh and unpolluted, and for a moment I grasp why people would purposely leave their homes and force their bodies out into the wilderness like this.

But there'll be time for admiring the scenery later – now, it's time to dispose of the mutant arachnid.

At the side of the path there's a low fence, the sort that's only an ancient piece of wood two feet higher than the ground. It's more of a suggestion rather than an actual barrier, since the ravine doesn't look at all dangerous.

I ignore the sign reading, 'CAUTION! DO NOT CROSS THIS BARRIER!' and drag my sleeping bag right to the edge. I carefully lift it over the low fence, then gently shake it, trying to dislodge its occupant.

Nothing happens, and I wonder if I've already lost the spider. But just in case, I shake the sleeping bag harder, giving it a good jerk. It makes a sound like a sail catching the wind, and then a leggy black form comes skidding out of the opening and tumbles down into the ravine.

Success! I begin to cheer…just as the backlash from shaking the sleeping bag too hard pulls it right out of my hands and into the ravine.

Ahhhhhh…

I bite back the scream that nearly spills out, then slowly check behind me to see if any of the others spotted my colossal mishap. No one's in sight, but there's no time for relief. No one must know what I've done – this is worse than simply letting Connor deal with the spider in the first place.

My body is tense with determination as I lean over the low barrier. From here I can easily see my sleeping bag, its red shape outstretched over the massive boulders that fill the bottom of the ravine about fifteen feet below. The same boulders create an easy but awkward pathway to the bottom. Itt wouldn't pay to fall in, but even rule-following Connor wouldn't leave the sleeping bag down there.

"That would be littering," I tell myself righteously. Also, I'd have no bedding, and that would really suck.

So I step right over the 'DO NOT CROSS' sign and begin the climb downwards.

Several minutes later I reach my sleeping bag. I grab it with a huff of satisfaction – step one in being a new, more capable Demi – then begin to quickly shove it into the attached carry-bag. It'll be much easier to climb up again if I'm not dragging a six-foot-long pile of fabric with me.

But I've only just pulled the drawstring tight when I hear voices above me.

"Where's Demi? I saw her come this way," I hear Tara say.

"Probably gone to use the bathroom," someone else replies. "It's the last proper one till we finish the trail."

I don't recognize the second voice, but I lean against the side of the ravine, determined to stay out of sight. But the comment about the toilet situation makes me scowl. If scenic beauty (and impressing one's coworkers) is a good reason to come, then the lack of facilities is a better reason to leave quickly. Even the 'proper bathroom' reeks.

Tara laughs. "City girl. If she hates the compostable toilet, then wait till she has to dig a hole in the ground."

I stand still and indignant until I hear them move away. Tara's probably the friendliest of all my coworkers, but she's not exactly Bear Grylls herself. I don't need her making fun of my struggles. I'm not *that* soft. I'm just civilized.

As their footsteps fade, I awkwardly try to climb back up the ravine. But I quickly realise that it's a lot harder to climb out than it was to climb in. The boulders seem a lot slipperier from this angle, and I can't get a foothold.

After several attempts I'm starting to panic, wondering if I'll have to swallow my pride and call for help. Before we left for this trip my dad made me read about all of Mount Freedom's known risks, including the fact that in the last thirty years, at least seven people have gone missing here.

The latest was a number of years ago; some college guy who went mountain-biking and was never seen again. They found the bike, but not a sign of him. I figured he'd been an idiot and wandered off the path, because how else do you go missing when everything's so clearly signposted? But now…well, case in point. I desperately don't want to become one of those missing idiots.

So I try moving a little way down the ravine to where some of the rock has formed an indented natural shelf. If I push myself up *here*, and crawl in *here*, I can get past the worst of the ditch.

I sit at the edge of the shelf to take a breather, my head on an angle so I don't knock myself out, and with my precious sleeping bag's drawstring cord looped over one wrist. I'm still very much hidden from sight, and very much not where I want to be. But it's something.

In fact, from here this space almost looks like a partial cave. Someone could live down here, if they were really desperate for shelter and didn't mind the climb. I even notice how inside the cave-ish section, the rock's texture almost looks like writing.

Just then I feel a slight tickle on my hand. I look down to see a big, dark, hairy shape crawling across my fingers where they rest on top of the bundled sleeping bag.

"AIIIEEEEEEEEEEEEEEEE!"

I fling out my hand and the sleeping bag – and mutant spider – go flying away to land in the deepest section of the rocky shelf I'm sitting on. I let out a growl of frustration, since I know there's no way my scream went unheard. I'm just going to have to explain what happened, try to make it sound like a joke, and practice having no dignity.

Sigh.

I crawl across the low rocky area, my bare palms pressing against the textured rock floor as I do so. By the time I reach my sleeping bag (again) I've realized that the rock isn't naturally textured at all. The deep clefts and lines are precise enough that someone must have carved them here on purpose. It's not writing of any kind I recognize; more like the kind of symbols aliens supposedly leave in cornfields.

I go to grab my sleeping bag, but as I move to get it, my other palm grazes across one of the carved symbols. There's a sharp pain and my palm starts to bleed. I stare at it for only a moment, one hand on the sleeping bag, the other on the rock. Then a weight seems to press in on my head, the world swaying around me, and-

Liam

The room's quiet when I wake up. Faint grey light streams through the high, narrow windows that we haven't yet blocked in, telling me it's morning. I can see two other small shapes huddled together nearby under the piles of patchwork cloth we call blankets. Jesse's little face is exposed to the chill, so I gently tug the top layer up until it half-covers his dark curls.

The fire pit in the centre of the room has burned down to embers, so I take a moment to gently blow on it until they spark brighter. I place a single dry stick on the embers but don't wait for it to catch.

Then I go about getting dressed in silent efficiency. I grab my makeshift armour and a hunk of breadish from the mostly empty bowl, and check once over my shoulder before heading out. I'll put my armour on before I leave home base. I can't risk Bianca waking up before I go – Jerrold's disappearance is hard enough without having to deal with her tears on top of it. She'll know where I am.

I make my way down winding tunnels irregularly lit by orange tubes along the ceilings and walls. There are piles of hoarded goods stacked all the way along, some of which I collected myself. Others could have been here for a hundred years but never found a use. That's the trouble with living in the remains of a destroyed alien civilisation. Half the time we can't even identify the things we find.

When I finally reach the compound's northern exit, I take the time to methodically put on my armour from shins right up to helmet. I tighten each piece almost to discomfort, since I can't risk them falling loose at a critical moment. Then I take my spear and lean against the door, listening for the telltale sounds of scavs on the other side.

I hear nothing but the wind, so finally I let myself out, setting a slab of wood against the door to avoid unwanted intruders. Scavs will make their way into any small space, but they aren't very strong, so shouldn't be able to force their way in.

The northern exit is closest to the Gate. That's my first destination, since Jerrold had headed there yesterday when we last saw him. I quietly trudge along the rocky ridgeline in the same journey I've made a thousand times, watching out for any sign of movement on the steep hill below. Any shape or colour that will show what I'm looking for – an old man wearing Mad Max-style gear and with a Santa-sized beard – or what I'm avoiding, which is the plague-ridden creatures that inhabit this area.

Why did Jerrold have to insist on checking the Gate alone?

Why did I *let* him?

My mood is low, bordering on desolate as I scan every last cluster of rocks, every faint shadow that might hint at where he's gone. Maybe he fell and twisted his ankle, and he's hiding out till he feels strong enough to head back. That'd be the best-case scenario.

But I know the truth. This world is brutal even for those who are prepared, and it's unlikely I'll be bringing Jerrold home in one piece. The real best-case scenario is that I find him alive, if I can find him at all. But chances are he's gone missing, just like Dominic did last year. Just like Sigge did the year after I arrived.

Well. We found Sigge eventually, not that it did him any good. Better to find a body, I think. Not knowing is the worst thing.

I huff out a soft, humourless laugh. No, the worst thing is watching our little group of survivors grow smaller year by year. No one's come through the Gate since I arrived, and I'd love some company – preferably young and female – but that would be damning another poor soul to this same desperate existence.

And when has what I wanted ever made a difference, anyway?

I come up over the ridgeline to the open area where the Gate stands. Its tall, blocky pillars reach high into the air; the only noticeable sign of intelligent habitation in this area. It's grey. The rock around it is grey too, as is the mist that fills the steep chasms on either side of the ridge.

A blob of red arrests my gaze. It's right under the base of the Gate, between the two pillars, and I come to a halt. Surely it's just a male scav with its colourful feathers, since there's a horde of the dangerous animals living around here. But then I see it's far too big to be a scav, and for a dismayed moment I think I'm staring at a battered human body.

But then it moves, and I realise in amazement that I'm looking at something quite different.

Another survivor.

Demi

Cold. So freaking cold.

I shiver in my sleep, wrapping my arms around myself and trying to find a more comfortable position. But the bed is hard and lumpy underneath me, and I seem to have lost my pillow. There's a biting wind cutting right through my clothing, and when I try to pull up my blankets, I come up empty.

My hand hurts.

It's that last thing that finally makes me open my eyes. In front of me is grey, stretching out as far as I can see. I blink, trying to make sense of what I'm looking at. Oh, that's right, I'm camping. Is it my tent wall?

I look down at my hand to see a nasty graze across the palm, and finally I remember why I'm here. I was getting my sleeping bag from the ravine...the spider...cutting my hand.

Ugh. I must have fainted, I realise. It's the first time I've ever done so, and the timing isn't good.

I struggle to sit up, my head swimming at the movement. It's still hard to make sense of what's going on around me, since the greyness seems to stretch in every direction, and I could swear I was just crouching in that mini cave-alcove down in the ravine. I rub my eyes. Maybe I hit my head and now I can't see properly. Sheesh. That would just make my day, wouldn't it?

And why is it so cold all of a sudden?!

Just then I see a bright red shape sitting just to my right. "My precious!" I cry, grabbing the sleeping bag and pulling it possessively into my lap.

But then as if the sleeping bag is some kind of talisman, the world around me comes into focus.

I'm not surrounded by grey walls at all. It's fog, stretching off into the distance, but it seems to thin even as I stare at it. Now I can just make out faint lines showing that I'm sitting on what looks like a rocky hilltop. In front of me, where the ravine would have been, the ground drops away sharply. Unlike before, there are no convenient boulders blocking the space from being truly dangerous or acting as a sort of staircase. I can't even see how far down it goes.

I look around, squinting to make sense of the world through the thinning mist. Boulders behind me. Carvings underneath my hands…pillar of rock to my right.

I do a double-take. Yep, that's definitely a pillar. It reminds me of those ancient obelisks that every second European country stole from Egypt and refuses to give back – tall, square, covered in carvings. But this one doesn't end in a point. Instead it stretches up and up, as tall as a two-storey building, then makes a sharp right angle turn to stretch well above my head, far out to my left, then down to the ground in the near distance. It's a gigantic rectangular archway.

That *definitely* wasn't there before.

I realise that the carving I'm sitting on stretches from one pillar to the next, creating a complete loop. I stumble to my feet, transfixed, and make my way to the nearest pillar. I touch my fingertips against it – making sure it's not my imagination – but it's as solid as can be. In spite of the cold, its rocklike surface is warm to the touch. I press my palm against it completely – and the moment my injured skin hits the surface, I'm hit with what feels like a jolt of static electricity.

I squeak and pull my hand away, rubbing it defensively. Then I add together 'giant archway', 'electricity', and 'completely different scene', along with the fact I can no longer hear or see anyone else at all, and come up with 'bad news'. It's clear something serious has happened. Something really, really serious – even worse than looking bad in front of my boss or getting a bug stuck in my hair (which till now had been one of my worst fears).

The mist has thinned even further, clearly revealing that I'm now on the top of what seems to be a mountain ridge. Barren and rocky, void of colour except for me and my sleeping bag, and empty except for the colossal archway that I somehow find myself underneath. And now I see that where the ground falls away…well, it keeps falling, and falling, and falling. I squint downwards for what feels like half a mile, only to see that the grey rock disappears into more mist.

I swallow. "Alright," I say to myself, hearing my voice tremble. "Don't fall in."

Now I'm shivering, so I tug my sleeping bag back out of its holder then wrap it around my shoulders like an enormous poncho. I have to find everyone – I have to find out how I got here – but it wouldn't do to freeze in the meantime.

Just then I see a flicker of colour. I turn to see a…*thing*…crouched on the ground about two body-lengths away. It's the size of a three-year-old, and it looks like someone dressed up a tailless monkey in an extravagant parrot costume, complete with bright green feathers and small roundish beak.

It squats on two gangly legs with its long, thin arms splayed in front of it, and its parrot-monkey face cocked to the side. Its bulging eyes don't seem to focus, but I get the idea it's looking at me.

I blink at it. It's cute…kinda…but it's not like anything I've seen before. "This is getting weirder and weirder," I breathe,

15

shaking my head in disbelief. "What are you supposed to be?"

The parrot-monkey blinks back, its googly eyes moving independently of each other, rather like a lizard. Then it lunges at me.

I shriek and stumble backwards to land hard on the rock, but then see it wasn't heading for me. Instead it grabs a big, black, leggy shape from the ground right by my foot and shoves it into its mouth. I catch a glimpse of a greyish maw lined with rows of tiny spiked teeth, right to the back of its throat. Apparently it hasn't got the memo that you should have either teeth or a beak, not both.

It doesn't look so cute anymore, even if it has destroyed my greatest enemy, the spider that was in my sleeping bag. Hard to believe I'd actually forgotten about the beast in the chaos and confusion of these past few minutes.

The parrot-monkey chomps down the spider as if it's starving, then turns to look at me again. It hops a little closer, letting out a hopeful croak/belching noise. Its skinny, clawed paws scrape against the ground, and I can see a hairy, segmented leg stuck in that mouth.

Ugh. Definitely not cute anymore. "I don't have any more spiders," I tell it shakily. "But if I did, you'd be the first to know."

Really.

An explosion of sound makes both me and the creature jump. "GET AWAY! SHOO!"

A hail of pebbles comes raining down, narrowly missing me, but hitting the parrot-monkey. It screeches and flees across the ridge line, then stops some distance away, turning back to hiss in my direction. Another rock – not a pebble – nearly hits it, and it disappears into the mist.

I turn to stare up at the new arrival, a guy of about forty

who's managed to come right up to me without me noticing. My rescuer/animal-abuser has straggly black hair and a big, bushy beard, but it's his mismatched eyes that catch my attention. One is glassy light grey, the other dark brown. Around the grey eye is a trio of thin red scars, running from his eyebrow through to his cheekbone. They look like they barely missed his eyeball. His skin is pale, his cheekbones sharp, and he's dressed like a survivor of a frozen apocalypse with a mishmash of tattered fabric, random pieces of plastic, and what might even be fur.

He's also holding what looks like a spear.

I take all this in in about three seconds, then he lets out a hiss not unlike the parrot-monkey. "Get up, girl!" he snarls at me, his voice as rough as his appearance. "The others will be here any moment, and I can't fight them all off."

I just gape at him. "What...?"

"The scavs," he grits out. "The thing I just chased away. A horde lives here, and their claws are toxic." He grabs my arm, yanking me off the ground. *"Please."*

He's stronger than he looks – not that I can tell his build under the wildman-style clothing – and I let him drag me to my feet. He tugs at my hand, and I stumble along after him as he races down the ridgeway, clutching my sleeping bag to my chest with my other arm. The path ahead is partly obscured by mist but definitely heads downwards, and I can now hear more of those croaking sounds around us and behind us.

The fear of being mobbed by more of the parrot-monkeys/ scavs makes me focus on keeping upright and keeping up with him. We haven't run for long when a rock wall looms up ahead. I catch a glimpse of a high, dark doorway, partially covered by scraggly greenery. He pulls me through then turns to grab the slatted door. "Help me shut this. Quick."

The guy's tone is harsh, but I don't take offense. My heart pounding, I move to help him close the door. It's huge, probably eight feet tall, and made of what looks like chunks of scrap metal. It slams shut, leaving streams of light coming through the small gaps, and he shoves a deadbolt-style lock into place. "We've got to block the door," he orders, gesturing at a pile of what looks like scrap and good-sized rocks. It's hard to tell in the dim light. "If they all come at once, they can force their way through."

Then suddenly the croaking and screeching noises rise to a crescendo. It's not just my panic – I can see writhing shapes through the small gaps in the door, and grey or colourful clawed fingers clutch at empty air. I gasp, but move quickly to drag anything I can find and shove it against the door. I'm moving mindlessly, shifting one piece of something after another, and it's not until the guy puts his hand on my arm that I even realise what I'm doing.

"We're OK," he says. "You can stop now."

I stare at him, my unnamed rescuer. Face to face, he's about half a head taller than my average height. His features are partially shadowed, and the dim light from the doorway flickers across his face with the movement of the still-screeching scavs. The light makes his pale grey eye gleam like silver, and he blinks, breaking eye contact as if he's uncomfortable.

"What just happened?" I manage to ask. My voice sounds surprisingly normal.

"Do you mean, what just chased us? Or where are we?"

"Both! One moment I'm in a forest, and the next I'm on a mountaintop! And what *were* those things?! Are they really...do they really kill people?"

He meets my eyes again, and his expression is solemn.

"Like I said, we call them scavs. They can kill, if enough of them get you, and they'll eat anything." He taps at his eye, and my eyes are drawn to the distinct fine cuts...clearly fresh, and just the same size as a small, clawed paw would leave. "If they scratch you, the cut gets infected. I'm lucky I didn't lose my eye."

I wonder if his eye was always grey, or if that was a side effect of the infection. But instead I ask, "I've never heard of them before. Where on earth are we?"

The guy smiles wryly, a sharp twist of the lips only. "That's the thing. We're not on Earth anymore."

Chapter 2

It's a girl. A lady. Now we're out of immediate danger, the shock of seeing someone new hits me.

She's young. Younger than Bianca; young enough not to have lines around her wide dark eyes. Her hair is straight and black and falls around her round, olive-skinned face with a snub nose and full lips.

She's on the short side of average, wearing incredibly fresh, tidy-looking clothing without even a rip in it. It startles me even though my memory whispers that this is normal.

She's so pretty. So *clean*. She's like a perfectly shaped piece of fruit compared to us battered and bruised rejects. It's...startling.

"Not on Earth?" the girl echoes, curling her lip in what might be amusement or disbelief. She even has perfect teeth. So *white...* "Then where are we?"

"Great question," I say, still unable to take my eyes off her fresh, clean skin. "You've come through an interplanetary gate – which we just call the Gate – and it seems to be activated by blood..."

I tell her as much as I know; the basics I've been taught in case I ever found a new survivor on this side of the Gate. But in all the years I've been here in this place we call the Wilds, this is the first new person to arrive.

It's a dangerous life here, I explain, and every step has to be made carefully since the landscape is full of lethal drops, and the local animals can be vicious. The scavs are the worst. If they scratch you, you'll get sick. Eventually it'll kill you. That's what took Alby just after I arrived – a long, much delayed infection.

I just manage not to raise my hand to my own scarred face as I tell her that. "So don't go running off unless you have a death wish," I finish. "But once you know this place, it's safe enough."

The girl just stands there in the dim light cast by the cracks in the doorway. She's clutching the big red cloth she'd been carrying – a sleeping bag – and her expression is still amused and disbelieving. "Safe enough except for the death pits and the rabid animals, huh?"

I look away, scratching my beard uncomfortably. "Well...I'm actually out here looking for someone right now. Jerrold didn't come home yesterday. You haven't seen an old guy with a big grey beard, have you? European, probably wearing what looks like a garbage bin lid on his chest?"

She looks me up and down and her smile spreads. "Like you, but grey-haired?"

"Uh...I suppose so." Not a decent description, was it? Maybe I need to shave.

"No. Sorry. I haven't seen anyone except the parrot-monkey. I mean, scav. And a spider – but the scav ate it." She blinks at me. "This is really interesting, but I need to go now. Everyone will be wondering where I am, and I don't want to hold them up."

I freeze and my heart sinks. Haven't I told her the worst part?

"You don't need to worry about them," I say as gently as I can manage. "The Gate is one-way. Once you're here, you're here to stay."

Demi

You're here to stay.

I blink at the guy, my face feeling frozen. "Pardon?" I manage to say. "Stay how long, exactly?"

He shifts, his bicoloured eyes flicking away from mine. "Hard to say. Until the Gate reopens, you're stuck here. We all are."

"Well, when does the Gate reopen?" I persist, hearing the pitch of my voice rise. "Tomorrow? Next week?"

"Uh…" He scratches his neck, looking incredibly uncomfortable. "It opens every quarter, but we haven't quite worked out how to move all the way through yet. If we had…well, I wouldn't be here talking to you. I'd have already gone through."

"Every quarter?"

"You know…four times a year. So it'll be at least three months till you can go back."

My breath catches in my throat, and I look blankly at the speckled light on the dim tunnel walls. I don't know whether to believe him, but does he really have any reason to lie? "I have a job," I tell him. "I can't stay here for three months because I'll lose my job. They'll think I ran off, or that I died."

The wildman shrugs helplessly. "Better than actually being dead."

Fair point, but it's still hard to accept. I decide not to argue with him right now. "So…what now?"

"I have to keep looking for Jerrold – the guy that's missing. So I'll take you back to the others, and you can get to know them while I'm gone."

He starts to move away from the door, but I don't move with him. I don't want to meet the others, whoever they are. I want to rewind the last twenty minutes of my life, right back to where Connor asked if I wanted help with my sleeping bag. I should have said, 'Yes, and would you please squash this spider for me?' Then they would have laughed at me for being soft, and I would've been a bit embarrassed but would've got over it.

But now I don't seem to have any other choices except to go with the wildman, unless I want to brave the pack of scavs still trying to get in through the barricaded door.

The wildman introduces himself as Liam, which is a nice, normal name for a decidedly abnormal person. He does have a normal voice, though, completely unlike his appearance.

I follow him along the wide, high corridors of what seems to be an abandoned underground mall/bomb shelter, avoiding tripping on piles of rubble and trying not to look too hard when I see the outline of fur or hair. If it turns out this guy's a cannibal, I'll be *really* upset.

I introduce myself too, trying to ignore the way he keeps staring at me as we walk. It's not an admiring stare, more a shocked one (or possibly a Hannibal Lecter-type one). I try not to stare back, since he's probably the oddest person I've seen in real life, and instead focus on the information he's rattling off.

Don't go outside alone.

Don't go out unless you're fully prepared.

Make sure you eat something and carry water with you.

Always cover your back and move silently and vigilantly.

Never throw anything away, because you never know when you'll need it.

You can trust any human you meet, since there are only five of us here in the Wilds-

I pause mid-step. "Wait, what?"

"Just five, now," Liam the wildman says. "You, me, Jerrold, Bianca, and Jesse. You'll meet Bianca and Jesse soon."

"Are they your family?"

He pauses, then shrugs. "They are now."

"Oh."

Liam stares at me again, his gaze flicking over me from head to toe, then turns to carry on down the hall. "You're taking this quite well," he tells me, clearly not realizing he's leaving me behind. "I lost it when they told me I'd be stuck here for a while. Punched a few people. But you're...calm."

I nod again. It's warmer in here out of the wind, I think, but suddenly I'm shivering.

"I'm going to get into my sleeping bag," I announce.

I shake it out, not waiting for him to notice I've stopped. Then I proceed to shuffle inside, boots and all, then zip the sleeping bag up all the way to my neck. The shivering doesn't stop though, and the bag is the sort that can zip up completely until you're sealed in like a caterpillar in a cocoon. I make use of it, closing the bag right over my head, then I sit down on the ground. Demi the cocoon feels a lot safer than Demi in the open.

It's nice and dark in here, even though it's hard to breathe, so I close my eyes and focus on the sound of my own breath.

In...out. In...out. Peaceful.

"Er...Demi?" Liam says, his voice a little muffled by the thick fabric. "What are you doing?"

I ignore him. Most things go away by themselves if you ignore them long enough. Maybe even the spider that caused all of this mess would have gone away by itself, had I just waited long enough.

The thought occurs that maybe the spider never existed. Maybe I'm dreaming, since that would be more logical than accidentally leaving Earth while trying to rescue my sleeping bag from an excessively large arachnid.

Or maybe there *was* a spider, but I fell and hit my head in the ravine. Even now, I could be waiting to be rescued and brought out of this creative coma that I'm clearly in.

Yeah. That makes sense. *Hurry up and rescue me, guys!* I'd even take a condescending Connor rescue right now, and that's saying something.

"Demi," Liam says again. He sounds a little impatient now. "We can't stay here. I need to keep looking for Jerrold, so I need you to be safe and stay with the others."

There's a pause, and I hear what sounds like a muttered, *"Damn it, I can't handle another person who needs babying!"* Then more clearly he says, "That means you need to walk."

Nope. Demi the cocoon – AKA Demi in denial – does not walk.

Liam sighs heavily. "Fine. Let's hope you're lighter than you look."

Excuse me?!

But I don't have time to do more than gasp in outrage when I suddenly feel myself grabbed around the middle and hoisted into the air, then slammed down over a metal slab. Or so it feels

– presumably that's Liam's shoulder.

Then I can feel we're moving, because I'm being jiggled up and down with every step. Kind of hard to keep my peaceful, in-denial attitude when I'm being carted around like a bag of potatoes. Not a small, easy-to-carry bag of potatoes either – the extra-large sort you need both arms and a supermarket trolley to move around.

After a few minutes Liam says, "Are you ready to walk yet?" He sounds strained.

I ignore him. I happen to be within my BMI, thank you very much, and if he's struggling, then it's his fault for insisting on moving me in the first place.

Then something occurs to me. "You're the idiot mountain biker." My voice must have been muffled, but I feel us stop moving.

"What?" he asks.

"Mountain biker," I repeat. "Years ago. You left the path, didn't you?"

There's a slight pause, then Liam shifts his grip, grunting in exertion. "In Mount Freedom National Park? Yeah, I did. I was showing off for my friends, and I ignored the barrier. But you must've done the same, or else you wouldn't be here."

"I wasn't showing off for my friends," I mutter. But then it hits me – I kind of was. The only reason I'd gone into the ravine was to avoid looking bad in front of my coworkers, which wasn't far from showing off.

Dang. When I wake up, I'll have to take this as a warning. Better to swallow my pride and look stupid than actually *be* stupid.

We trudge along in silence, and eventually I feel myself turned upright again, then set down on the ground.

"We're ten minutes from home base," Liam says. "Either you walk the rest of the way, or I'll find someone to help carry you. And trust me, you won't live that down. Jerrold still calls me Fisticuffs when he thinks he's being funny."

Then they can call me Cocoon, because I'm definitely not getting out of here.

And when even his dire threat doesn't make me budge or reply, I hear him sigh – again – then there's the sound of footsteps disappearing off into the distance.

Alone. Hooray.

I sit for a while in the dark, my breath hot against my face, since the sleeping bag is made for an icy winter, rather than whatever this is. It's so dark in here that I literally have no idea where I am. I can feel something solid against my back, but the floor under me is hard and flat.

I don't know if I fall asleep – or wake up – but a slight noise startles me. I jolt in place, briefly panic at the lack of air, then remember where I am. I fumble for the sleeping bag's zip, then pull it down just enough to expose my face.

Air. Glorious air. It rushes in, cold and fresh and with that slightly musty dirt smell you sometimes get in old buildings. It's dim down here, although not fully dark. I'm clearly in some kind of hallway. It's faintly lit with what looks like thin lines of gleaming paint at floor level and repeated about ten feet in the air.

Then a small face pops into my view. It's a kid of about five or six years old, skinny and with tangled, curly black hair around a wide-eyed, brown-skinned face. A boy, I think, who needs a haircut. "Who are you?" he asks.

At this point it seems unlikely I'm dreaming, so I'm going to have to deal with the current situation. "Demi. Who are you?"

"Jesse." He barely pauses before announcing, "Liam says you're in shock an' won't get up. He thinks you're gonna freak out soon."

I narrow my eyes. "I was just having a rest. I'm not going to freak out." Surprisingly, that statement feels true. Panicking will just make me feel worse, so I may as well keep calm until this is all sorted.

He seems to take that into his stride. "Liam says you're a girl."

"Liam would be right." And Liam apparently has a lot to say.

I hear other footsteps approach, then a middle-aged woman comes into sight. She's mixed race and wiry, with grey-streaked hair pulled up on the top of her head and skin a couple of shades darker than Jesse's. She has similar dark eyes, but shadowed and tired-looking, and her cheeks are hollow. She wears apocalyptic-chic just like these other two. I quickly note her colouring, then Jesse's, then Liam's paler tone, and conclude they're a little family.

Shame Liam can't get his staring problem under control if he's got a partner, I think self-righteously.

"Hi Demi," the woman says in a voice that's as weary as her appearance. "I'm Bianca. Liam thought you might want some company."

The wildman himself is nowhere in sight. He's left me with these two instead. The fact that they're a woman and a child rather than a couple of men makes me feel safer, but I'm suddenly very aware of the fact I'm sitting in a hallway, while in a sleeping bag, which happens to be zipped up to cover everything except my face.

Exit Demi in denial…enter Demi the dignified. I unzip the

sleeping bag and shuffle my way out of it as smoothly as possible. "Thanks," I reply, getting to my feet. "But I don't need company. I just need to find my group. They'll be looking for me, you see. We were about to start walking for the day, and there was this thing with a spider, then I dropped my sleeping bag in the ravine and went looking for it. Then there was the parrot-monkey-scav and Liam, and now I'm here."

Bianca and Jesse stare at me. Perhaps not Demi the dignified after all.

"Did Liam not explain the Gate to you?" Bianca asks finally. "That you've-"

"Come through an interplanetary portal and I'm stuck here in the Wilds for at least three months till it reopens?" I cut in. "Yes."

I don't mention that I can't accept the three-month thing, because it's way too long to be stuck out in the middle of nowhere with a bunch of strangers. Just because they haven't managed to reopen the Gate doesn't mean that I can't do it myself somehow. But I can tell that once I even hint that I'm planning to run, they'll be watching me like hawks.

"OK," Bianca says slowly. "That's...good. Will you come home with us? It's got heating."

Heating does sound nice. "Where did Liam go?"

"He's looking for my father-in-law," Bianca replies. Then her face crumples, and tears begin to stream down her cheeks. "Jerrold has been missing since yesterday, ever since he went to check the Gate. We take turns just to make sure no one's come through...but I'm so worried about him."

She looks so upset that I feel worried for Jerrold too, never mind that I haven't met the man. Could he be Liam's dad? I reach out and hesitantly pat her on the shoulder. "There, there.

I'm sure Liam will find him."

Actually, I'm not sure at all, but I don't say that either, since I do know how to keep my mouth shut sometimes. But she doesn't respond, and Jesse just watches her with a worried expression. Then he takes her hand and starts heading away, down the hall.

I bundle up my sleeping bag again and follow the two of them the rest of the way, past more organised-looking piles of junk and hallways blocked off with manmade barricades. I notice that Bianca moves slowly, as if she has a limp or a bad hip. Jesse takes this into account and paces his steps accordingly.

We eventually come out into an open area that reminds me of an old warehouse. There's definitely natural light here, streaming in from windows high above us. A fire pit is in the middle of the room, with what might be chairs made of odds and ends placed around it. Everything seems to be made of odds and ends – it's a total trash palace.

Lovely. I've been growing more and more uncomfortable the longer we've walked, till I'm practically jittering in place. It feels so…wrong being here, like someone's grabbed me off the street and said, 'here, play this role' without giving me the chance to say yes or no.

This doesn't feel real. I know it is, but it doesn't feel like it, and I can't relax into this place in any way, shape or form. I need time to *think*. "Can I use your bathroom?" I blurt out.

Jesse scrunches up his face. "You want a bath?"

"The lav," Bianca corrects. She sits down with an audible sigh of relief, then begins massaging her knee. "Jesse, please show Demi where it is."

Jesse leads me down a hallway that comes off the main room, then he points to a random door that's half propped open.

It looks like an elevator door, metal and smooth. "In there. Don't forget to wash your hands."

"Thanks," I reply dryly. I'm still carrying my sleeping bag, but I don't care. It can come into the lav with me, because I'm not willing to give up my last connection to normal life.

The 'lav' turns out to be a reeking long drop. I don't look down the hole, but the cold breeze coming up tells me where it leads. It's built from an unfamiliar dull grey substance, clearly machine-made rather than thrown together like the rest of this place, and when I compare it to a toilet back home, it must have been made for a giant. Whoever built the complex must have been pretty damn tall, although they probably didn't intend it to be used by random, much shorter squatters (pun intended).

There's also a tall, narrow window jammed open. After I use the facilities, I take the chance to look outside.

I see we're not underground after all. Or this part isn't, anyway. Instead I'm looking out at the most colossal, terrifying drop I could imagine. I quickly realise the grey below is actually clouds or mist rather than the pit's base, and that it must be another section of the pit I saw from back at the Gate. Home base is clearly built just around the corner from the Gate itself, on the edge of this vast hole. Cavern. Basin. I can only just make out the other side…

Well, it's definitely not Mount Freedom National Park. My last small hope that I'd just got lost (or stolen by some crazy mountain tribe) fades.

I let out a long breath, pushing back the intense urge to run screaming back to the Gate. This is pretty bad – but I remind myself that I can handle anything if I know there's an end date.

But still, I take several minutes to squat on the grubby floor, my arms wrapped around myself as I focus on breathing evenly, waiting for my heartrate to go down again.

It's OK. I'll be OK.

Breathe.

When I finally come out of the bathroom, Jesse's gone. I take a moment to check that no one's watching me, then immediately set off in the opposite direction from the main room. I follow the hall past dozens of rooms and other halls, all lit by either glowing paint strips or orangish, slightly inadequate lighting from overhead, and test random doors as I go along, looking for sounds or any breeze that would indicate the outdoors. I can make out faint chittering sounds, like there's a malfunctioning machine in the walls, but don't see anything that I care to recognize.

Then I find an exit. It leads right out to the side of the colossal pit, but there's a proper pathway and a set of safety-rail-enclosed stairs leading upwards. I take a moment to scavenge my own makeshift armour, but it's harder than I expected to turn random pieces of plastic or metal into something that will stay attached to my body.

In the end I just unzip my sleeping bag and turn it inside out so the grey, warm side faces outwards, then sit it over my head and shoulders like a big, thick hooded cloak. I grab a weird shaped, vaguely metallic stick-thing to use as a club, then set out. Liam's warning about the dangers of this place rings once more in my head, but I resolutely move forward.

I'll be careful, because I can't stay here.

Ten minutes later, I've managed to make it to the top of the outdoor stairs without tumbling to my death or freaking out too much. I'm now in another part of the scrubby, thin-treed forest, this time with a solid view of that same horrendous pit –

henceforth to be called the Pit of Despair. (As in, even looking at it makes me want to give up and collapse in a heap.)

But to my other side, the forest continues on into somewhat flat land. I can see the drop of yet another pit in the distance, and the occasional window sticking up from the barren ground hints at the rabbit-warren complex underneath.

It's cold too, of course. And not too far away, the stark shape of the Gate stands out against its surroundings. So naturally I head for the Gate.

It looks like it'll take a good hour to get there from the exit I've taken, but the way seems clear. I heed Liam's warning about this place though, watching every step and listening out for scavs lying in wait. I walk for about thirty minutes without incident, keeping the main pit to my left and the forested area to my right. There are faint sounds around me, perhaps birds from the forest and the ever-present wind from the pit, but I don't see anything alive. I'm feeling pretty good about myself – an inch away from being Demi the wilderness expert – but then I hear a scuffling noise in the bushes to my right.

I pause, pushing back my sleeping bag/hood so I have full vision, and hold my makeshift weapon out in front of me. Then I stare into the scrubby vegetation, watching for movement.

A grey shape shuffles its way into sight. It's about knee-high, with beady eyes virtually hidden under a mass of fur. It has four legs, a snoutish face and not much else to recommend it. It looks kind of like a dog and a boar mixed together.

I wave my weapon at the animal, trying to work out whether it's dangerous. "Shoo. Go away."

It shies away, backing into the undergrowth a little, but doesn't leave entirely. Then I hear a sound behind me, a much louder sound.

My blood chills. Suddenly a movie scene comes to mind where the character runs into a small animal, only to turn around and see its much larger, more dangerous parent behind them. Hmm…more than one movie, actually.

I turn around slowly, the feeble stick my only hope.

Then I see what was behind me.

Chapter 3

I can't believe what I'm seeing.

Demi is unmistakable with her shiny black hair above the unzipped, inside-out sleeping bag, hints of its red surface visible as she moves. She's wearing it wrapped around her shoulders like a cloak, but her neck and face are exposed to danger.

Worse still, there's a boggart not five feet away from her. Its hackles are up but it stands almost dead still, which for a boggart is a clear indicator it's about to attack.

Then Demi turns towards me. She's holding some piece of junk as if it's a weapon, and her whole posture speaks of aggression and fear, her eyes wide.

She's turned her back on the thing, but the moment she sees me, she relaxes. "Oh, it's just you! I thought for sure you were some kind of-"

She screams as I lunge towards her, spear outstretched, and catch the boggart in the throat before it gores her legs. It keeps fighting – boggarts will fight till they win or die – so I push her away and stab at it again, my jaw taut and my only focus on getting it to stop moving.

If scavs are the biggest danger here, then boggarts are the next biggest. They're fierce and fast, and they'll eat anything

35

they can catch. We'll return the favour though, and this'll be dinner, tomorrow's breakfast, and an addition to our blanket pile.

The boggart finally goes still, and with the immediate danger out of the way, my fear bubbles over into anger. "What were you thinking, turning your back on that thing?!" I shout-whisper, because I know better than to really raise my voice out here. "And what are you doing out here alone? Are you *trying* to die?!"

Demi's wide-eyed expression turns indignant. "I didn't know it was going to attack me-"

"And that's why you shouldn't be out here! I *told* you to stay with the others – and you couldn't even last an hour?"

Her eyes narrow, and she folds her arms. "You gonna stab me with that spear, Wildman? Pick me up and drag me back to your cave? Because if not, you can't make me do anything. You're not the boss of me."

Her voice has steadily risen in volume throughout the confrontation, and her cheeks have turned pink. She looks an inch away from clubbing me with that junk she's still holding. The fact that she called me Wildman catches me short, and I step back, abashed. No one's called me anything except 'boy' for years, since except for Jesse I was always the youngest of the group. *Was.* Obviously I don't look like a boy to *her*.

"Sorry," I mutter. "Can you keep your voice down, please? I don't want to fight off anything else."

Demi glances down at the unmoving red and grey shaggy pile in front of her and visibly recoils. "Sorry," she echoes in a much quieter voice. "Ah...and thanks for stopping that thing."

I shrug, bending down to pick it up by one leg. "Human life is precious. Boggarts, not so much. And you're welcome."

"Bogart? Like, Humphrey?"

"No, boggart like...well, like nothing I suppose. I think it's some kind of mythical monster. I didn't make up the name." I feel a little defensive for some reason, so I focus my attention on tying its feet together. Easier to carry that way.

"What are you going to do with it?" Demi asks. "Eat it?"

She looks horrified, and I almost laugh. It's probably better not to mention what our staple food breadish is made of, if she can't handle this. "Among other things. I'll leave it inside the nearest doorway then keep looking for Jerrold till we run out of light." I pause. "You can come with me if you refuse to stay inside where it's safe...but you have to *listen*, alright?"

Demi's eyes flick from my face, to the dead boggart, to the bloodied spear hooked to my armour. "I want to go to the Gate," she says quietly, almost nervously. "Please."

I sigh, because of course she does. "Then it's lucky that's where we're heading."

I tuck my impromptu hunting spoils into one of the half-hidden compound entrances we keep open just for that purpose. There are a dozen useable doors scattered around this area (some of which used to be windows). We keep them all unlocked for human hands but blocked enough to keep out the wildlife, since you never know when you'll need to sprint for one. Then we head for the Gate...again.

Demi asks questions all along the way, wanting to know everything from the refrigeration available for meat (none), through to Jesse's age (five), through to the dangers out here. I've already told her a bunch of them, but I recount everything I know anyway, starting with 'don't turn your back on a boggart'.

"Or a scav, for that matter," I add quietly as we trudge

along. I'm moving as close to the pit's edge as I dare, watching out for glimpses of anything that doesn't belong. Any sign that Jerrold might have fallen or been chased down here, but there's nothing. "They'll go for you, and their scratches never really heal. You can die of an infection years later, from an old scav scratch."

Demi turns sharply at that, staring at the left side of my face. "Years later, you say?"

Ah. That didn't exactly fit in with what I told her already. "Or so I hear," I say mildly, although it's not a mild topic. "I'm going by what others have told me."

"But *you've* been scratched," she persists, as if I hadn't noticed until now. "And recently too, by the look of it. Are you saying you might die from it?"

"I'm hoping to get home and get antibiotics before it becomes a problem," I reply, not meeting her eyes. "But in the meantime I watch it carefully."

Yeah, right.

We pass the last boulders that mark the nearest compound door to the Gate, the same one I fled to with Demi not two hours ago. The fog sits thick and low, almost blocking out the structure up ahead, so I come to a halt and indicate for her to step back quietly with me. "This is a danger zone," I murmur. "A scav pack lives in this area – you already met them – so we don't go unless we have some visibility. We'll give it ten minutes then try, OK? Quickly go in, look around, then come straight back here."

"But if you're that quick, how can you test how the Gate works?" she whispers back.

I pause. Good point. "With difficulty."

"But nothing's more important than getting home! Maybe you need some kind of diversion. Draw away the scavs, then send someone to test the Gate."

So many questions! Had I recently been wishing for more company, specifically female? Maybe next time I'll wish for a mute, or someone who doesn't ask questions. I scratch at my beard irritably, then realise I probably look like I have fleas, so forcibly stop myself. No need to reinforce the wildman stereotype.

I pull my biggest card, pointing to my pale, damaged eye. "Staying alive is more important than getting home straight away."

She stares at the eye as if I've given her permission, but there's no disgust in her gaze. "Did that happen when you were scratched?" she whispers. "In this world, after you came through the Gate?"

Now that's another awkward subject, but for a different reason. "I was out hunting with Dominic," I say slowly. "Jerrold's son. We were caught out by a pair of scavs. I…I wasn't paying enough attention. One moment I've got this thing in my face, and I can feel it's cut me and can hear Dominic fighting the thing off, and the next there's this bright light." I glance at her sidelong, checking to see if she believes me, but she seems to be listening raptly. I swallow. "It must've been a hallucination, because I passed out. Then when I woke up, Dom was gone, and I was all scratched up with my eye the wrong colour. Lucky to be alive, though."

Sad story, but it's not the whole one. It's all I'm willing to tell at the moment, though. I know well that too much truth too quickly helps no one.

"What happened to Dominic?" Demi whispers. "I didn't meet him today."

I turn away, looking out to where the ever-present mist

39

partially covers the Gate in the distance. "I don't know what happened to him," I say flatly. "That was three years ago. People have a habit of going missing around here." Hence my current search for Jerrold.

"*Oh.*"

There's enough of a silence that I think the conversation's over. I haven't talked this much in years, not since Dominic disappeared. It's surprisingly uncomfortable.

But then she says, "But the cuts around your eye, they're red. They look fresh. Are you saying they're *three years old*?"

I shrug awkwardly. "As I said. The cuts get infected, and they don't really heal." They're actually quite good, compared to how they can get, since they're closed over.

"Ah." Demi's nose is wrinkled as if she doesn't know what to make of that. "And…you said Dominic is Jerrold's son. What about his mother?"

"Elizabeth died in childbirth, long before I ever arrived."

"Here?" Demi's eyes widen. "How long have people *been* here?!"

I shuffle in place uncomfortably. "A long time, for Jerrold. He was more focused on survival than, er, working the Gate. It's better now there's a few of us."

It's complete BS, but she seems to accept it. "Died in childbirth," she murmured. "How medieval."

"This world isn't the safest place to give birth," I agree. It's a massive understatement. "So it's…ah, best not to get pregnant here."

Demi lets out a short laugh. "Yeah, that won't be a problem."

Right. I try not to react to the reminder – again – that she doesn't find me at all attractive.

But then her lips turn into a tight line. "So Jesse...is he yours, or...?"

"Dom's," I say a little too sharply. I hadn't realised she'd been thinking down that track. "There's nothing between Bianca and I." Nothing except guilt, obligation, and the intense protectiveness that comes from having such a tiny human population. "But we all look after Jesse. Bianca and I, and Jerrold, who's a real doting grandad. If we can find him."

"Do you think we will?"

I don't answer. "The mist's thinning. Come on, let's go while we can."

Demi

Liam hasn't answered my last question, I notice, and I'm trying to come to terms with his comment about how long some people must've been here.

Long enough for this Jerrold to become a father then a grandfather? Sounds like he wasn't trying hard enough to make the Gate work. But then some people seem to like the survivalist lifestyle.

And Bianca and Liam the Wildman aren't together, I note. I'm not sure whether that's better or worse than them being a couple, since I don't want his attention on me in that way.

But then we move out into the barren, open area where the parrot-monkeys-scavs live, and staying alert keeps all my attention.

Well, most of it. My mind keeps turning back to Jesse's grandmother Elizabeth, who'd died after giving birth here. How freaking *medieval*. It's a terrifying thought...but for the first time

I'm glad I can't have children.

I stumble on some loose gravel and grab hold of the nearest object, which happens to be Liam's junk-armoured shoulder. He stops, glancing back at me with those disconcerting bicoloured eyes, but then turns back and keeps walking.

It's probably a good thing that I won't be here for long, because the only available guy isn't exactly my type. I prefer men younger, more clean-cut and less like Tom Hanks in Castaway.

Although he does have nice cheekbones. Maybe if he had a shave...

I brush that idle thought away and focus on our location. The Gate stretches up ahead of us, taller even than I remember, and so very alien in appearance. I lurch forward – looking for what, I don't know – but Liam sticks out his arm, halting me.

Oh yeah, that's right. Dangerous animals inhabiting a dangerous area. I raise an eyebrow at him, lifting my hands with my makeshift weapon at the ready.

He starts to move forward, looking around cautiously and with his own spear held out in stab-something position. After a few moments he gestures at the Gate. "Go ahead."

I give him a quick glance then hurry up ahead until I'm standing under the high archway, right on top of the carvings in the ground.

It's freezing cold up here, the wind cutting straight through my sleeping bag cloak, but I expected that. And now I'm here, I'm not sure what to do.

I crouch down, trying to remember what I'd been doing when I'd arrived. Fleeing from a spider...crawling across the ground...cutting my hand. It's a light graze which has now scabbed over, and I wrinkle my nose at the idea of reopening it.

I've never been fond of pain.

"You said blood activates it," I call softly to Liam, who's pacing around the area like we're about to be imminently attacked. (It's not at all reassuring.)

"I also said it only works every quarter, and that it won't work for you now," he replies just as softly. "If you cut yourself now, you might feel a tingle or two from the Gate but it won't let you go through. You'll just attract a bunch of scavs instead."

"But it hasn't let anyone back through yet. That's what you said before."

He shrugs, lifting his spear. "We're still here."

Still here, long enough for a child to be born and grow to school-age. I know Liam's been here for at least three years, since he was with Jerrold's son Dominic when he disappeared. But when I think back on the old story of a mountain-biker going missing in Mount Freedom National Park, I'm *sure* Liam must have been here for six, seven years even. It strikes me as weird that they've only just worked out the Gate's function now, when surely that should have been their only goal this whole time.

But I can't focus on that thought. Instead I try touching the Gate. Its stonelike surface feels almost warm against the freezing air, but it doesn't feel powerful or otherworldly or whatever I need to take me home.

I run my hands over the carvings on the vertical pillars, then back over the same place I'd been touching when I came through. Nothing happens – not even a hint of a tingle. "I had a spider with me," I suggest. "Maybe I need one to get home too."

Liam looks at me incredulously. "You think you need a spider to make the Gate work? I told you it won't work today."

I don't want the spider anyway. But even though I've been

told otherwise, I stubbornly stay by the Gate for as long as I can get away with, touching it and trying to recreate the circumstances that brought me here. On the off-chance the Gate is supernatural rather than science, I even – ugh – scratch my palm as a sort of minor blood offering.

"Maybe I need more blood," I suggest reluctantly. The idea of injuring myself worse is really unpleasant, but I'll do it if I need to.

"We've tried that. As I said, all it does it bring scavs." Liam shrugs. "We think it might need a particular type of blood to get back, or something mixed with blood. Or maybe there's a different exit than entrance, which I look for every time I go out.

"But nothing's going to happen now, and there's a man lost out here, possibly desperate for me to find him. Now are you going to come help me search, or do I need to take you back to home base?"

I get up from my prone position, feeling as guilty as he probably intended. I'm not too upset about the Gate not working, since he already told me it wouldn't. But I had to test it for myself before I settle in to play Survivor for the next three months. (Damn it!) "I'll help."

Several hours later, the darkness is setting in. We've walked for miles and my feet ache like crazy, but it's not any worse than the camping trip I'd set out on. I'm hungry too, but I don't complain, because Liam's posture and mood have become noticeably darker.

It's clearly because we haven't found Jerrold. I keep thinking about Bianca and her tears earlier today, and I dread giving her bad news. Or being with Liam when he gives her the bad news, which feels like the same thing.

The weather improves just enough for a glowing shape to emerge over the horizon, clearly visible in the dimming sky. "Is that the moon?" I exclaim.

"Looks like it."

I ignore his lifeless reply, enthralled by the sight. It's about the same size as Earth's, round too, but there are faint lines and swirls glowing on its surface in irregular patterns. It looks unlike anything I've ever seen: gorgeous and alien all at once. "Odd," I remark. "I would have thought an alien planet would have two moons, or maybe half a dozen. Are there any others?"

Liam shrugs. "I haven't seen any, but the sky's usually too cloudy to see even this one."

"Oh." We keep walking, and the distinctive outline of a doorway appears up ahead. It's yet another entrance to the compound they live in, and it looks fairly ordinary, just too tall for humans. "I wonder if this is a parallel universe," I comment as the idea occurs to me. "One where there's an Earth-like planet with a single moon, but the locals and the wildlife are all different. The locals must be giants, of course. Have you ever found any bodies?"

Even in the half-darkness I see him stare at me incredulously, and I realise what I just said. We've been hunting for a body…maybe. Or maybe he just thinks the parallel world idea is stupid. "Alien bodies," I elaborate. "A giant alien body, I mean." Because that would be incredibly interesting – maybe even worth getting temporarily stranded for.

He huffs out a sigh. "No aliens, Demi. Whatever built this place is long gone."

He opens the door and I bite back my next question as he picks up the hairy dead thing from earlier, then barricades the door behind us.

We tramp along the endless tunnels in silence. I try to keep track of where we're going, but it's a lost cause and I've never been great with directions.

I've made some sense of this compound, though. It's a massive underground set of buildings, largely built into a hillside, with multiple exits and windows that look out to the sky. Home base – AKA that big area at the apex of multiple halls – is quite deep into the complex, and pressed right up beside the Pit of Despair. But beyond that, I'm lost. I'll just have to trust that Liam is a decent guy underneath his uber-rough exterior, and that I won't ever need to flee.

Back at home base, Bianca is still sitting on a makeshift bench next to the fire pit. She sees how we have a hairy dead animal as opposed to a human (also possibly hairy and dead, by the sound of it). Her shoulders slump and her expression falls – I've never seen such despair on someone's face. She starts to sob where she sits, and Liam just drops the dead thing and goes to embrace her. Jesse hugs them both around the legs, and I hang back at a distance, feeling useless. What kind of life have they lived that a child would respond in a more controlled way than a grown woman?

I'm upset too, damn it! But my upset at being here pales to the possible loss of a human being.

"We'll go out again first thing in the morning," Liam tells her in a low voice. "Demi has a good set of eyes. If he can be found, we'll find him."

I startle at the mention, surprised that he noticed. I might be a semi-unfit office worker who had to be paid to venture out in the wilderness, but I do have perfect vision.

"I want to come," Jesse says. "I want to find Grandad."

"You need to look after your mum," Liam replies. "She

46

needs someone strong and brave to help with her bad leg, remember?"

The boy pouts but doesn't argue. Honestly, this is the best-behaved kid I've seen in my life. The comment about Bianca's leg makes sense, though. When I first met her, I noticed her distinctive limp. I wonder if she's been injured or if it's something like arthritis.

As for me, I'm feeling more and more useless. "Is there anything I can do to help?" I ask.

Liam looks back at the dead hairy thing, which is lying stiffly at the side of the room. "That boggart needs dressing and draining as soon as possible, since it should have been done earlier. How are you with a knife?"

My jaw drops and I stare at him blankly. "Uh…"

He sighs. "Jesse and I will do it, won't we?"

"Yeah!" Jesse cheers. "I love meat!"

Great. Of course he does. As for me, I'll eat meat if I can't see where it came from, but I'm just as happy with a decent vegetarian meal.

I flee to the bathroom, mostly just to stare out the window at the view. But of course it's fully dark now, and the view seems ominous. I catch glimpses of stars, but that fantastic glowing moon is nowhere in sight.

By the time I slink back to the main room, the boggart is a pile of something I refuse to look too closely at, and there's the smell of roasted meat. Kinda reminds me of a barbeque, and I figure that if I don't have to look at the thing's face, I can manage to eat it for dinner.

"It'll be ready in about an hour," Jesse says in a matter-of-fact way. He sits next to a separate fire pit, turning chunks of meat on a metal spit system that's been rigged up. "It has to be cooked for a long time so we don't get sick."

"Oh." It smells and looks ready now, and cooking it more will surely turn it into something resembling boot leather. I think for a moment about how steak back home only needs a few minutes to cook. But then most cows don't potentially carry a deadly disease, do they? If they did, we wouldn't eat them. "Is there anything else?" I ask, feeling like a prima donna. "To eat, I mean. That's not…meat."

"There's breadish," Jesse suggests. He points to a canister nearby. "We usually eat that, but meat is nicer."

That's not reassuring, but I open the canister anyway. Inside are chunks of a grainy, dark brown something that might be bread…ish. I pick one out gingerly and give it a sniff. It doesn't smell like anything, just faintly musty like the rest of this complex.

I take a seat near Jesse and nibble carefully at the breadish, quickly deciding that it doesn't taste like anything either. Not bread, maybe more like if cardboard and sand were ground together and baked.

But Jesse's comment about meat has brought back to mind an uncomfortable idea I had earlier, one inspired by post-apocalyptic and disaster films. It's probably nonsense, but I have to check. Because what if Liam hasn't been staring at me because he thinks I'm nice-looking? What if I just look meaty to wildfolk who live off this cardboard rubbish?

I lean in and lower my voice. "Do you eat a lot of different types of meat here? Besides boggart?"

Jesse nods in that way that can mean either yes or no. "Boggart's my favourite, but we eat other sorts too."

"Like…?"

He shrugs.

Thanks a lot, kid. I'm going to have to ask outright. I check around me to make sure neither Bianca nor Liam are nearby, then whisper, "Do you ever eat...people?"

Jesse's eyes bug and his jaw drops. "Nooo..." he whimpers, leaning away from me. "Why would you say that? Do *you* eat people?"

"No! No, of course not," I reassure him hastily, feeling my cheeks heat. I'm relieved to be so clearly proven wrong, but now I feel pretty damn stupid. "It was a joke, haha! Nobody eats people... I thought I was being funny."

"I don't think you're funny," Jesse declares. His lower lip is sticking out, but he's no longer staring at me like I'm a monster. "That was a bad joke."

"I'm sorry," I say repentantly. "Forgive me? I'll tell a better joke."

"OK..."

Thinking quickly, I hold out my hand, palm upwards, fingers partially curled in deceased-bug pose. "What's this?"

He studies my hand with a frown. "A hand?"

I flip my hand back up the other way so my fingertips rest on my knee, then wiggle them slightly like my hand is a crawling insect. "A dead one of these."

Jesse stares at me blankly, and I persist. "Geddit? It looks like a bug. Alive...dead...alive again."

"You're weird," he declares.

I sigh. "My ex-boyfriend would agree with you." The no-kids thing wasn't the *only* reason we broke up. I may also have a fear-based fixation on insects...and I may be a bit odd.

But if I'm going to be stuck for a while with a kid who thinks I'm weird, a sobbing widow, and a staring wildman, at least I don't have to worry about being eaten too.

Chapter 4

Demi

I'm still figuring out how to keep Jesse quiet on my 'are you a cannibal' misstep when Liam comes over. He's lost the makeshift armour, but his clothes underneath appear just as makeshift, hanging off his rangy frame. His vest looks like it's made from an old tarpaulin.

"Good job, Jesse," he says. "Do you need a hand?"

"No," Jesse replies, sounding proud of himself. "I've got it all sorted." Then he indicates to me a little accusingly, wrinkling his nose. "Demi doesn't want to eat the meat. She wants breadish instead."

"Well, I wouldn't go as far as to say *wants* breadish," I argue, relieved that he hasn't mentioned that *other* topic. "But I was thinking how if the boggarts can all make you sick when you're alive, maybe they're the same when they're dead."

Liam grunts. "Nobody here's died from eating boggart meat."

I notice he doesn't say no one's been sick from eating it. "I'll try it next time," I say politely, thinking I'll have to be much hungrier before I'll risk eating tainted meat, even if these people don't mind. "This breadish is…um, interesting. What's it made of – some sort of grain?"

Jesse opens his mouth and Liam suddenly slaps his hand over the boy's lower face. "Cover your mouth when you sneeze," he tells him. "Especially when you're cooking."

Jesse looks startled, and I don't blame him. He didn't look like he was about to sneeze. Besides, surely it's just as unhygienic to put your hand over someone's mouth.

But to me Liam says, "Yeah...grains, of a sort. Breadish is made in a machine here in the complex, ingredients and all. We figure it's the leftovers of some ancient bomb-shelter kind of tech, but it keeps us alive." He grimaces. "So best learn to like it, I think."

Alien bread from alien grains, by the sound of it. "I'm sure I'll get used to it," I agree generously. "It's kind of like crackers mixed with really, really wholegrain bread."

Jesse wrestles himself free from Liam's grasp. "What's crackers?"

I brighten – finally, a subject I'm an expert on. I launch into a detailed description of different types of crackers and what you eat them with, but when that leads onto 'what's cheese? What's jam?' I give up. "Well, what do *you* like to eat with your breadish?" I ask Jesse, making a point of ignoring the wildman who's gone back to staring at me from his seat across from the boy.

Jesse shrugs. "Meat!"

"There's not much of a dietary range here," Liam says. His eyes flick over me like they've done repeatedly today. "No fruit or veges. And although we've found a few roots that are edible, we don't find them often. What did you do back on Earth?"

"I'm a business analyst for a telecommunications company," I reply, deliberately wording it in the present tense. I am *not* staying here. No matter what I've said to these guys, I'm not resigned to the 'three months until the Gate opens' timeframe. "I came out here – to Mount Freedom, I mean – as part of a team-building activity. My boss thought it was a good idea to get us away from our desks."

And my boss has no idea how thoroughly I've achieved that goal.

"I've never had a real boss," Liam says. "I was a student when I came through the Gate, and I worked casual jobs before that, whatever was available. My last one was to go through comments on internet articles for a news website and delete any that broke the rules. The things some people would say…well, I won't repeat them here." He laughs with the first true humour I've seen him show, shaking his head. "I remember there was talk about updating controls so people couldn't say those kinds of things online. Did it ever happen?"

I look at him pityingly, trying to imagine him ever sitting in front of a computer. It's not an easy image. "Nope. The internet's still as full of trolls and bad behaviour as ever." A smile curves my lips as something else occurs to me. "Hey, want me to tell you the craziest stuff that's happened in the last few years?"

I run through a list of the oddest world moments in my twenties, which is basically the whole time he's been stuck here. And man, the world is a strange place…Earth, I mean, even without the interplanetary gate.

But Liam mostly knows what I'm talking about, since he asks relevant questions and shows the appropriate dismay when I describe some of the political and international shenanigans that have taken place. He cares more about the reality TV star who became president than about who the British prince married, but listens attentively when I tell him about both.

Jesse, on the other hand, watches with increasingly glazed eyes. I finally notice and take pity on him. "Enough from me for tonight," I say. "Why don't you tell me about your day, Jesse?"

But he just looks from me to Liam, then back again. "Are you and Liam going to get married?"

Now my jaw drops. He's clearly getting me back for the cannibalism question, because I did *not* see that coming. "What? No, of course not. We hardly know each other."

"But Mum and Dad got married," Jesse persists. "And my grandad and grandma got married too, Grandad says. And you're the same age, not like my dad and mum."

Hmm, it sounds like there's an interesting story there. I file that away to ask about later.

"Men and women don't always get married," Liam tells him quietly, avoiding my eyes. "Even if they have things in common. Sometimes they date. But most of the time, they're just friends."

"What's date?"

"Dating," Liam corrects. "It's…being friends with someone, except with…ah, kissing."

That's a good enough explanation in my books, but I'm so uncomfortable with the subject even being raised in relation to Liam. Just…no.

"We'll talk more another time," Liam adds. "I think the edges of the meat are cooked enough, don't you? Go on and take some to your mum."

Jesse complains but does as he's asked, leaving me alone with Liam in the aftermath of one of the most awkward conversations I've ever had. And whew…I've had some *awkward* conversations.

Liam

As a wingman, Jesse has let me down. I'll have to teach him about subtlety...but is there any point? I'm literally the only adult man on the planet, and Demi couldn't turn me down fast enough. To be fair, it was a casual proposal of marriage via a five-year-old, but still.

If I hadn't noticed her repeated comments about my appearance by now, this would have dashed any of my lingering hopes. And to my irritation, it turns out I *do* have lingering hopes.

Well, she's literally the only woman on the planet who's not old enough to be my mother. And we did only meet this morning.

I turn back to Demi. "We've taught Jesse a very simple way of looking at human interaction," I tell her evenly. "Based on the people he's known here, although most of them are gone. He didn't mean anything by it."

"I know," she says, her eyes fixed on the meat which appears to be burning on one side. She reaches forward and begins turning the spit, proving that she has some degree of common sense. "Kids say the darndest things, right?"

I force out a smile, then change the subject. "But forget all of that. If you're coming out with me tomorrow, you're going to need more protection than a cloak made from a sleeping bag."

An hour later we're chewing on the remnants of dinner and watching as Demi puts on increasingly ridiculous-looking outfits. Even Bianca's stopped crying enough to watch from a distance, and she shakes her head as the latest helmet slips and falls forward to cover Demi's face.

"I told you the bucket would be no good," Bianca says. "It's the wrong shape."

"Everything's the wrong shape," Demi mutters, trying to lift the thing off. "Can't I go with the first option?"

Meaning the platelike piece of metallic stuff which could be tied to her head but not reshaped.

"It doesn't cover your neck," Jesse half-sings, half-shouts, which for him means he's both overtired and overexcited. "You need to cover your neck!"

"You need to cover your neck," Bianca and I agree in unison.

"Not much good you replacing Jerrold if you get your throat slashed by a scav the next day," Bianca says darkly.

I shoot her a look. Demi doesn't seem to have heard (the bucket on her head probably dulls her hearing, which is a mark against its safety), but Bianca and I have already had this conversation. She pointed out earlier that Demi had come through the Gate a day after Jerrold disappeared – quite a coincidence, considering that there's an average of nine years between Gate-travellers. Maybe they swapped places.

That's nonsense, of course. Bianca's too panicked and grief-stricken to think straight, since we hadn't lost a person when I came through, or when Sigge and Bianca arrived together a few years before me.

The deaths came later.

"And you got what you wanted, Liam," Bianca adds quietly, her tone tainted with what sounds like malice. "A younger woman without any baggage."

My lips tighten. My relationship with Bianca is complicated

to say the least, and I've been wondering how she feels about Demi's arrival. I'm not surprised she's unhappy, because it's her general state of being since Dominic…disappeared. She blames me for what happened with him, while at the same time resenting me for not pursuing a relationship when there are no other choices. Dom hadn't minded the age gap, but I do. That, and my guilt over what happened.

"I haven't got anyone," I reply just as quietly. "And everyone has baggage. Let's just focus on finding Jerrold, alright?"

Bianca doesn't say anything else, which is a relief. She doesn't usually pursue arguments, though. None of us do. With so few of us here, all relying on each other to survive, we can't afford to have arguments or domestic spats. We can't afford to fight over anything nonessential or upset each other if we don't need to.

Which is why I don't tell her that Jerrold must be dead. He can't have gone through the Gate; we've never managed to send a living person through…or a dead one. Poor Sigge proved that.

And I know Jerrold would have come back if he could. There's a part of me that hopes he's still out there, just waiting for the chance to wander back. But in my heart I know he's gone, and that hurts.

I push the pain aside and focus on our newest survivor. Clueless, soft Demi with her sleeping bag attached at the hip and her apparent hatred of bugs, germs and eating anything that didn't come out of a packet. Heaven forbid we tell her what's in the breadish until she's too hungry to say no. I barely stopped Jesse from blurting it out earlier.

But then I know well that some lies are told out of kindness, because some truths are too harsh and painful to hear until there's no other option.

And I'm not talking about the breadish.

I don't sleep well that night. I never do, but this time I'm kept awake worrying about Jerrold, thinking about Demi. Wondering what will happen to Jesse. Not wanting him to be alone, but knowing it's inevitable with the infection in Bianca's leg and the age difference. Thinking of how Demi will be so destroyed when she hears the truth, and how I'm so ashamed that I'm glad she's here.

She thinks I'm a weirdo, a savage wildman, but I'm still thrilled she's here. And that's even after what Jesse told me she said last night.

I'm up as soon as the faintest morning light reflects its way down the mirrored skylights. Demi proves harder to wake, and the other two are stirring by the time she crawls out from under her sleeping bag. Still, soon enough we're on our way out for another day of searching.

"We'll go in the other direction today," I tell her. "We've checked everywhere Jerrold should have gone and he's nowhere to be seen." I pause. "Oh, another rule: make sure you tell someone where you're going, and don't go anywhere else. Then we can find you if you go missing."

Demi makes a grunting noise that might be agreement. She hasn't said much all morning, and I stop to look at her properly. Her new helmet/neck protection is attached, and she's finally given up her sleeping bag in lieu of a hastily built spear, bag and shield set. But her eyes are half-closed, and her movements are slow and graceless.

"Oi. Are you even awake?"

She grunts again. Not like a pig, more like a sullen teenager.

Hmm.

"Demi," I say in a low, urgent tone. "There's a spider."

Her eyes pop wide open and she looks around in a panic. "Where!? Where is it?"

"There's no spider," I say, not hiding my amusement. "I just wanted to see if it would wake you up properly."

"That's just mean." She rubs her free hand over her eyes, still studying the land around her suspiciously as if my threat of a spider might have conjured one up. "I was already awake. I just don't like to talk before eight a.m."

"There are no clocks here," I point out. "How would you know what time it is?"

"It *feels* like it's before eight." She scowls. "Any chance of coffee? I'm starting to get a headache from caffeine withdrawal."

A whole day without coffee, wow. "Nope. Sorry."

"Figures."

We trot along in silence for a while. I think on how being out here with company reminds me of all my old hunts with Dominic. I've been so used to walking in silence, but now someone is listening, suddenly I have plenty to say. "I used to be a night owl," I say casually. "Stayed up late watching TV or on the 'net, slept in till midday. Exercised if I had to. But now I'm up with the dawn."

Demi shoots me a half-smile. "Hard to see you as anything except what you are now."

"A fitness god and survival expert?" I joke. I shoot her a sidelong glance. "Not a cannibal, though."

Her eyes widen and an expression of panic comes over her face. "Uh…"

"Jesse told me about your bad joke," I continue, more

calmly than I felt when he first recounted the tale. "I assume you've decided we're safe now, if you're out here alone with me."

There's a long silence. Then Demi says defensively, "I have to prepare for the worst. You could be the best people in the world – not that that's saying much – but I don't know that. And if you do turn out to be dangerous to me, what can I do to stop you? Beat you with my tinfoil hat?"

It wasn't tinfoil, but whatever. "Yet you're out here with me," I point out.

She sighs. "Yet I'm out here with you. You seem like a good guy, Liam, and I won't forget that you've probably saved my life a couple of times-"

"I *definitely* saved your life."

"Fine, definitely. But if you do turn out to be a creep…"

"You'll beat me with your tinfoil hat," I say dryly, trying not to be offended. I mean, I am a stranger to her, and I can't convince her of my good intentions just by my words. I have to show them through my actions over time. "Understood. And if *you* turn out to be a creep, then I'll make you use the outside loo."

Demi raises an eyebrow. "What constitutes being a creep for me? And do you even *have* an outside loo?"

"Telling children horrifying jokes is pretty creepy." I wave an arm at the wilderness around us. We've travelled well away from the compound by now, and I'm doing my best not to lose focus from our dangerous surroundings. This area slopes steeply downwards, covered in scraggly forest and interspersed with ancient ruins. "And this is the outside loo. Just choose a tree."

She laughs harder than I expected, enough for me to check around us for any animal reactions. Even though it's too loud, it still makes my spirits lift.

Maybe she *does* like me a little.

Demi

Liam's comment about outdoor loos makes me think of Tara and her threats about 'the last real toilet on this track'. If only she knew where I am now.

I've been away a whole day now, assuming time passes the same as back on Earth. They will have surely noticed I'm missing, at least because I haven't helped take down my tent.

My mood drops. My disappearance will ruin their trip; there's no question of that. But it's not as if it's within my control. I just need a way to prove where I've been once I get back through the Gate…

The ground underfoot becomes steep and a little unstable, with loose rocks poking out from the clay soil. I turn my attention to watching my footing, and we're silent for some time.

The pervasive mist has drawn back, revealing a landscape that somehow manages to be both scrubby and overgrown. The glowing moon is still full and visible over the silhouetted horizon even as the morning sky lightens, but its visibility is fading by the minute.

Up ahead is a looming outline that I make out as some kind of building. Liam's walking slightly ahead of me now, and he pauses to look back at me. "We'll need to keep it down now," he murmurs. "I've set a trap up ahead, but sometimes something else gets to it before I do. We need to be prepared."

I nod, but nerves heighten my senses. I grip tighter onto the spear he made me last night, checking our surroundings warily. I'd thought we were out looking for Jerrold, but it seems to be a hunting trip as well.

Maybe *every* trip is a hunting trip.

Liam has just reached the edge of the overgrown building when I hear a strange sound. It's like when you blow across the top of a bottle, crossed with this weird rattling instrument I had as a kid.

I tense. "Did you hear that?!"

Liam doesn't respond, which makes me think that a) he doesn't want me to talk or b) he didn't hear the sound. I shuffle as quietly as I can to where he's standing, but I don't hear it again. It was probably just a bird or the sound of the wind. Wind can make all sorts of strange noises.

He points down at what looks like a pile of sticks and an empty loop of cord with a bit of grey fluff attached. "Whatever was in here got away, or something else got it, see?"

Ugh. I nod, but I'm secretly hoping that it was the first option. I might be OK with killing things when it's them or us – I think – but I'm not so good with targeting some small fluffy creature for dinner. "I'm not much of a hunter," I admit. "I don't like killing things."

"You don't say."

Just then my stomach growls violently, reminding me I haven't eaten properly in over twenty-four hours. "Except I guess I'll have to get used to it," I say glumly. "You can't be the only one bringing home the bacon for four people, haha."

"Five if we find Jerrold," Liam says, but his tone lacks sincerity. He reaches into his pocket and holds out a handful of something brown. "Breakfast."

"Thanks." I take the breadish, although if he's pulling something brown out of his pocket, I'd much prefer it was chocolate. "I guess I'll get used to this too."

But a few seconds later I almost throw the food away from me in horror. "It's got a bug's leg in it!"

"Let me see." Liam examines the tainted brown lump, then picks off something long and thin and tosses it to the ground. He holds out the remainder. "I'd say it was extra protein, but I don't think you'd find it funny. Go on, it's safe now."

It most certainly is not. "If there was a leg in there, then a whole bug must've fallen in," I explain tersely. "A big one, by the look of that leg. It'll be ground up in the mix, and I really don't plan to eat bug today."

He lets out a long, slow breath through his nose, looking at his feet. Then he lifts his head and holds out the other lump of suspicious brownness. "Have my piece if it bothers you so much, but you'll have to get used to things not being supermarket-clean. Breadish is from ancient alien machinery, Demi, and bugs *are* going to fall in once in a while. If you don't eat it, you'll starve. Anyway, haven't you heard that back home, people eat eight spiders a year in chocolate bars?"

"That's a myth," I tell him. "Someone made it up to prove that people will believe anything if they see it on the internet. Case in point."

But I take the breadish anyway, because he's right. If I don't eat it, I'll eventually starve. I'm already feeling slow and cranky from hunger (and lack of coffee), and if I don't eat, I'll probably get sneaked up on by some horrible, oddly named creature.

As Liam resets the trap, I nibble at the food and take the chance to study the building we're up against. From this close I can see that beneath all the overgrowth, the walls are in surprisingly good condition. Plain, blocky, definitely not wood or brick, but still solid.

"I think this is a door," I say in surprise. I poke at the curved indentation in the wall. "Have you been inside?"

"There's nothing in there except junk," Liam replies, not looking up from his work. "Feel free to go in, but make sure you go spear-first, and carefully, OK? That means-"

"Check for sounds, smells, and anything that looks out of place," I cut in, echoing his earlier instructions. "I hear you."

It's a bit of effort to work out the door handle – sort of pull, push, pull again – and then I'm in. But the inside of the building proves to be a disappointment. It's one big room, maybe the size of home base's main room, and it's empty except for a wall full of unused shelving and a fine layer of debris on the floor. There's one boxy shape in the room's centre, kind of like a kitchen island or low cupboard. I open its smoothly swinging door to find it's empty too.

I poke at the scattered debris with the end of my spear, checking there's nothing alive in there, but it's clear that this place has been pretty well sealed up.

Maybe the debris is what's left of whatever was stored here. Maybe the junk filling home base's corridors came from places like this.

"It might be a mess," I muse aloud, "but it really is fascinating." The remnants of an alien civilisation. All I need to do is find a pyramid or two – perhaps with a tomb full of treasure in a handy size to take home – and my adventure will be complete.

I glance at the open door. I can't see Liam from here, but I've no doubt that he'll call me if he wants to leave. He seems that sort of person. I lay awake last night thinking about him, and about the others here. Unsurprisingly I couldn't sleep after everything that had happened.

I've been trying hard to hold it together; to stubbornly think of this as an impromptu camping trip rather than a miserable ordeal. That means not pondering how long I'll be stuck, but instead deciding that I *will* go home. It means not thinking about the lack of amenities and even groceries, but instead resigning myself to an odd diet for a while, and maybe dropping a dress size or two. It means not dwelling on how upset my family and friends will be to hear I'm missing, but instead planning how I'll explain my absence to them once I'm back.

I'm still not sure how that will go. I don't even know how to explain it to myself.

But I've come to a few conclusions about this place…about the Wilds. Liam's been here for years. Jesse's father was *born* here, so the Gate can't be that easy to use, or they would have left already. Which means I'll be lucky if I can get back anytime soon, or even in three months at the next quarter like Liam said. It might even take a few tries, which means…I could be here a while….

I find myself staring at the grubby alien wall, my lip sticking out like a toddler about to burst into tears. It's all very well to decide not to be upset, but it seems my body is still catching up with the idea. Underneath all this 'holding it together' is a monumental tantrum and panic attack just waiting for the chance to explode outwards.

Breathe. Breathe. Breathe.

Yep, breathing. I turn away from the wall and determinedly fix my thoughts back on what I *can* control. Not much, really, although I can ask Liam and Bianca what techniques they've already tried with the Gate so we don't waste time with double-ups. But it's a shame Jerrold is missing. Obviously for his own sake, but also because I'll feel like a jerk asking about the Gate before his situation is resolved. Either we'll find him...or we'll declare him dead.

Hopefully the first one.

The wind whistles through the open door, making that odd rattling noise I heard before. I move to the doorway since I haven't heard Liam in a while, but then I see him.

I almost can't believe my eyes.

Liam is frozen in a partially bent over position, his eyes half-closed. He's covered in a net of tiny glowing spots, with faint lines between each one.

He's also floating through the air in best horror movie tradition.

I suck in a long, eye-bugging breath, ready to scream for an exorcist. But then I see the ball hovering above him. About the size of a soccer ball, pale grey and utilitarian in appearance, it carries him sideways just above the ground. It flickers in and out of sight as if it reflects its surroundings, and it seems to be making that sound I'd mistaken for the wind.

Shite. There *are* still aliens around here – because this is surely some of their tech!

I haven't moved up till now. I haven't even called out – I've been too shocked. But now I realise that this alien ball thing is taking off with the one person capable of defending and hunting for the other three of us, and who knows what they're planning to do with him?

I spring into action, gripping my spear in clammy fingers, and creep after it. Should I stab it? I wonder. Bash it with a rock? I feel terrified and useless and strangely numb.

Everything seems to be happening in slow motion as the ball comes to a halt over a nearby flat patch of ground, just out of sight of where it caught Liam. I can now see other, smaller balls in a circle around it, like a sci-fi version of Stonehenge. The ball seems to release Liam and he slumps forward, but then the same lit-up net appears from the new balls. The lights brighten and the sound gets louder, and I panic.

I race forward and whack at the nearest balls with my makeshift spear. With a *whsst-zzz* sound, the closest one falls away. But then the spear is yanked right out of my hand and pulled into the network too.

Ahhh!

The light-net is growing brighter, and the buzzing noise is increasing. Now I can feel it vibrating through the ground. My heart pounding, I throw myself at Liam's fallen body, grabbing him by the nearest piece of armour. I try to yank him away from the light-net but the sound increases until it's all I can hear, until it's vibrating through my body; and just when my teeth start to rattle...I let go.

There's an intense flash of light, and the sound stops. The light dies. And as I blink to clear the spots from my vision, I see that the hovering balls have vanished...

...and so has Liam.

Chapter 5

Demi

First I run around in circles, checking on each side of the small building and behind scraggly trees as if Liam could have been deposited there. I do find my spear nearby, seemingly rejected by whoever makes these decisions. (To teleport or not to teleport?) Then when it becomes clear he's gone – really, truly gone – I sit down in a heap on the dry ground.

Didn't see this one coming. Although, it looks like the aliens prefer rugged, competent wildmen to whatever I have to offer.

Or they're coming back for you, inner Demi suggests unhelpfully.

Oh GOD. Please no. I wonder what they're planning to do with him, and a dozen nasty options spring to mind, mostly involving probing or experiments.

And what about Bianca and Jesse? What's going to happen to them? Who's going to hunt until we manage to reopen the Gate?

Can we reopen the Gate without Liam's help?

I swear fervently inside my head, then again under my breath, since I don't want to attract any boggarts, scavs or…aliens…

A strange sound cuts through my quiet rant, sending chills

down my spine. I turn slowly to see the first hovering ball directly to my left, barely an arm's length away. It doesn't have any eyes – nothing except a faintly glowing gold-grey surface – but I swear it's looking at me.

My hand tightens on my spear, then in one panic-fuelled move I swing it. The hoverball proves to be lighter than it looks – I barely feel my spear connect and it goes spinning away through the air.

Then I scramble to my feet faster than I even know I can move, and next thing I'm scrabbling at the nearby door of the abandoned alien building, the one I was exploring when Liam was taken. I throw myself inside then try to slam the door shut. But it's heavy, and it closes slowly – oh so slowly – before shutting with an unimpressive *click*. I lean back against the door, panting for breath and feeling as though my heart is going to pound its way out of my chest.

The hover-ball is nowhere in sight. Maybe I've lost it?

Then I hear the sound again. The strange, could-be-wind kind of sound that accompanies the ball. And next thing I can see it in the corner of my eye – it's come right through the wall.

"Go away!" I cry. "Leave me alone!" I swing at it with my spear but it just moves neatly to the side, dodging all my blows. The faint humming sound grows louder, just like when Liam was taken.

Oh, no you don't.

I swing at it once more – missing yet again – then run for the blocky furniture/kitchen island in the centre of the room. I duck behind it, then scramble inside the cupboard-like alcove underneath. The little door swings shut after me, and then I'm in darkness, my knees pressed against my chest and my face against my knees.

I hear the sound again.

"Please, please," I plead into the darkness. "Just leave me alone. And give Liam back! But leave me alone."

The hover-ball sound comes again, but I don't see it. Instead everything around me is buzzing and rattling. It's worse than coming through the Gate. The darkness takes on a new quality; like a faint, yellow-grey light. I feel like the whole world lurches underneath me, a terrible sense of displacement combined with that bone-rattling noise and growing light. Everything goes bright white for just a moment before settling back into cramped, quiet darkness.

Then the little cupboard door swings open.

I should have known before seeing that something had changed. The sound here is different – the very air feels different. But instead of looking out into a dim, debris-filled abandoned hut, through the door is an entirely new scene.

The cupboard and I are now in a much larger, brighter room, as big as a warehouse, but there are boxes everywhere of all shapes and sizes. Everything looks so clean and cold and sterile in comparison to where we've just been, and I can't tell if it's all really bright white or if it's just my eyes playing up. I can't identify anything in particular, except I see more of those grey spheres zipping around. They don't seem to notice me.

Then I see Liam. He's lying on the floor just across the massive room, as if he's just another parcel being transported. He's definitely unconscious, but the light-net is gone along with its mini hover-balls. Instead he's surrounded by a sheer wall of light, like a transparent box. The square of floor he lies on is marked with bright orange instead of white, like a direction to 'lay abductees here'.

I rush over and shove my hands straight through the light wall, grabbing him by the shoulder. It feels like pushing through a thick, warm layer of paste, but I ignore it and shake his prone body. "Liam. Liam. Liam. Wake up."

But he doesn't move at all; his eyes in a creepy half-open state that makes me cringe. I grab him tighter and try to pull him away from the light box, but he may as well be made of concrete. I can't move him an inch.

"LIAM!!" I bellow. I try to move my hands away from his armour, intending to give his bearded face a good, revitalising slap, but realise my skin is sticking to him. I pull my hands away with a gasp of dismay, and a stringy, gluey mess stretches between us for a few seconds before springing back to his body. Ugh – he's being covered in a clear, sticky gel that's crept up from the ground underneath us.

I cry out in disgust and shuffle back. The gel is tacky under my knees and boots too, making each step feel like walking through well-used chewing gum. Something hits the back of my calf and I almost trip over. I turn to see it's yet another grey hover-ball.

This time I'm certain someone's watching me. I've got the sense of presence, of not being alone, but nothing else happens. I stare at the ball warily for a few more seconds, then glance back to Liam.

I gasp. The shiny gel has spread to cover Liam's face and hands, and he now looks like he's been set in varnish. "You can't preserve him!" I cry accusingly to the hover-ball. "He's still alive!"

Isn't he?!

I try to grab him again – more out of stubbornness than expecting a good result – but suddenly the light wall turns solid. My hands are slingshotted out of the space and slap me in the chest and the face. Then there's that terrible buzzing sound and feeling again, a burst of orangey-white light, and Liam vanishes.

Again.

I slowly turn and stare at the single grey sphere still hovering behind me. Maybe I'm in shock, but in this moment I feel no fear. If it's going to cover me in glue, knock me out or even drop me in the depths of the Pit of Despair, I can't change it.

"This is kidnapping," I tell it fiercely. "And you're being a terrible stereotype. You should put us both back right away, back where you stole us from." I pause as a thought occurs. "Unless you know how to open the Gate. Then open it…then put us back, alright?"

The hover-ball hovers silently. I've no idea if it's registered my words, or even cares. I brace myself, waiting for the buzzing to come back and for me to be teleported somewhere else, but it doesn't move. Somehow the inaction is worse than any violence.

Then the ball vanishes too.

"Typical," I mutter, but I'm relieved to see it go.

But it's too soon to sigh in relief. Footsteps sound behind me, and I turn with trepidation to see a huge figure. Clad in white, just like everything else, with two arms, two legs and a head in all the usual places. But its eyes are glittering black ovals that take up half of its otherwise blank face, and its naked, glossy skull curves backwards and arcs down to connect with its back.

The thing has to be eight feet tall…and it's looking at me.

I'm petrified. For a moment I can't move – frozen into place and unable to turn away from that thing's shiny blank face. This must be what it feels like to be a possum in car headlights.

I don't want to be run over. *I don't want to be varnished like Liam!*

Then in the next moment, a jolt of energy sizzles through me.

OW-

Part 2:
The Rule of Law

Chapter 6

Liam

Everything around me is white. The whiteness fills my vision, blinding me. My limbs are stiff and immobile, and my whole body feels wrong. So very wrong.

There's an itch on the back of my leg, but I can't move to scratch it.

This is a nightmare, but nothing changes when I open my eyes. Or were they already open, I wonder?

A few moments pass and the whiteness clarifies itself into walls around me. I realise that I haven't been hit on the head, and I'm not covered in a white blanket or even under a rockfall as I first thought. Maybe I'm hallucinating, but this feels pretty damn real.

I appear to be in some kind of…room? Or a space, anyway. It reminds me of a giant shower cubicle from back on Earth;the clean, shiny sort that's a cold white from top to bottom. Except I can't see any joins in the walls.

The last thing I remember is crouching over the sprung trap, putting the pieces back in place and wishing that Demi would take the time to learn rather than explore empty shacks. I didn't say anything to her at the time, although I decided that I would. And then…

...then there might have been a light, or that might be my imagination rather than memory, just based on where I am now. I recall there was a bright light when Dominic disappeared three years ago. But either way, it's starting to dawn on me that I haven't come here by accident.

Demi's comments about aliens come to mind, and I remember telling her that they were long gone. Now I'm having to eat my words, and they're even less palatable than breadish.

Oh, and I still can't move. I wiggle my neck, trying to look down, but don't manage much more than a sideways shuffle, complete with squeaking sound.

My neck isn't supposed to squeak when I move.

There's no pain, though, so I wiggle around more, managing to turn (squeakily) until I catch a glimpse of someone next to me out of the corner of my eye. It's another man, spread-eagled against the same wall and looking back at me with what I imagine is the same sense of dismay I'm feeling. He's wearing white – or something pale – and he's clean-shaven. Young, then, but with dark hair.

"Hey," I croak. "What's going on?"

The guy's lips move too.

"What? I didn't- Oh."

It's my reflection. What a doofus. But I haven't seen my face without a beard since just after I arrived on this world, and I'm sure I never used to have so much pale, hairless skin.

Has someone *shaved* me?

The indignity of the idea gives me energy to wiggle more forcefully, until I can turn my head properly sideways and even glance downwards. I can't see much, but I can see enough.

They *have* shaved me. Whoever brought me here has

depilated me as hairless as a preteen boy. Maybe even a preteen vampire boy, because I had no idea I was so pale. I'm actually not wearing anything except a pair of white briefs and my own skin, which hasn't seen sunlight in many years in the Wilds' cold, overcast climate.

And those aren't *my* briefs. My single pair fell apart a year or two after I arrived, and well after I should have stopped wearing them.

I can't see my hands and feet. They disappear into the wall, as if the whole thing is made of modelling clay and someone decided they wanted me to stay put.

It's working.

"Hello?" I call out again. My throat feels odd and thickly coated in something. It isn't painful, more like I've been eating custard but haven't bothered to swallow it properly. "Hello? Can anyone hear me?"

There's a faint chiming from somewhere, and the wall in front of me turns transparent. I can see it's still there, but I can also clearly see through to the person standing on the other side. It's a bald Caucasian guy with a mad grin on his face. He looks short from where I'm hanging, and he wears a stiff, baggy white T-shirt/tunic thing that looks like it was made for a much larger person. There's a deep dimple creased in one cheek, and his perfect teeth are as white as the tunic.

Why so much freaking white?

I have a few moments of absolute confusion. I know this guy – why do I know this guy?

Then I realise who I'm looking at, and my jaw drops.

Demi

I don't want to be varnished! I don't-...wait.

I'm now lying on the floor, my face resting on the back of my hand. I sit up, pulling my hand away from my cheek, and my skin peels apart with a distinctive sound, like your legs do when you get up from a plastic chair while wearing shorts. I stare down at my hand in dismay. It looks like I'm wearing a thick mitten made of shiny, clear dried glue. I can't even wiggle my fingers, and it doesn't take long to realise my whole body has been given the same treatment, clothing and all.

I pat at my face, and while my mittened hands are useless for detail, I can feel my face is also layered in this same gunk. Fortunately I can breathe and open my mouth just fine.

But damn it – I said I *didn't* want to be varnished!

At least I'm alive, I remind myself. That probably means Liam is too.

And I see I'm not in the shipping warehouse-type room anymore. Now there's a brightly lit wall just an arm's length from my face. I turn to see one in every direction – and high above me, too.

I'm in a box. A bright, shiny white box. Apparently there are no other colours available here. The walls aren't quite opaque as I'd thought – as I move closer to them, they turn somewhat transparent. I stumble forward and press myself against the barrier, squinting to see through.

Two hulking figures come into focus, and I lurch backwards in dismay. But I can't unsee them. They're clearly alien, identical to the first bug-eyed figure I saw, except that one is a little shorter than the other. The taller alien is gesticulating wildly at the shorter one, whose arms are folded in an unimpressed manner. Their facial expressions don't change at all – as blank as ever – but I get the idea they're arguing. The shorter one doesn't move, and finally the taller one throws its arms in the air and storms away.

Then the shorter one turns towards my box-prison. Even with no nose or mouth I can tell I have its attention, and as it moves closer, I step back fearfully. Thinking of it as 'shorter' was deceptive – they were both further away than I'd realised. Now, with it right outside my box, it's tall enough that my eyes are only level with its abdomen. It's easily seven feet tall...maybe more.

Gulp.

I don't want this thing's attention. I'm shrinking back, shaking worse than any time out in the Wilds, because I know that animals might kill me, but it'd never be with malice. Intelligent beings can be so much worse.

I'm waiting...shaking...for several minutes, and I don't dare close my eyes for fear of what it will do when I'm not looking. But the alien just stands there, its buglike black eyes seeming fixed on me.

I start to feel silly at my fearful reaction, so I stand up straight and study the alien right back. Apart from its size and face, it's remarkably humanoid. It even has what looks like a normal-shaped hand within a translucent mitten.

I raise my own gooped-up hand in a brief, shaky wave. "Hi."

The alien cocks its head to the side. The mittens show it's wearing some kind of suit, and I start to recognise its posture as possibly 'exasperated'. A bit tense in the shoulders, with hands on hips. Kind of reminds me of my mother.

"Do you speak English?" I try again. I'm aiming to come across as friendly but intelligent, i.e. the sort of being you wouldn't want to perform experiments on. I've also heard that if you're kidnapped, you should try to connect with the kidnapper. Make sure they see you as a person. Surely it can't be any different if you're kidnapped by aliens. "I'm Demi. A human with, um, thoughts and feelings and dignity and nerve receptors and all that. And, ah, I'd appreciate if you didn't...probe me, please?"

As I speak, the giant alien's appearance begins to change. Its smooth, blank white face recedes into its black, buglike eyes, which then disappears over the curve of its domed skull and then into the back of its neck.

It dawns on me that the whole thing was a helmet. Obviously. And underneath the helmet is something that looks far more...human.

It – he – looks male. His skin is yellow-brown with a sheen to it, like polished oak, and his features are sharper than any human I've seen, with precise lines around the bridge of his hawklike nose and his jaw, almost like he's been crudely carved from wood. He has small ears and a short silver wedge on his head where a human would have hair. It's shiny too, and it doesn't move as he leans forward, down to where I'm standing close to the barrier.

This close, he seems even more giant. Gianter. Giganticus. His face alone must be twice the size of mine, and my eyes widen till they hurt as they hold his. His irises are as silver as his hair-wedge, and stand out startlingly against the contrasting tone of his skin.

He taps once on the barrier between us, and it all flashes green for a moment. Then his lips move, and a robotic voice echoes through the chamber. *"Yuuu-maaan."*

My mouth goes dry. That doesn't sound good.

Liam

I stare down at that bald, pale, familiar stranger grinning at me through the transparent wall, and my brain seems to short-circuit. *"Dominic!?"*

"Yes!" bald Dominic shouts, his grin still splitting his face. If I thought I'd been shaved hairless, they've done far worse to my friend. Even his eyebrows are gone. "Liam, I thought you were dead!"

I jolt at that. "No, you can't have," I argue. "I thought *you* were dead. Dom, you just disappeared! Have you been here all this time?"

"Yes! And I *did* think you were dead, because last I saw you, you were bleeding from the face, and the aliens wouldn't tell me anything, and I was *ssooo* worried about the others- um." He slams his hands up against the clear barrier, then presses his shiny, happy face between them. "I'm sorry you're here...but I'm glad you're here. I *missed* you."

Joy is bubbling up inside me in spite of the terrible situation. It's really him. My best friend who's so naive and clueless that he says whatever he thinks; who doesn't understand how terrible humans can be because he's never experienced a real human society. Who fell in love with the first woman he ever saw who wasn't his mother. Who I assumed had been dragged away and eaten by animals after our awful argument three years ago.

He's been here…like a lab rat in a cage.

Damn. Looks like aliens can be terrible too.

"They wouldn't even talk to me for ages," Dominic continues rapidly. "I've been here all alone in this room the whole time, wondering about you and Dad and-. And I *missed* you, but I was happy you weren't here because you were safe, and now you're not…" Tears begin streaming from his blue eyes, and his grin twists into a grimace. "Ah, I'm sorry you're here, Lee."

He'd given me the nickname even though Liam doesn't need shortening, just because 'that's what friends do'. But with every word, my blood grows colder. "What have they done to you, Dom?" I ask quietly. "Did they hurt you?"

He's silent for a long moment. Then when he finally answers, his tone is dull and quiet. "They would put me to sleep. And then I'd wake up, and I'd be sick. Or…different." He wiggles his fingers at me, and I notice for the first time that the tips of several of them are an odd silvery colour rather than his usual beige flesh tone.

My breath catches, and I start to notice other abnormalities. Not just the hairlessness – they've done that to me too. But more odd patches of silvery skin. Even the tip of one ear. His too-white teeth – this, a guy who'd never once visited a dentist or even had access to toothpaste. The skin on his forearms looks odd, like the light falls across it and gives it a whiter criss-crossed texture.

"The marks on your arms," I say. "Is that just the light…?"

Dominic looks down at his pale forearms, where fine

crosshatching covers every inch of exposed skin. His smile is now completely gone. "It's not the light."

It's scarring, I realise. What have they been doing to him?!

His lips tighten, and he whispers, "Don't trust them, Lee. They're *cruel*."

I won't. And I realise in that moment that we're in a world of trouble.

Crap. I hope they didn't spot Demi. I haven't missed that Dominic hasn't mentioned Bianca, Jerrold or Jesse, or even asked about them either. Surely he's trying to keep their existence secret from the aliens, but he doesn't know about Demi.

And Jerrold's missing anyway, presumed dead. I consider my words, then decide there's nothing to lose. "Your dad didn't come home from checking the Gate two days ago," I say casually. "I was looking for him when I was...captured."

Dom's expression suddenly brightens, enough that I jolt within my restricted position on the wall. "Oh!" he exclaims. "Dad's here, Liam! He's in the room on the other side of me!"

Relief washes over me and I slump down on the wall as far as my restraints will allow, which isn't much. "Thank God." I was convinced he was dead, and I'd been searching because I had to at least try to find him before telling the others he was gone forever.

"He's not here right now," Dominic says more seriously. "But they should bring him back soon." He looks over his shoulder, then moves away from the barrier between us. It turns back into an opaque, frosted white.

A minute passes, then Dominic reappears at the barrier. "He's back," he announces. "But he's asleep, stuck on the wall just like you."

"Does he look…whole?" I ask with dread.

Dominic's lips tighten. "It could take a while to show if they've given him the virus. Besides, his hands are hidden, just like yours."

Shite. True. I wiggle my fingers in sudden panic, but they hardly move inside whatever's holding me to the wall. And is that an ache in my wrist, or am I imagining it? "Did you say virus?"

"It's the scav sickness." He shrugs. "They call it something different, but that's why we're here. The aliens are terrified of catching it because it makes them really, really sick. So they gave it to me, then tested all sorts of cures."

"Bastards." I mutter. I've seen what the scav sickness does to humans over a period of years – infections that appear everywhere and never really go away. Kind of like leprosy, but fatal before you'd lose limbs.

That's what Jerrold said happened to Alby, one of the earlier survivors. I've been waiting for it to happen to me too ever since I got scav claws to the eye, but I never get more than the occasional infected spot in random places.

Bianca hasn't been so lucky. Her knee is wrecked, even though the original scratch was on her hip. The sickness gets into the blood.

"Do any of the cures work?" I ask.

Dominic looks down at his hands with their silver-tipped fingers. "I kept getting sicker and sicker, and I'd wake up and find more silver patches where I'd been…hurt."

Where he'd lost flesh to infection, he clearly means.

"That was their way of fixing me. But I haven't had any injuries or sores in the last few months," he continues. "There's a new alien running this place now, and things have been a bit better since he arrived. They used to ignore me completely, although there's a kind of translator that works sometimes so I hear a bit of what they're saying. This new one tried to talk to me directly once, like I'm a real person, but his English wasn't good." Dominic shakes his head. "A few months sore-free doesn't mean I'm cured, though. And I wouldn't trust the new alien as far as I could throw him. He's exactly like the others. A monster."

For all of our sakes, I hope Dominic is wrong. One less-monstrous alien might make all the difference to our survival.

Then Dominic crooks his head to the side, looking at me curiously. "Lee, is one of your eyes silver?"

I go to touch the eye in question, but of course I can't move my arms. I tell him about my experience of the day he vanished – presumed dead – and how I'd woken up with scav wounds and a weirdly pale eye. "I figured I was lucky to be alive," I say, "but now I'm not so sure. Why would the aliens take you and not me?"

He's still staring. "Probably because you'd just been scratched by a scav and they knew you were tainted. That's what they call it when someone has the scav sickness. But it was good of them to patch you up back then, even if they left you behind." He scowls. "They're not usually that thoughtful."

"Patch me up?"

He wiggles his silver-tipped fingers. "Silver means you've been fixed in some way."

The answer dawns. "I've got a fake eye," I say in shock.

A fake *alien* eye. It works perfectly, because my eyesight hasn't changed.

But that's just one more shock on top of all the others. Some shocks are good – like my friend is alive, when I thought he'd been dragged off and eaten by animals. Jerrold, my second dad, is alive too. Some are bad – we're at the mercy of unmerciful beings. Bianca and Jesse are alone in home base. And Demi's nowhere to be seen.

Figures that when I finally meet a girl, not only is she uninterested, but I get abducted by aliens the next day.

Demi

"Pardon?" I squeak.

"*Yuuu-maaan cheeldah,*" the robotic voice says in low, ominous tones.

My eyes bug even wider, and I feel my lip quiver. Oh God. Please. No. Whatever he's threatening – no.

His eyes widen at my expression, then he frowns and begins swishing a hand madly through the air. "*Z'foh. N'yost. Nyet. Non. Nein.* Ah… No."

He leans in towards me again. "Do you understand me now?"

The voice echoing through my chamber now sounds far more normal, both in tone and pace, and I perk up a little. He doesn't sound half as frightening with this translator voice, and it'll be easier to beg for my life (and dignity) if he knows what I'm saying. "Yes! I can understand you." But my lips are still trembling. I can't help myself. "Are you going to hurt me now?"

To my shock, the alien man's face creases into an intensely sympathetic expression. "Most certainly not! The Perfected laws forbid harming children, even those unlike us."

Oh. My anxiety levels immediately drop. Giganticus has a conscience, then. And...er...thinks I'm a child. Really, it could be worse.

"Although," the alien continues, "there are those who do not follow those particular laws, who I would not trust with an infant *polcaht*, let alone a sapient creature, let alone a human child." His silver eyebrows lower into a worried expression. "We'll get you cleaned up, little Dee-mee, then we'll decide what to do."

I realise that's what he was trying to say earlier when he sounded so terrifying – 'human child'. He's at least got my species right. And he remembers my name, sort of. "Thank y-"

Suddenly I'm blasted with a cloud of pale smoke that tingles and burns like air from a freezer. I suck in a breath of the stuff and it burns on the inside too. I bend over, coughing and spluttering, and finally the cloud dissipates.

"Apologies," the alien says softly. "Testing for cleanliness. Ah." There's a faint chiming sound and a flash of green light that briefly transforms my little chamber. "Good news, Dee-mee. You are entirely syn-free."

I look up at the alien in disbelief. "I am?"

I mean, I'm what most people would call 'a good person' since I keep my hands to myself and try not to hurt others, but I wouldn't claim to be entirely sin-free. But then who could?

"The synaptic ynnsshelppnn*[no-translation]* nucleotide virus," he continues, watching me with earnest silver eyes. "Syn, yes? You do not have it."

"Oh." I wave a hand, even though I'm still off-balance from the sudden acid cloud bath. "Translation issues. Um. That's good news." Another virus, huh? We have enough of our own on Earth. I wonder if that's what Liam calls the scav sickness.

Liam! I'd almost forgotten him! "My friend!" I burst out suddenly. "He was taken just before me, and I saw him out in the warehouse – that big white room. Where is he?"

"The small, hairy adult male? He is also being cleansed. Unlike you, he *does* carry syn, so will need much longer."

It does make sense that syn and the scav sickness are one and the same. (Small, hairy) Liam told me he had it. "What are you going to do with us?" I ask. I can't help cringing a little at the whole situation, because in spite of this one's apparent friendliness, we've still been kidnapped and detained by non-humans. The whole situation has gone from bad to worse.

Giganticus shuffles and crouches so he's eye level with me, like I'd do to get friendly with a cute dog or a small child. "Dee-mee," he says, and his lips quirk. "You will not be harmed. And I will do everything I can to get you all back home."

'All'? Surely he only knows about Liam and I? "But I wasn't taken from my home," I reply carefully. "My home – my friend's home – is through this big square archway we call the Gate. That must be your people's technology, and we don't know how to work it. Can you open it and truly send us home?"

"That is my intention. Your people do not belong on our world."

He says it matter-of-factly, and I couldn't agree more. But my heart leaps in cautious hope. I'm so desperate to trust someone – anyone – who can help us, but is this alien even trustworthy? I hope so.

I meet his earnest silver eyes, and I don't look away. Feeling like the child he thinks I am, I ask, "Do you promise?"

"I promise, Dee-mee," the alien replies earnestly, and for

the first time I realise his mispronunciation of my name translates as 'little one' on the room's translator. "I will send you home, if it's the last thing I do."

Chapter 7

Liam

Dominic moves back and forth between my cell and Jerrold's, which appears to be on his other side. Then he bounces back to my side. "Dad's awake!" he tells me, pressing his palms flat against the wall between us. "I told him you were here too, and we're both very concerned about our pet dogs back home." He wiggles his non-existent eyebrows urgently. "The bitch and the puppy, left alone to fend for themselves. Do you think…do you think they'll be alright?"

For a few seconds I'm baffled, since I'm used to hearing 'bitch' in quite a different context, and we obviously don't have any pets. Dom's never even seen a dog – although Jerrold must have told him about them in glowing terms, since he seems to think they're a cross between a loyal bodyguard and a cuddly blanket.

But his urgent tone and worried expression gives away his real meaning, and I almost laugh in spite of our situation. So that's how he's choosing to discuss Bianca and Jesse without naming them. When this is all over – assuming it's ever over – I'll explain that he probably shouldn't compare his lady to a female dog.

"They're smart dogs," I say evenly, pushing down my own worry at Bianca and Jesse's situation. "You know there's the food dispenser."

We'll have to get back to them, though. Now I'm getting a sense of our location, and now we've got such good news and I don't need to be searching for Jerrold's dead body, our focus has to be on escaping. Bianca is injured, and Jesse's just a kid. They're both easy targets if anything goes wrong.

And never mind Demi. I actually forgot about her for a moment.

"But J- the puppy is so young," Dom persists. "And the bitch is injured."

This time I do laugh, because this conversation is so ridiculous, and because it's exactly what I was thinking.

"Is that funny?!" he asks in outrage.

"No, just…" I sigh, still half-laughing, but it's a grim laughter. "We can't do anything right now, can we? Nothing at all until the aliens get bored with us and send us home." Or we manage to escape ourselves, which is looking like a long shot. "Ah…is it just Jerrold on the other side? Is anyone else here?" Dominic looks baffled. "No. Why would there be?"

That means the aliens may not have found Demi, and I don't dare mention her now, not even as 'our new puppy'.

Dominic and I stare at each other for a while. My nose starts to itch, but of course I can't scratch it. I say so.

"Yeah, you'll get used to that sort of thing," he says knowingly. "I'd often get put in the wall after my…tests. It fixes you up, but it's horrible if you're itchy."

Dang it. And now my nose tickles even worse, because I know I can't touch it.

His lips twitch, then curve into a smile. "You do look so strange, Liam, all shiny and pale and stuck to the wall. I've never seen you so hairless."

I'd arrived through the Gate with two days' stubble, and

hadn't shaved since. "Back at you," I retort with a grin. "You look like a happy grub." So bald and pale and *white*.

He laughs. "At least there's something to smile about. It's been a while."

I can only imagine what his life has been like. We've had so little to smile about at home base, and at least we were free.

"Dad looks strange too," Dominic continues. "They cleaned him up and shaved his beard and most of his hair – I almost didn't recognise him."

"Say hello to him for me, will you? And tell him to warn me before he gets abducted next time. It's been a nasty couple of days, wondering where he was."

Dom takes me at my word – because of course he does – and disappears from his spot against the barrier. Thirty seconds later he returns. "Dad says something about a pot and a kettle. He asked if you're still stuck to the wall like a cut-price messianic figure. I said yes."

Now I'm grinning, because that's so like Jerrold. The man has spent most of his adult life as an involuntary survivalist/ hermit, but he hasn't lost his sense of humour. "Do you even know what that last thing is?"

"Nope."

I go to explain – and probably would have said something about religion, political figures and Superman – but then a bell chimes through my chamber.

It must've sounded in Dominic's too, because he stands up straight, all hint of a smile gone. "They're coming," he says. "Whatever you do, don't make them angry."

"Who's *they*?"

But Dominic disappears from the wall again, leaving it blank and frosty-white.

Then a moment later, someone appears at the wall directly in front of me. No, two figures. They both appear male, and they're simply enormous. Easily seven and a half, eight feet tall, and clothed from head to toe, with only their heads exposed. One wears white, right down to gloves and hood, and his yellowish eyes stand out from a glossy gold-brown face with sharp, unhappy features that are otherwise fairly humanlike.

With the other, I get an impression of dark blue fabric with ornate gold decorations, but it's his eyes that capture me. They're neon purple, a colour that would be stunning if it wasn't in such a malignant expression. This alien looks a lot like the one in white, but his features are a little narrower, his hood edged by golden tassel.

He's also looking at me like I'm something stuck on the bottom of his shoe.

I don't like this guy. I don't like him at all.

Purple Eyes' lip curls and his mouth moves. Then I hear a slightly robotic voice through the chamber's speaker. "This is the new one, Jud'or? It is visibly damaged."

A translator being piped directly into my prison cell. How useful.

"Mostly healed, High Priate Sy'lis," the yellow-eyed one replies, and it's translated in the same way. "He was with our original subject when we retrieved him three years ago, but we left this one behind since he was newly tainted. It looks like Peh'tra must have gone back and replaced his eye."

That confirms Dominic's theory about my silver eye. I decide like the alien in white better –Joodor – just because he's said 'he' rather than 'it'. (Also, whoever Petra is – thanks!)

"That was an unapproved use of valuable resources," Purple Eyes says coldly. "I expect she was reprimanded." He doesn't wait for a response before squinting at me. "And how long before we can expect to see a change in this one?"

"He was given Priate Krys'tof-Atem's new greyce formula this morning. The priate suggests improvements should be seen immediately."

"Hmm." Purple Eyes – High Priate Syliss – waves a hand, and I squint as a flash of red lights up my chamber. "Red light. Still tainted, even hours after being given the formula." He scoffs. "Krys'tof-Atem's so-called cure is a failure, as I expected. That Perfected is a disgrace."

White-clad Joodor bows respectfully, but doesn't comment on whoever is being verbally slaughtered. "We usually allow up to six days before declaring any new formula a failure."

Syliss makes a disparaging noise that doesn't translate well, and moves as if to leave.

But I'm over my initial shock at seeing these two, and I'm getting sick of being talked about as if I'm not here. I don't want to lose this opportunity. "Hi," I call out. "Syliss, was it? Joodor?"

Both aliens stop and stare at me with identical appalled expressions.

"By Atem," the High Priate says. "Is it talking to us?"

The second alien clears his throat. "Priate Krys'tof-Atem arranged for translators to be built into the quarantine chambers, so it will have understood what we're saying, yes."

That was a helpful little explanation. I soldier on. "Yes, I do understand, and I am talking to you. I'm Liam. Nice to meet you. And if you've given us some kind of cure to scav sickness, then thank you, but you can't just kidnap intelligent beings and keep them prisoner. We have a home, and we'd like to go back to it as soon as possible."

They're still staring, and I add belatedly, "Thank you."

Better to be extra polite with the alien captors, right?

"Quite a list of demands," the High Priate finally bites out. "Is there anything else it would ask of us, I wonder?"

He's looking at Joodor, not me, but why not? "Actually, I'd like to come down off the wall," I say.

The priate waves a hand, and with a slight sting, my hands and torso are abruptly released. But my ankles are still connected, and I spill away from the wall to land face first on the floor, hard. "*Ow...*"

A moment later my feet are released, and I fumble to my hands and knees. My head is spinning; my cheekbone and shoulder aching from where I landed. The cuts over my eye sting, and there's a harsh smear of black on the clean white floor where I landed. It lines up with where my face hit. I raise a hand to my eye area, and my fingers come away red. The old scav wounds have split open again – but the blood is showing *black* on the cell floor...

"That darkness symbolises the taint the creature carries," the High Priate says in much the same cold tone, as if he knows what I'm thinking. He's looking at Joodor, but it's clear the message is for me. "The greyce formula may one day clear it of the syn virus, but it will never be clear of that taint. It was saturated with it when it came into our world, the filthy little barbarian. So it's in no position to make demands of we Perfected. It will stay here, serving our superior race until its frail body gives out and is discarded with the rest of the refuse."

I sit in shocked silence as the High Priate steps away from the wall, followed by the second alien, and it reverts to plain, cold white.

That...didn't go well.

Demi

The silver-eyed alien's name is Kris. It's actually something longer, but his real name didn't translate well.

And boy, he's nice. So, so nice, and I lap it up. Perhaps the disastrous last few days make him seem extra-wonderful in comparison, but I'm drawn to his kindness like a struggling plant reaches for the sunlight. I can only hope it's not an act.

He talks to me while I'm in the chamber being blasted with tingling air some more – not for cleansing this time, but for practical purposes. With the small room's helpful translator, he tells me exactly what's happening. It's not half as scary when I know what's going on.

The tingling on my skin is the protective coating shrinking down from ultra-thick and awful to an ultra-thin coat layer like he's wearing. Kris says the coating is normal, and it stops skin particles, hair and germs flaking off.

A hygiene thing, then. I could've guessed these aliens have a hygiene obsession, just judging by the cold whiteness of everything around us. A single speck of dirt would be glaringly obvious against any of these sterile-looking surfaces.

The gunky glue coating is removed except for a thin layer that leaves my longish dark hair as malleable as a roll of clay. I twist it into a bun on the top of my head, and it stays, just as if it's been glued into place. Maybe Kris has hair after all, rather than that wedge of silver, but it's so glued you can't tell otherwise.

And when my skin is almost clear of the coating and I can wiggle my fingers freely again, there's another puff of spray and my bright white clothing changes colour. Within seconds it's a sunny shade of yellow. For children, Kris tells me, since white is for patients and researchers. I even have a pair of matching booties, a bit like babies wear back home. Classy.

As I'm being cleaned up, Kris tells me about his people, the Perfected, who are at terrible risk from the syn virus. Apparently it hits them a lot harder than humans – and it sounds like it hits us hard enough too.

But he's just been appointed as 'priate' of this cleansing facility, Halfway Point, which sounds a lot like the lead doctor or scientist of a lab or a hospital. He says he's created something like 'greyce' formula which is both a cure and a vaccine. It should help Liam and I, and also change the lives of the entire Perfected race. A miracle cure, really.

It turns out that all of this stuff we've been pulled into – it's all because of syn. All the cleansing chambers, all the gluey skin and hair, and even the way everything is white – it's all designed to detect, prevent and cure the virus. Syn terrifies the Perfected, because catching it means being isolated from your people until you die a slow and painful death. And there hasn't been any cure till now.

I feel so lucky at hearing that. Imagine if we'd arrived before the cure had been created. Imagine going home through the Gate – because we will! – and taking such a terrible sickness to our own world. Better to get killed by scavs here than bring such an awful thing to our own people.

I tell Kris about my own arrival, about being found by Liam who protected me from various wild creatures and kept me from being scratched, something I haven't truly appreciated till now. I tell about home base, about living in the remnants of what was surely the Perfected's civilisation.

Kris makes a grumbling sound at the mention of those ragged buildings. "We lived there many lifetimes ago," he says. "Back in the age of Atem, before the Great Disaster. But one day we will reclaim those lands."

He's mentioned this Atem guy a few times. There's so much information coming at me that I don't get a complete understanding, but Atem seems to have been instrumental in creating an incredibly restrictive yet 'safe' place the Perfected now live in, along with the cleanliness laws that run their lives. The name of this shiny, futuristic place translates as 'Rule-of-Law'. I think it's a city? A country barricaded from the rest of the wounded world? Hard to tell. All I know is that Halfway Point, our current location, is outside Rule-of-Law, and we can't leave here till I'm ready.

"Great Disaster?" I echo.

"You called it the Gate," Kris explains. "But for us, it almost caused our destruction."

Oohh. This sounds like an interesting story...

"And now you are ready," he continues. "Time to leave the Halfway Point and enter Rule-of-Law, yes? Don't mind the jolt."

"Wha-"

But now my whole body is tingling in what I now know means some kind of teleportation. I squeeze my eyes shut as a flash of orangeish light shines even though my eyelids, and the ground seems to lurch.

"Ah, heeere we *fzzt* are," I hear Kris say. His voice sounds much closer than before, but there's a garbled echo to it, like I can hear his own language and the English translation at the same time. "Welcome*fzzt* to *ah*-Rule-of-Laww."

I open my eyes, and there he is right in front of me. Instinctively, I let out a squeak of surprise and step back, because if he seemed large from behind the barrier, in person he's colossal. My eyes really are level with his midriff.

"I trussst the translocator did not *ftt* givve you t'much troubllle?"

It takes a few moments to understand what he's saying. "Translocator? Like, teleportation?"

He frowns and says something like, "Trnssloccator, mooves you*huh* frmm one place*zzt* to anothrr."

I cringe. "Sorry, but the translation here is awful. I can hardly understand you because I can hear the words in your own language as well."

Kris steps away, giving me time to take in my new surroundings. I'm in a new room, perhaps only as big as my living room back home. The ceiling is high, unsurprisingly, and it's mainly white. But unlike the place I just left, this is homey, with furniture, colour and pattern. I look down to see I'm standing in the middle of an orange circle about two metres wide. It's similar to the marking in the warehouse where Liam was, where the light-net had made him disappear. It occurs to me that maybe I was never in the same room as Kris. Maybe he was here, in this place, talking to me via a screen while I was in the cleansing facility.

Weird.

Even weirder, some patches of wall are slightly reflective, and I see myself. I look...odd. My honey-brown skin is now glossy and an odd yellowish shade, perhaps reflecting my clothing, and my dark hair looks like a plastic cat poo- um, spiralling bun on my head. I look almost like I could be one of Kris's people. But a child, of course, if you ignore my non-childish body shape.

That makes me wonder exactly what *they* look like without

all this junk. Are they something like gigantic humans?

Speaking of gigantic, Kris is bustling away to what looks like a narrow desk coming out of the wall. He taps at it, opening draws that I couldn't even see were there. Then a few moments later he turns back to me, holding out his hand. Pinched between his massive forefinger and thumb is a shiny blob about the size of a marble, with a glimmer of silver on the inside. "Trraanslatrr," he says, pointing at his ear. "Ths'shd help-ts greatlysh."

I gingerly take the blob from him. It's firmer than it looks, but it takes a bit more gesturing before I finally get brave enough to lift it to my ear canal and give it a gentle poke. It immediately sticks onto my skin, slipping partially into my ear. I squeak at that too – because I'm really not very brave – but relax as the sound around me changes.

"Herre is the ssecond one," Kris tells me, holding out a matching blob.

This time I hear the translation clearly through the blobbed ear, while the mangled echo continues in the other. So I put in the second one, there's brief discomfort as it slips into my ear canal, and suddenly, there's blessed silence.

"Ooh," I say. "That's good. Lucky you had these."

"Actually, I just put them together," he replies, sounding a little apologetic. "I did not think that the translation here in Rule-of-Law would be faulty. But then I did not account for such a situation as this."

"Neither did I," I say dryly. I couldn't have imagined it in a thousand years.

"Do be aware that the translation may not go both ways," Kris adds. "I myself have been working on a decent translator ever since taking on the position of Halfway Point priate. I knew that we had a human, you see, and I wished to communicate. Now I wear a built-in translator of my own, but other Perfected will not have the same abilities."

He opens his mouth as if to continue, then hesitates, grimacing. "Most Perfected will not notice your translators, for that matter, assuming you cross their paths. I…recommend that you keep any special abilities secret. It is better to be underestimated by your enemies, even if you must humble yourself, for then you have the advantage."

My eyebrows shoot up. I don't the idea that I have any enemies! But it's interesting that he has some among his own people. "Thanks for the advice." Then I think back to what he'd said. "Wait…did you say, you had a human here? Do you mean today, when you took Liam?"

Kris frowns. "No. Not Lee-am. The other one."

There was another human!? He must mean Jerrold! I'm just about to burst out with excitement – and some indignation too, at so many kidnappings – but just then there's a chiming sound. A pleasant voice says, *"Visitors approach, Krys'tof-Atem. Technical Specialist Jud'or-Atem and your lord and master, High Priate Sy'lis."*

Kris lets out a hissing breath through his teeth. "I did *not* programme the greeter to call Sy'lis that." He turns to me, his expression anguished, and rattles off, "I regret that I do not have explicit permission to bring you here, little Dee-mee. While the law can be interpreted to allow a clean human child to enter Rule-of-Law, Sy'lis will not be so generous. If you wouldn't mind hiding…?"

I don't know 'Syliss', but I already dislike the guy based on Kris's reaction to his impending arrival. So I let Kris hustle me over to a nearby wall. He presses a hand against it, and a small square hole opens near the bottom. It reminds me of a dog door, and it's just about big enough for me to fit inside.

"Ventilation passage," Kris says. "Safe but small. My apologies for this situation. I will see that it doesn't happen again."

There's another chiming sound. *"Technical Specialist Jud'or-Atem and your lord and master High Priate Sy'lis request access to your domicile."*

Kris looks panicked, and I hurry into the small space, refusing to think about the size of it, any claustrophobia, or how I feel like a golden retriever being banished to the doghouse. He whispers, "Don't go through the airlocks!" and then I'm in darkness.

Liam

I push myself into seated position, my cheek throbbing from where I landed on the ground, along with the usual sting of my open cuts. I'm still stunned by that awful alien's awful words. Something like, 'You'll be here till you're dead, so get over it'.

Dominic's pale face appears at the wall to my left, and I turn to look at him. "Was that normal?"

He shrugs a shoulder, but his blue eyes are wide. "Syliss never spoke to me directly before."

"He didn't speak to me directly, either!" In fact, Syliss had very deliberately addressed his comments to his alien colleague in white, even though they were clearly meant for me.

"Yeah...but he's never had so much to say. He usually stares for a while, sneering, then walks away. But if I make him mad, I end up regretting it." Dominic brushes a hand softly over one arm's worth of scars. "I used to shout at the aliens, beg them to let me go, sing obnoxious songs you and Dad taught me – you know, like the one that never ends? *It just goes on and on, my friend. Some people started singing it, not knowing what it was-*"

"Yes, yes," I cut in, before he sings the whole bloody thing and gets it stuck in my head too. "So you'd sing annoying songs, and get stuck full of needles as a result. But the aliens never spoke to you like that?"

Dominic shakes his head, still wide-eyed. "I mean, I figured they were going to keep me here a long time, but I thought...I thought they might get sick of me one day and just...send me back. But if Syliss has his way, we'll die here. All of us."

We exchanged appalled gazes. *Then we'll have to escape,* I mouth, not daring to voice that aloud. Dominic gives me a decisive nod, then disappears off to see Jerrold, no doubt.

Damn. Escaping will be a miracle – but what choice do we have?

Just then there's another chiming sound (*bing bong bing!*) and a flash of golden light. "Activity time," a pleasant, slightly tinny voice tells me.

I get up and look around me suspiciously, expecting an alien version of a personal trainer to show up, complete with alien whip. If they think I'll participate, they can think again. I don't care if-

Bonk. There's a soft noise against the wall to my left. I look up to see Dominic against the wall again – but this time he's near the top of it, well above where he should be able to reach. He appears to be *floating*. "Activity time's the best!" he shouts. "But it doesn't last long!" Then he pulls away from the wall and vanishes.

My eyebrows raise. Could that be anti-gravity!? Perhaps

activity time is more of a treat than a threat.

I step forward cautiously, and the white walls of the chamber peel open around me, falling away to reveal an expanse of starry night sky. I start to rise into the air…then panic and stop abruptly, and the chamber walls immediately reappear as if they'd never left.

Huh. That…seems like an illusion. But Dominic did call it activity time, didn't he?

Then I notice the harness that's been stealthily connected around my torso, arms and legs, and realise I'm certainly not going anywhere. I hadn't even felt it touch me, and I hadn't seen the chamber walls turn so quickly and smoothly into video screens.   Clever.
I step forward again, adding a little hop to my step, and suddenly I'm rising in the air again. Or at least I seem to be as the walls of the chamber open up again and I float out into the endless night sky.

It's incredible. The clouds of bright stars on a purple-blue background look as real as if I was out in the desert on a clear night back on Earth. I reach for them, cycling my legs as if I'm running through the air, and the scene changes around me as if I'm truly moving. An enormous, shimmering silver sphere comes up from one side – this world's moon, covered in swirls and sparkles. I reach for that too, and I zoom towards it until each swirl and sparkle becomes visible as rows of buildings or structures, strung together like pearls on a giant necklace. Each spherical structure seems to be bigger than a football field, and is lit up with faint strips and rows of cats' eyes in pale blue, green and gold.

"Rule-of-Law," the artificial voice tells me pleasantly. "The last bastion. The home of the Perfected and the children of

Mighty Atem. Rule-of-Law keeps us safe. Keeps us clean. Keeps us happy."

Does it, now? It *does* look like the home of someone who thinks white is the only shade of value. And who's Mighty Atem?

But the voice has nothing further to tell me. The scene's still changing though. Closer and closer to the moon I come until I see the fine details of all these massive buildings with vents and tunnels and lights everywhere. Then I reach the side of one and its surface turns sheer, revealing hundreds of rooms within, and what looks like tiny furniture...beds...people.

I want to look closer. I want to see those people properly, even though I'm already certain of what I'm looking at.

The aliens live on their moon.

The freaking *moon*, people. Moon people! And at a guess, you could fit many thousands of people within these buildings. Maybe even millions, depending on how far these structures go. If they're built all the way around, then there could even be *billions*...

I desperately want to see more, but the programme stops just outside the buildings with a brief glimpse of what's inside, and finally I give up and turn back the other way.

I'm greeted with a devastating view. Against the vast backdrop of space is a planet: grey and brownish-green, mottled with white. Like Earth on a bad day. But this planet is also *wrecked*. It looks like a big apple that a fussy toddler tried to eat but gave up after taking a dozen timid bites: covered in pock marks and dents through the swirling grey that covers most of its surface.

That's got to be the Wilds. I'd guessed the world of the Wilds was in a bad state, judging by my own damaged little corner of it, but this is so much worse than I'd even imagined.

And right between me and the ravaged planet is a hulking grey shape. It spins gently in the empty atmosphere, lit up on every edge with cats' eyes just like the moon settlement. But while those were gold and blue and green, these ones are a foreboding red and orange. *Don't come here*, it seems to say. *Evil is held within.* Because isn't evil always in red and orange?

I run towards it anyway, because it's not real, and because I have a sneaking suspicion that's where the programme brought me from.

Then as I get closer to the space structure/ship/station, its walls turn transparent and reveal dozens of rooms within, proving my guess right. Inside, it's a clean, cold white in comparison to the dark exterior. I catch glimpses of hundreds, maybe even thousands of tiny boxes, each glowing red against the ultra-bright background.

Each box could be a prison cell, just viewed from a distance…

"Halfway Point Quarantine and Research Facility," the voice tells me. "Preventing the spread of the SYN virus, and dedicated to finding a cure."

I scowl at the screens and run faster, trying to get a look inside. How many people are here anyway? How did they get us here, to the middle of nowhere? What's the way out?

Oh God, what's the way out?!

But just like with the shining moon structures, I can't get closer. I can't see details. I cycle my legs madly, swiping at the air with my arms as if I can drag myself closer. I'm panting, covered in a light sweat as my heart begins to pound, but I don't give up. Maybe if I just try harder, if I just push a little more, I can find our exit-

I stop with a jolt as the scenery suddenly vanishes and is replaced with those same cold white walls. They hurt my eyes after the darkness of the video projection, and I struggle in annoyance, trying to get the activity moving again. But I can't. My hands and feet and torso – all of me – are now stuck to the wall.

Again.

"Activity limit exceeded," the pleasant, tinny voice scolds me. "Time for a cool-down."

"I don't want a cool-down!" I shout. "I'm fine! I want to keep going!"

"Time for a cool-down."

"Look," I tell it in a more controlled voice. "I know my limits, and I certainly can run for more than a couple of minutes. If you'd just let me go again, I'll pace myself-"

"Time for a cool-down," the voice repeats in exactly the same tone.

Great. I guess it's time for a cool-down.

I try to slump in place as a show of irritation, but I can't even do that. It feels kinda...light in here; my body isn't even dragging at the bonds.

But I have worked out one thing. We never saw aliens in the Wilds – assumed they were all gone, in fact – because they weren't on the planet at all. They were on the planet's moon.

And us captive humans? We're stuck somewhere in the middle, with miles of freezing, airless space between us and our salvaged home in the ruins of their civilisation.

This is worse than I could have imagined.

Chapter 8

Demi

I'm stuffed inside the ventilation shaft. It's fairly wide, but not quite high enough for me to sit up, so my head is pressed awkwardly against my shoulder.

It's also pitch-black, and I can't see anything at all in any direction. Kris said not to go through any airlocks. I don't even know what an airlock looks like, even if it was light enough to see in here.

But I can hear just fine. There's yet another chime, and then I hear a *whoosh* and Kris saying, "Sy'lis. Jud'or. What brings you to my home?"

"Your failure," a new voice snaps. It's male, a touch higher than Kris's, and clearly displeased. "And it's High Priate to you, Krys'tof-Atem. I examined Halfway Point's latest acquisition just now. Your greyce formula is a complete and utter let-down, and now I hear you're holding a female barbarian in the facility?"

There's a long silence. Then Kris says coolly, "The High Council appointed me as Halfway Point's priate for a full ten years. I do not require your opinion on anything I do during that time, Sy'lis."

I suck in a mostly silent breath. Kris doesn't pull any punches.

There's a brief pause in response – I imagine it to be startled – then Syliss replies nastily, "Your manners are as poor as your

107

scientific methods. But while you may ignore my *opinions*, as you call them, you may not ignore our laws. Any tainted creature must go through due process and be isolated from Rule-of-Law and from people, for fear of spreading the virus. The female must be registered and put with the others of its kind where it cannot cause harm! Are you going to spit on a thousand years of tradition and wisdom in this matter?"

"The law also states that a child must be treated with care and not subjected to the same conditions as adults," Kris snaps. I can hear his irritation in his voice. "This female is a juvenile. Moreover, she is entirely whole, unblemished, and untainted. *I* will take care of her – and by our own laws, she goes free."

I've never been so happy to be called a juvenile, and I decide that Kris is more than just friendly. He's a big alien hero, like Superman but without the tights.

But I'm starting to think that this new guy – Syliss – doesn't know I'm now here, in the same room. And that's the second time I've heard 'others' in relation to humans, so it does seem like poor old Jerrold made it. Thank goodness.

When Syliss speaks again, his voice is a hiss. "You will hand over the female, Krys'tof-Atem, or son of Atem or not, you will regret it."

I hear a chime again, perhaps a swish of fabric, and then Kris mutters, "Good riddance to him." Then his tone changes. "Jud'or, when I was appointed, you vowed to assist me in every way. Why are you then bringing that *[untranslatable]* into my very home?"

Damn. If there's still someone here, I'll have to stay in the vent longer, and my neck is starting to ache from this awkward angle.

"Apologies, Priate. When High Priate Sy'lis makes a request, one does not decline." This third male voice sounds a lot like Kris, although there's something different in his tone.

"You told him about the human girl against my express orders," Kris persists, sounding exasperated. "What good could come of that, Jud'or? He's trying to get my greyce formula pulled before it even has a chance to work! One day and he calls it a failure? We need longer! And you know that once it's proven-"

"I know that *if* it works, it will change our lives," Jud'or cuts in. His tone is sharper than I'd expect for someone speaking to their superior. "Of course. But it has to work first. And it has to be proven to work on the human test subjects before we're free to test it on Perfected, who really matter. And so we need to have those human test subjects. You've been freely testing on the others, Krys'tof, small as they are, and now you're holding back on us because you think this one is *cute?*"

I freeze, blood rushing into my head, and I miss what Kris says in return.

He's been testing on the others. *Others,* so presumably both Liam and Jerrold are being treated like lab rats.

A sense of betrayal overwhelms me. Even though I just met Kris, and I knew he was part of this set-up, I... I thought I could trust him anyway. But how much can I trust him if he's hurt and degraded other humans by kidnapping them and experimenting on them?

Clearly I've been a fool. I've wanted someone to save me, to offset the terror I've felt since coming through the Gate, so I've let him play that role. But he never deserved the faith I so quickly put in him.

I'm clearly not a good judge of character.

Tears burn at the back of my eyes and I try to shuffle

backwards, away from the room. But of course there's nowhere to go, because the vent tunnel runs parallel to the wall. So instead I reach out sideways in the darkness to find more flat, smooth space.

I shuffle-crawl my way along the tight, dark tunnel, head down and shaking. I don't want to see Kris again, and I'm damn well not going to trust him to care for my wellbeing if he won't care for Liam or other humans. My faith in his motives has been shattered. What if he's not a friendly, fatherly alien after all, mistaking me for a child? What if he's a pervert who thinks I'm the wrong sort of 'cute'?

My thoughts spin, growing darker, even as the space seems to grow a little lighter. How long have I been crawling? I haven't been able to hear the two aliens talking for some time.

Suddenly I see a light grey patch up ahead. It doesn't take long to identify it as another vent cover like the one I entered through, and my heartrate picks up in excitement at the thought of an exit. When I reach it, I pause and listen carefully. There's a faint hum that could be machinery, and the subtle smell of something fresh wafts through the opaque vent cover.

After waiting a few minutes and hearing no other sounds, I push at the cover gently. It doesn't budge. I try again with more force, but I may as well be hitting a solid wall.

Damn.

I try prying at the corners, pressing my hands against it, even whispering at it to open in case it's voice-activated. But I have no success, and finally I give up and move on. The next vent will be better, right?

I crawl in the darkness for what feels like hours. A few times I think I hear a faint 'Dee-mee!' but that could just be my imagination, or the air moving through the vents themselves. I pass dozens of covers, each with their own scents or sounds coming from the room beyond, and I even listen in on a few different alien conversations. But none mean much to me, and not one cover will open.

This could be a problem. I'd really rather not have to crawl backwards all the way back to Kris's room's vent – even if I could identify it.

Then finally the shaft tilts upwards. I've been crawling at a slight slope for ages, but this is a distinct tilt and I have to brace my feet against the smooth floor to avoid slipping back down. I can hear a faint roaring noise like the sound of a quiet fridge motor back home. There's surely another vent up ahead, but unlike the others, no light shines through its mostly opaque surface.

Something different, maybe. A real way out?

Re-energised, I push forward into the darkness as the faint roar becomes marginally louder. And just as I'm wondering where the blasted thing is, I hit a new surface, forehead first.

"Ow."

I've said it out of habit than real discomfort, because the surface is spongy rather than hard. Maybe even a bit jellylike. I reach up, patting the space ahead of me, and identify that yes, I've reached the end of the shaft.

I swear under my breath and sit up. This seems like the end of my little journey, except that the roaring/machine sound appears to be coming from behind this barrier. I can't give up.

I push my palm against it and it gives a little. "Aha!" Next thing, my hand is moving through the barrier, disappearing up to the wrist. My fingers are free on the other side and I wiggle them a little. The air on the other side is cold enough to chill them even through their thin coat of varnish.

But what's a little cold compared to being a lab rat or an alien's pet? I brace my feet against the ground, take a deep breath, shut my eyes, then push into the barrier head-first.

It parts around me, dragging a little at my glazed hair but not hindering my movement. Then finally I feel myself pop through to the neck. Damn, it's cold. I open my eyes and take a deep breath. I get an impression of greyish darkness broken by sparkling blue and white lights, the scent of sulphur and-

I can't breathe. *I can't breathe!*

I try to suck in another breath but it feels like my chest is caving in. It's on fire, and the shock is so intense and horrible that it consumes my attention. I thrash around, trying to pull back through the barrier while my chest seems to be collapsing and I CAN'T BREATHE, and the pretty lights swim in my vision and my face is being crushed and-

Liam

After an interminable twenty minutes stuck against the wall – again – I'm finally allowed down again. I launch back into the virtual reality/video programme they've got set up, but this time I take care to go slowly and steadily. I don't want to risk being immobilised once more.

But this time the programme takes me to a pretty field full of symmetrical yellow flowers under a massive gleaming dome. The dome is opaque, reflecting a vaguely blue and white sky that seems fake even for this virtual environment.

I pass the massive field and reach a new one full of symmetrical green plants, tall and with perfectly shaped leaves

– also under a dome. Then beyond that in an even larger dome, there's a shining, futuristic city of white spires and connecting bridges. But perhaps to the aliens it's not futuristic. Perhaps it's just ordinary.

The artificial voice informs me that this is the 'enduring and beautiful capital of Rule-of-Law'. I ask for more information – because why not – and I'm given precisely nothing. No chance to go back to my first video either. I decide I'll just have to wait till next time.

All up, activity time lasts about an hour. After the video stops working, the harness disappears and a few moments later Dominic reappears against my wall. I tell him about my video and how I'm sure we're stuck somewhere between the shining moon and the Wilds planet, and he nods.

"Yep, looks like it. But the programme never lets you get close enough to really see detail."

Damn. Figures Dom would have already checked that out – he's naïve, not stupid.

"Maybe the new priate will come talk now you're here," Dominic continues. "He's an alien, so I don't trust him. But he doesn't seem as bad as the ones before him, because I never got activity time till he started." His lips curve distinctly downwards. "It's just…my pet dogs, Liam. I can't stop thinking about them being all alone. Maybe…I should risk talking to him about them."

My heart clenches, because it hurts for me as well to think of Bianca and Jesse all alone. And Demi, fresh to the Wilds and so terribly soft and clueless, maybe still out there by herself. Or maybe picked up by the Perfected as well – but if so, where is she?

And Dom doesn't even know about Demi. It definitely

doesn't seem the right time to mention her, either. "Better that they look after themselves, huh?" I say soberly. "Or maybe we can talk to the, um, priate." He surely can't be as bad as that Syliss.

"Maybe." But Dominic's tone is flat, and his shoulders are drooped, his head low.

I can't stand seeing him like this. "Hey, did Jerrold ever tell you about Saint Bernards?" I ask casually. "On Earth, they're one of the biggest dog breeds around."

His head lifts. "Not Great Danes?"

I remember how Dom's memory is excellent for random facts. Probably because he never got any formal schooling or ever watched TV, there's plenty of room in that brain of his. But he's always been interested in details of a 'normal' life that he'll never know for himself.

"No, those are the tallest breed," I explain. "Saint Bernards are big, fluffy and drool a lot…"

I go on to tell him about my uncle's pet Saint Bernard, and how as children my cousins and I once put a saddle on it and tried to ride it like a horse – with limited success. And in spite of the circumstances, I see my friend's posture relax and his expression lighten.

This guy. I decide in that moment that if we ever get back to Earth (and that's a massive, chasm-sized 'if') then I'll buy Dom a dog. The fluffiest, friendliest one on the market.

But in spite of Dominic's suggestion about the friendlier new priate, no new visitors come to our cells. Hours pass and we catch up on conversation, diligently avoiding certain topics and with him acting as middle-man between Jerrold and I.

Then dinner appears. I mean, it really does appear – one

moment I'm in a plain, empty room, and the next this shelf slides out of the wall. It contains a tray divided into segments, each filled with a small, squarish block of something. There's a mottled light green block, a rough-looking dark green block, and a beige block. A fourth block is transparent and ripples like a bag full of water.

Next door, Dom exclaims in excitement. "Yum, light brown! My favourite."

I poke at the beige block. It looks like a cross between uncooked tofu and potter's clay, so 'light brown' is a good enough description. "What does it taste like?"

"Mmmf," he replies through a full mouth. "Schweet."

It does taste sweet, I decide when I take a bite. Dense and soft, with a slightly rubbery texture that reminds me of haloumi cheese. It's quite literally the first time I've eaten anything besides breadish and meat since coming through the Gate. For a moment I'm not sure how I feel about it...then I hoover the lot, including the watery block which turns out to be – wait for it – water, complete with edible packaging. Besides the water, the rest of the meal is unidentifiable, and I can't argue with Dominic's system of naming by colour.

"I'm still hungry," I announce, then stare longingly at the now empty tray as it recedes into the wall. "Do you ever get seconds?"

"Nope."

Damn. Not too different from home base then – except there, you don't usually *want* seconds.

Just then, there's a faint tingle and warmth to the air, and my chamber is briefly lit with a flash of red light. I pause, then look at Dominic quizzically. "What was that?"

"No one's ever explained it, but I think the red light means we're still tainted. You know. Still have the virus."

"Oh." Well, I hadn't expected it to be fixed in a day if Dom hasn't been fixed in three years. Now I think of it, I think my cell flashed red earlier today, but I didn't pay attention. Enough was going on. "What colour is the light if we don't have the virus?"

He shrugs. "I have no idea. It's always red."

Of course it is. But somehow, I'm still disappointed.

Shortly after that, the wall between Dominic and I turns opaque and he's cut off mid-sentence. A moment later the lights dim and the artificial voice says, "Sleep time."

"Thanks, but I'm not tired," I tell it. Well, maybe I am just a little tired, but as a grown man, I can damn well decide to go to bed. I also kind of need the bathroom, but I can't see anything like that. No bed, either, although I'll be fine sleeping on the floor. I've done it for years in home base.

"Sleep time."

Suddenly I'm pulled backwards flat against the wall, in the exact same position I've found myself in several times today. But this time there's a soft yet firm barrier holding my head in place. My hands and feet are strapped into the mouldable walls, and my tunic thingy disappears as the mouldable 'briefs' reappear. Then there's a faint tingle in the briefs section, and I find I don't need the bathroom anymore.

Hmm. Efficient. But… "There's no way I'm going to sleep like this," I say.

In response I hear a faint *pfft*, then there's a weird scent in the air. Huh. Reminds me of this 'ocean-scented' air freshener we used to have in my old apartment. Don't know why anyone would want to smell like brine…

Demi

"Dee-mee. Can you hear me? She still looks unconscious, Petra, but the med-chamber shows she is alert- oh. Her eyes are opening."

It's not that bright, but I still blink at the light invading my eyes. I'm lying down, I think, and that semi-familiar voice continues in the background as a semi-familiar face looms into my vision. It's shockingly strange, with oddly carved features and too-bright silver eyes, but then my memory clicks in and I remember who it is. Kris, the alien. Except...I'm mad at him, aren't I? He did something...

I suck in a breath, gasping, then cough convulsively. My chest feels strange, all numb right through to the inside, and while I can feel myself breathing, it's strangely muted. Just like my vision.

"Don't try to speak yet, little one. Your body is still adjusting to your new lungs."

New lungs!? I raise my hands and hit a hard surface a few inches above my body. Then I realise that the fogginess is some kind of barrier that goes all around me. I can't turn my head, but am I in a glass coffin...?!

"It's a medic-chamber," Kris continues, his voice slightly warped by whatever pipes it into my coffin-box. *"Here, I'll open it up just as soon as we're sure your lungs can handle it. We nearly lost you yesterday."* He shakes his head, the image blurred by the barrier between us. *"I said no airlocks, little one. Then I find you hanging halfway out of one, head-first in an airless environment! We are remarkably fortunate to have found you in time."*

Memories trickle in, of darkness and a terrible pain in my

chest, and I lift a hand to the body part in question. Why the hell would they have an airless space anywhere around their homes?! Or maybe it's a teleporter, um, translocator, to send their trash straight out into space. But the most important thing he said…

"New lungs?" I whisper, and the words come out easily enough. A little weak, perhaps. "In one day…?"

"Not quite new," Kris amends. *"But the medic-chamber taught your body how to fix all manner of injuries."* He grimaces. *"Your people do not value scars or the like, do they? I fear a length of time in a med-chamber will indiscriminately heal anything it identifies."*

I shake my head. I don't think I have any scars anyway – but I suppose if I *had*, they'd be gone now. "Heals anything…?"

"Almost anything short of death or syn virus." He pauses. *"For the Perfected though, it does reverse even clinical death in certain situations. But we would not want to test its full abilities on one as fragile as your small human self. Now, your readings look good. I'll open up the chamber and we'll see how you're feeling."*

He doesn't wait for my response before the barrier covering me slides aside and I see him clearly. I am lying down as I'd guessed, and he's all dressed in white, standing over me with his damn stupid wedge of silver hair and an intensely sympathetic expression on his stupid, lying alien face.

Behind him is another alien. A female, judging by the coil of shiny blueish hair on the top of her extra-large head. Presumably the 'Petra' he was talking to earlier. She wears white as well, and she glances over her shoulder at me long enough to meet my eyes with her vibrant green ones. Then she turns away dismissively.

Or maybe it's not really dismissive, but I feel like it is. I remember what happened now – why I was angry and upset.

Why I took off down the ventilation shaft rather than wait for Kris to let me out of my hiding place. A rush of the same emotions floods in. Anger...fear. Betrayal.

I push myself into a sitting position. "You kidnapped me," I say, and the accusation rings through my voice. "You stole Liam and Jerrold, and you're experimenting on them. On *us*."

Kris is shaking his head. "No. No-"

"Don't lie to me!" I cry. "I'm not a stupid child! I *heard* what you said to the other two. Silence and...Dude. You can't test your failed formula on your own *special, perfect* people until it's been proven to work on someone who doesn't matter! And that's stupid too, because we're not even the same species!"

"Dee-mee. Please."

I glare at him, putting all my fury into my expression. And glaring seems to be all I can do. I'm definitely weak, but I feel so helpless in this whole situation. Because really, how can I stop them? How can I do *anything* to help myself or Liam or even Jerrold? I've got nothing. Apparently not even my own pair of lungs any longer.

"Dee-mee," Kris says again in that stupid, mispronouncing way of his. "Please hear me out. Whatever you heard from *Sy'lis* and *Jud'or*, it is not the truth. It is their version of it, spoken by people who don't like your kind, who don't believe there'll ever be a cure for syn, and who never liked me in the first place. They'll never give the greyce formula a chance. But any cure needs more than a day, don't you understand?"

"You fixed my lungs in a day," I say aggressively. "Why not the virus?"

He looks down. "Syn...goes deeper than any injury. It goes into the very cells...the DNA of the afflicted. Syn must be destroyed from the inside out, and it is no small task."

My lips tighten. "And so you took Liam, and Jerrold too, I assume. And here I am too."

"The two recent males were intended to be rescues," Kris says softly. "I promise you, Dee-mee. On my honour. I had them brought here because their lives were so wretched down in the tainted ruins, and I knew that in time, the virus would kill them if they were left alone. Here, the greyce formula will cure them, I swear it!

"But I did not know about you until I saw you down with Lee-am, and I was so relieved to have rescued you as well." He frowns. "Of course, medicine and quarantine are necessary for all of you until you can be released, but it pains me that you feel so mistreated."

I study his face, wondering how good a liar he might be. He lied to Silence-Syliss's face…no, he didn't, I amend. He told that nasty alien that it was none of his business where I was. No lie.

But I *want* to believe. I *want* to trust Kris, but how can I take the risk when it will be so painful if he does turn out to be false? "You say you're not hurting them?" I whisper. "You won't ever hurt them?"

"I promise on my honour," he says again, putting a hand on his heart. "No, on my very life."

I want to believe that, too, but I'm not sure what to think. Promises are all very well, but his actions will prove if he can be trusted.

Kris continues, "The two new males are in quarantine but have not been harmed, and I will speak with them as soon as I am able. I will free them as soon as I am able! But I had no control over how the previous priate took the first male several seasons ago, and I confess he *has* been mistreated."

"First male…?" A faint memory pings in my mind. "You

120

have *three* other humans…?!"

"But of course. Would you like to see them?"

I scramble to my feet, lurching a little at the sudden movement, and buzzing with excitement. "Yes!"

Liam

"Time to wake up."

The tinny auto-voice speaks right into my ear, and my eyes pop open. I wouldn't know I even slept except there's a feeling of time missing. I'm not at all groggy, but I'm still stuck to the wall.

Sometimes in the mornings I wake up confused. But today, I know exactly where I am. Bad news – I've been freaking abducted by aliens. Good news – Dominic and Jerrold are here with me. Not quite safe and sound, but alive.

Unbelievable.

I look to my left to see if Dominic's pressed against the barrier between us, ready to make conversation, but it's opaque. Just a plain white wall, so I figure he's still in his 'morning routine' as well. I'd like to see his face again, and Jerrold's. It would remind me that all isn't lost.

"Good morning, alien overlords," I say dryly. "May this weak human be allowed off the wall, please? I'm eager to start a brand-new day."

Auto-voice doesn't respond to my sarcasm. Instead, there's a faint whirring sound, then a red light flashes through the chamber. I pause, waiting for more, and ten seconds later the tester light repeats before returning to the room's usual dull white light.

Red, so it looks like I've still got the virus. No surprise there, but I'm still disappointed.

I wait on the wall a few moments longer, then clear my throat with a short cough. Immediately, a tiny tube drops from the ceiling, like a miniature periscope with its opening pointed at me. It puffs a cloud of tingling mist right in my face.

I suck in a breath, startled, then sneeze in reaction, right back onto the tube.

That turns out to be a bad move. The tube emits a second, stronger puff of mist, right in my face again. I sneeze again reflexively…and it puffs even more mist at me.

This time I suck in my breath and hold it. But the tube just sits there in the air, a foot from my face as if it's waiting for me to sneeze again, and it can play this game all day. If it's me versus the mist, I guess the second will win.

After thirty seconds of non-sneezing – and when my face feels like I'm almost purple – the tube slowly withdraws into the wall.

I let out a long sigh of relief – and the tube pops out and puffs me in the face again.

"Argh!" Luckily this time I manage to hold back my sneeze, and when I can finally breathe normally, I say aloud, "I'm going to complain to management about this."

"You'll learn not to sneeze or cough." Dominic's helpful voice comes from the wall beside me.

I automatically turn to my left, and there he is, pressed against the now-transparent barrier with a bright smile on his face. Wow, he never used to have such white teeth.

"The spray never stops as long as you keep sneezing," he

continues, "and after a while it makes your throat hurt. Also, they keep you on the wall for longer if they think you're sick at all."

"Thanks for the warning."

But then Dominic glances over his shoulder to what must be the front of his chamber, and his whole posture perks up in noticeable surprise. "Oh, hello! Who are you?"

Chapter 9
Demi

Once the offer's made to take me to the other humans, Kris doesn't delay. I follow him along in my newly white clothing – the colour reflecting my recent status as a medical patient – as we walk out of the set of rooms that seem to make up his home, and out into a wider area.

Then we step into a narrow hall covered in tiles, and I squeak in surprise as the floor begins to move. Not the whole floor, just our section of tiles, moving like a tetris game. We pass closed doors that are set regularly along the hall's length, their oval shape odd enough to make me look twice. No one else is around.

The whole time Kris is tapping away at something I can't see. "I'm giving you general access to this section of the *Lystra* block, which is the complex we're in. Such access will allow you to operate most devices and open most doors, including vent covers." He looks down at me sternly. "This is for your safety and so that you may hide if needed. But please, *please* Dee-mee – do not go anywhere dangerous. No airlocks! Avoid people. Stay with me or Peh'tra until your position here in Rule-of-Law is safe. Is that understood?"

In spite of his strong words, his tone is gentle, and I don't take offense. It's clear he's giving me more freedom than the other aliens would ever do. Plus, I plan to go exploring as soon as I get the chance – forget the new lungs. It's hard to believe that even happened, except for the slight tightness in my chest that I can't shake. "Which devices and doors doesn't it work on?"

"The most highly secure ones. That is, the translocators between Rule-of-Law and the Halfway Point facility, as well as the doors to the quarantine chambers themselves."

Hmm. No teleporting, I see. "Quarantine chambers?"

Our moving section of floor comes to a halt outside a closed door. It looks like all the others, but this close I can see a series of symbols set in its surface, the sort I've concluded is alien writing.

But a moment later it slides open, and Kris steps through. I follow at his heels to find I'm on yet another tiled floor. This one doesn't move though, and Kris stands and waves at the wide wall in front of us. It turns transparent and we're suddenly looking into three identical chambers, the size of small bedrooms back home. They remind me of animal enclosures at a zoo.

Inside each chamber is a human man...and I don't recognize any of them.

"Step up close to the wall if you wish to speak to them," Kris tells me. "Otherwise, they will not see you." He's standing back behind me, I note, so must be out of sight of the chambers.

So I do step forward, right up to the middle chamber. Inside, a completely bald guy is pressed up against the wall between him and the person on the left. He's fair-skinned and wears a baggy white tunic, and seems to be caught up in conversation.

But a moment later he glances over his shoulder at me, and his eyes widen. "Oh, hello!" he says enthusiastically. "Who are you?"

His eyes are blue and his face is free of scarring, I see as he practically skips towards me, and he's clearly not Liam. A bit shorter, maybe, with a rounder face? (But who could tell under that massive beard Liam wears?)

"Are you an alien?" the man continues rapidly. "You look sort of like an alien, but sort of like a human, too. You're very short. I've never seen you before."

"I've never seen you before either," I reply, a little startled at this enthusiasm from a stranger. "I'm Demi, and I'm most definitely human." I'm not *that* short, either. "Are you Jerrold? Liam's been looking for you."

"No, I'm Dominic! Jerrold is my father!" The blue-eyed guy points at the chamber to my right, where I can just see an older man pressed up against the wall between the two chambers, much like Dominic had been doing. He wears a matching white tunic and his short white hair is slicked back against the dome of his skull, but by the way he's squinting, I suspect he can't see me over here.

"Dominic," I murmur. That name brings a ping of recognition – but didn't Liam say there were no other survivors? Just Bianca, Jesse, Jerrold...and someone who vanished, presumed dead, years before. "Oh!" I cry in sudden recollection. "You're Jesse's dad! Everyone thinks you're dead!"

I'm so excited that I don't notice the horror on Dominic's face at first. I rattle on, "Liam said something about a fight and a bright light, but I guess that was you being abducted, right? Oh, they're going to be *sooo* happy to have you back..."

Then I realise his frantic waving is a desperate plea for silence, and I close my mouth. "Um..."

"I miss my pet dogs," Dominic says stiltedly. The little colour in his skin has leached out, leaving him almost as white as his clothing. "My *puppy* Jesse. Though he'll be a big dog now, right?"

A big...dog? "Yes...?" I venture, because it sounds like what he wants to hear, even though it makes no sense. Was I not supposed to mention Jesse? "I wouldn't really know. I only just arrived myself."

"And you're stuck in a chamber just like us."

"Actually, no," I correct him, unsurprised that he can't see my surroundings properly. The zoo animals are there to be watched, not to watch. "I'm in a hallway. They say I don't have the virus, so I don't have to stay..." In prison? "...in quarantine like you."

Dominic seems to regain a little energy. "You're very lucky."

I guess I am. I lean in closer, not that it makes any difference to the sound which seems to be coming from somewhere above me. "Kris says you'll all be let out after the cure works," I tell him quietly. "He says we can all go back home, and that he's going to reopen the Gate and send us back to Earth."

Dominic stares at me. "Wouldn't that be nice." But he doesn't sound as though he believes it.

I fidget a little, because I don't need that kind of discouragement. "I actually came looking for Liam," I say, leaning a little to the left, trying to see into that chamber. From this angle I can't quite make out who's in there.

This new guy angles his thumb towards the left chamber, his expression brightening. "He's in there! But careful, he's still-"

His voice fades out as I step away from his section of the wall to face into the left chamber. And then I see inside, and...well...

...*That's* not normal.

Liam

Dominic's walked away from the wall between us, the jerk, and I have no idea who he could be talking to. It's not as if I can walk over and see for myself, either. I'm still stuck to the stupid wall without so much as a hospital gown, just with those white clay briefs covering my essentials. That's what I get for daring to clear my stupid throat.

But I figure if it's an alien, they'll be coming over to gawk at me soon enough.

And then a distinct figure appears at the clear wall outside my chamber where Syliss the heinous High Priate stood yesterday. But this one is much smaller, almost childlike, and feminine.

It's Demi. Her light brown skin looks rich and warm against the white of her clothing, and for a moment I think they've taken her hair too. Then I realise it's all plastered on the top of her head in a glossy black spiral. She's squinting through the glass, one hand pressed up against it. Her mouth moves, and a moment later I hear her voice through the speaker.

"Whoa…*Liam?*"

Demi's mouth is a dark circle of shock, and I'm sure I must look the same way. I suddenly feel horribly exposed, as inappropriately uncovered as a speedo-wearer two blocks away from the beach. Make that a speedo-wearer who hasn't seen the sun in two years.

I can feel heat rising up my face and neck, and I know I must be turning noticeably red – the curse of being both pale-skinned and a blusher. Apparently I never grew out of that habit.

But even though I'm stuck on the wall like a semi-nude, cut-price messiah (Jerrold's words), I nod and force a smile. "They got you too, huh?"

"Kinda," she breathes. "You look so different...and why are you naked?!"

My blush turns into a full-body burn. *Please* don't let these briefs be see-through!

Out of the corner of my eye I see that Dominic has reappeared at our connecting wall. He's jiggling anxiously, almost galloping on the spot. "You didn't say there was a new person, Liam!"

"I didn't have a chance," I reply as evenly as I can manage. "But here she is." I nod at her. "Demi, have you met Dominic? He went missing three years ago, do you remember me telling you?"

"I do!" she says brightly, her eyes sliding to the next chamber. "Lucky, right? You must be so happy he's alive!"

At the same time Dominic's saying excitedly, "She's a *lady*! She's *pretty*, Liam!"

Somehow my face heats at that too, because yes, Demi is pretty. And I'm still stuck on the stupid wall, without any dignity at all. Feeling flustered from the situation and from the two conversations I'm having to hold up, I snap, "Yes, Dom is a lady! And yes, Demi is alive, and I'm happy about it! But-

"Dom's a lady?" Demi asks, frowning. "I thought he was Jesse's- um... I mean Jerrold's-"

Dominic is still nattering at me from the other side. "You said you wished someone else would come, and-"

"ARRGH!" I let out an overwhelmed cry from my position on the wall. "Can you two *please* give me a moment to reply?! I can hear both of you, but you can't hear each other!"

129

Both fall silent. Demi watches me for a moment, then steps away from the wall, her figure disappearing entirely.

Hmm. Life is going to be difficult if she's so easily offended. And I'm *still* stuck on the wall, hairless and shiny and so horribly unclothed. "Please tell me you can't see through my shorts," I say miserably to Dominic.

But he's already stepped away from our connecting wall.

Demi

The aliens have put Liam in a box. They've stuck him to the wall with his wrists, feet and pelvis covered in what looks like chunks of white plastic, and he's…so shiny. So *white*. So…clean-shaven.

Holy moly. He looks like a pasty plastic doll. If not for the distinctive scars on his face and his near-black hair, I wouldn't have recognised him at all. He looks far younger than when I first met him, and it's clear that he's been living on a limited diet for some time. His muscles are lean and defined, but a touch underfed. As my mama would say, the man needs to eat a pie.

But that's not the worst thing. The worst is that while Liam and the others mourned Dominic as dead, Dominic was *here*. Held in a cage.

I cast an accusing glance over my shoulder to Kris, who's standing back and fiddling with his wrist control panel. He smiles at me then goes back to whatever he's doing. The smile doesn't reassure me, though. For Liam to be in this kind of condition…

Just then I hear him say grumpily, "Please tell me you can't see through my briefs."

I'm startled by that – because I swear, I hadn't even thought to look. I try not to sound accusing as I say to Kris, "Can you let Liam down off the wall and give him some clothes like the other two?"

Kris taps away at his invisi-screen, and Liam tumbles off the wall even as a tunic is wrapped around him and sleek white socks appear on his feet. I watch to make sure he's OK, and Kris says, "I have to go now – I've been called before the Council again – but I will come back for you as soon as I can. Please do not leave the *Lystra* section." He pauses, then sighs. "I also ask that you stay out of sight of any other Perfected, although I don't suppose it matters much now."

Because they already know I'm around, I figure. Those two yesterday just didn't know exactly where I was. "Stay out of sight. Don't leave this section. Got it." That still leaves me a lot of room to manoeuvre.

Kris leaves, and I go back to introduce myself to Jerrold. He's as shocked to see me as Dominic was, but I give him the briefest summary before moving back to Liam's chamber. After all, I walked off mid-conversation.

We quickly figure out that if I stand right between Liam and Dominic's chambers, I can chat with both of them. Dominic relays the conversation to Jerrold, who can't see me at all. (Sorry, Jerrold.) I resolve to make up for it later.

The two men talk to me in hushed, hurried tones. I try to listen and not get distracted by their looks – Liam, looking so pale, clean and different, and Dominic...well.

Dominic asks me in urgent tones not to talk about anyone else besides those already here, and when I see the fine white scarring that riddles his exposed arms and neck, barely standing out against his skin, I understand why. The injustice of it makes me seethe, and I wonder how much of this Kris could control. He said it was the previous priate, right?

It's disgusting, but only time will tell if he can be trusted. Either he's right, or I'll end up in another ten-by-ten room like these three, growing weaker from lack of sunlight, and scarred as they carry out their tests.

And it's not like we can just escape from the chambers, break a window and run off back to home base. According to Liam and Dominic, we're not even on the planet any longer. We're stuck on a space station somewhere between the planet and the moon, which is where the aliens now live.

I knew it. I *knew* that moon couldn't look so weird and sparkly for no reason. But they're wrong about one thing.

I'm not stuck on the space station at all, I explain to them. Even though I arrived on the station right after Liam, I'm now on the Rule-of-Law moon colony. We must be communicating through massive video screens rather than a single wall as it appears.

We're so far apart it's not funny. So we either need to make great friends with the aliens and convince them to return us to the planet in perfect health…or we need to take ourselves down there by translocator, which I don't have access to.

The others look downcast as we realise that, and Jerrold does too once Dominic relays the information.

"But we have something we didn't before," Liam says. "Someone on the outside."

I take a moment to realise he means me. "I'll do what I can. Do you have something in mind?"

Liam and Dominic exchange glances. "The exercise programme only shows a distant view of Halfway Point,"

Dominic says. "But if you can see what the aliens see…"

Then maybe I can find another way out, back to the planet. My heartrate picks up – excitement or fear, I don't know. "Let me see if I can work these screens," I tell them.

I step back and swipe at the clear wall, just like Kris did. And suddenly the view changes.

Half an hour later I've viewed the men's prison top to bottom. Halfway Point is massive – made up of a dozen warehouse-sized rooms stacked on top of and next to each other. Some are full of boxes of different sizes, and I manage to identify some of the contents.

There's metal, rock and perhaps even wood, looking like scrap from the broken civilisation of the Wilds, and hover-ball robots move the shipments via a massive translocator in different warehouse rooms. They seem to be reclaiming resources from their ruined buildings. Waste not, want not.

There's what looks like a control room as well, with a couple of weird-looking seats and wall-to-wall screens like the one I'm using. Everything's white, of course. It's clear that there's some correlation between the colour (or lack of it) and the Perfected's intense fear of sickness. Taking into account Liam's injury turning the floor black, I can see how that works. The slightest hint of sickness would be immediately noticeable.

There are a couple of space suits stuck to the walls, like the one I first saw and mistook for being an actual alien. They're huge, though, and I can't really see how to open them. I study them briefly then turn away.

And then there are the chambers. The warehouse-sized rooms that aren't full of boxes are full of chambers instead, like the ones holding my fellow humans. Hundreds of them, maybe even thousands, all stacked next to each other with narrow, even gaps on every side. The flat roofs are lit up red, orange, or yellow, reminding me of a typical warning or stop signal.

I quickly figure out that the yellow-lit chambers are empty. When I zoom in close enough, they turn transparent, like the men's earlier. At first I think the orange ones are empty too, except for long, narrow boxes running down the centre of each.

Then I realise that the boxes are coffins of a sort. Slightly transparent, I can just make out sleeping figures inside. Some of them look big enough to be adult Perfected like Kris or sullen Petra, while others are as small as me. They seem to float inside their translucent casing.

Maybe they're medic-chambers like the one I was just in…or maybe they really are coffins with people floating in embalming fluid.

Yuck. And there are *hundreds* of them: sleeping alien people in the orange-lit chambers.

The red-lit chambers, in contrast, contain real, living people. All Perfected, except their yellow-brown skin is mottled with black and green wounds. I can't look at them for long, but I can clearly see that whatever's affecting them is hitting them *hard*.

These ones don't seem to notice me, although a couple of them appear to be communicating through their walls, like the humans were. Except since there's a sizeable gap between each chamber, I conclude the walls must be functioning as video screens. I wonder if the men know.

I resolve to tell them once I find them. See, I've misplaced them during my virtual tour of these colossal rooms, and from a distance, all the red-lit chambers look the same. I've no idea which ones they're in. There's another cluster of red chambers on the far side of this room, so I swipe the screen to head towards it.

But somehow I overshoot, and I find my view zooming right through the outer wall of Halfway Point, into space, and then rapidly towards the glimmering sphere of Rule-of-Law. A second later my view shoots through one of the moon's structures, and then I'm looking at a narrow hall with a short, dark-haired woman in it, who's looking at a hall with a short, dark-haired woman in it...

Oh. I'm looking at myself, but from behind. (And my hair really does look like a curled-up cat poop.) But the images just go on and on, smaller and smaller, like a colossal set of Russian nesting dolls.

I scrunch my eyes shut, feeling momentarily nauseous from the recurring self-portrait, and swipe my hand randomly. I've got to get away from this mirror scene.

Then when I reopen my eyes, I'm somewhere new.

Well, not that new, I amend. These buildings all seem the same, a maze of gleaming halls and partitioned areas and closed doors. The only reason I know I'm on Rule-of-Law instead of Halfway Point is the colour scheme. That is, there's actually colour here – subtle greys, yellows and blues against the shining white.

I send the video down endless hallways. It almost feels like I'm travelling down them myself, flying, or being stuck in a giant video game, and I quickly realise that I must be steering one of the hover balls that I've seen used so many times.

I spot a couple of Perfected moving along with their shiny heads down, both studying images flashing at their wrists. One of them glances up as I whiz by. For a moment I freeze, waiting to be caught out, but they glance away again. Whatever they saw, however I'm making my way around these rooms, it's nothing out of the ordinary.

Around one more corner, and I'm in an entirely new hall. I know it's new because there's a green plant growing right out of the ground, just off to the side. It's about knee-high with big glossy leaves that shine under the bright lights, and there's something squishy around where its roots should be, but seeing it feels like a small miracle after the sterile, unnatural environment I'm stranded in. It's the only plant life I've seen since leaving the Wilds.

At the end of the hall is a greenhouse. There are these huge clear windows, and every last one of them is packed with the same type of plants I've just passed, only far larger. I can see rounded shapes amongst them that look a little like unripe corn, if corn husks were transparent and showed the pale cobs inside.

The small plant in the hall is clearly an escapee. Nice. My stomach rumbles, and I actually reach out for the nearest cob before remembering I'm watching a screen. My hand hits the screen, even though I can't see it, and there's a little sparkling burst where I touch it, before I pull my hand away.

Note to self – when Kris returns, ask him to provide lunch. Or breakfast, even. Now I'm aware of my hunger, my stomach feels like it's turning on itself.

I send the viewer straight through the clear windows into the greenhouse itself, and for a moment I just stop and stare. This is…incredible. The room is simply enormous, as big as the rest of the building I've just wandered around, and several storeys high. The artificial light in here feels a little different, and there's no dirt that I can see.

The plants are planted in levels, each with its own ambient light source. They stretch up in columns to the excessively high ceilings, and I can see small robotic shapes moving amongst the columns as if tending them. A perfectly straight aisle divides the high rows of plants, going far into the distance.

This garden room must be colossal. I wonder how many people it feeds?

I video-wander the aisles for a while, trying to make sense of everything I see, and wishing desperately that my new translator stretched to written text as well. I see some symbols here and there – reminding me of films with 'alien signs in a corn-field', actually – but I've no idea what they mean. Probably nothing much. I should probably get back to the guys. They'll be wondering what I've learned, and there's nothing of use to us here.

Then I hear voices.

"Jud'or, I can't believe you," a female voice says in a hushed whisper from somewhere just out of sight. At least her tone suggests she's trying to whisper, but her voice is as loud as if she was standing right next to me. Naturally, my ears prick up, and I send the viewer skimming around the aisles looking for her.

"You know how hard Krys'tof worked to get this position," she continues. "How hard we *all* worked. And now you're saying you want to give up, right before we have the chance to prove the cure works? You want him to be sent away when he's finally in the position to do real good?"

Ah, there she is. Female, as I'd thought, and I recognise her immediately. It's Petra, Kris's helper from this morning. Her varnished pile of blue-grey hair gleams in the bright lights of the greenhouse, similar to the shade of her clothing, and I can now see that her eyes are a light, bright grass-green, unnatural to any human, but seeming to fit her well.

If I didn't already know how huge she was from this morning, I'd think her short. She's talking to a male dressed in white as if from the facility, and she barely reaches his chin.

"I'm not saying that," a male voice replies just as quietly. He sounds a lot like Kris, or perhaps like one of the males I heard through the vents before the airlock incident. "I don't want to give up, and I don't want him removed. But we need proper authority brought back onto this project! He's not *sound*, Peh'tra! Some of the choices he's been making…"

"Are his right to make," Petra snaps. "He is priate of Halfway Point, signed and sealed by the council. And he will remain so until his tenure is complete. Leave him to do his job, Jud'or. The last thing we need is you bringing in *kzthaka* High Priate Sy'lis who gets in the way of every decision Krys'tof makes, and is trying to pull the formula before we get a chance to see if it works!"

Ooh. Now this is interesting. I gently move my view so I can see the male speaker's face too, and when I see him, I do a double-take.

Joodor looks just like Kris. In fact, if not for his eyes being a distinct gold rather than Kris's silver, I'd say he was the same person. Maybe taller, although it's hard to judge on these screens. Could they be brothers?

"There's no need for name-calling," the Kris lookalike says tersely. "I *do* want the greyce formula tested, and used, because maybe it'll work. Maybe. We all know Krys'tof-Atem is talented – brilliant, even. But he's not sound-minded, Peh'tra! You're too biased to see it! He refuses to follow the laws, and touches tainted things, and-"

"What laws has he broken?"

"He's letting one of those filthy creatures run around freely on Halfway Point," Joodor retorts, sounding very self-righteous. "And he won't cage it properly, and he lets it wear people clothing. Who knows what diseases it could be spreading?"

I finally realise he's talking about *me*. A filthy creature, huh? If I could operate this properly, I'd drop a bucket of fertiliser right on his stupid shiny head.

Petra's expression closes down. "I'm not going to talk about the human child. This is about you, Jud'or-Atem, undercutting our society's best chance to defeat syn in a thousand years."

Joodor's eyes narrow. "Why, because he's supposedly immune to syn, so I should just let him stomp all over our heritage? I want to respect him, Peh'tra! But I need him to behave respectably. Not like a madman who makes mad promises." His voice lowers. "I heard him say he can reverse the Great Disaster. Make the planet liveable again. Surely you don't believe that comes from a sound mind?"

There's a long silence, and I find myself holding my breath. This is what Kris said to me earlier, and I know it relates to the Gate. Reversing the Great Disaster…sending us humans home.

Then Petra says quietly, "Krys'tof-Atem is special, even among the sons of Atem. If it can be done, he'll do it."

"*If* it can be done," Joodor repeats, emphasising the first word. "And if it can't, then he'll be the madman who promised everything, failed, and was cast out. And you'll be the fool who believed him."

There's another long silence. "You need to go," Petra says finally. "Do not bring in the High Council again. If Krys'tof-Atem is to fall, let him fall. Do not trip him then call him clumsy."

Their conversation's over, and the two turn to leave. I reverse my view out of the greenhouse and back to the nearest hall as the tall Kris lookalike leaves, his steps wide and his familiar face as expressionless as if he hadn't just been stabbing his boss/brother in the back.

He passes the rogue corn plant where it grows out of a crack in the hall, and pauses, staring at it. He taps at lights on his wrist, and a moment later, a sphere whizzes out and zaps the plant. It's severed at the roots, and a second light blasts the place it had stood. A moment later the plant vanishes, and the hall now matches all the others. Shiny, clean, and devoid of life.

Then he looks up at me. Right at the camera, of course, but he seems to be staring me right in the eye for a long, uncomfortable moment. Then he turns and walks away.

I stand in front of my video wall, eyes wide and heart pounding, and cursing myself for being careless. I should have remembered that another Perfected saw me earlier, so I'm not truly invisible to the people walking these halls. But I'd started to feel that way.

He would have only seen a hover ball, I remind myself. He wouldn't have known who was on the other side. But still, I shiver. It feels like if Jood knew a 'filthy creature' was watching him, he'd cut me down and make me disappear just like that out-of-place plant.

Slowly, carefully, I zoom out my view, right out of Rule-of-Law's perfect corridors, out of its string-of-pearl buildings, and away from the whole moon. I steer myself back to the floating hulk of Halfway Point, so small against the massive backdrop of the ravaged planet.

Kris is the only person who's treated us well…but even his own people don't seem to trust him.

Chapter 10
Liam

Demi's been gone ages. Now she's finally back, but she's not giving me the right information. Not what I want to hear. "So you're saying that even the alien's own people think he's a crackpot," I summarise flatly. "Wonderful."

"I don't care if he's crazy, as long as he doesn't hurt us," Dominic ventures. "Maybe he *will* send us home." He looks at Demi, and his gaze stays on her too long. "Back to home base, I mean."

I try not to be irritated by his open interest. I have no right to be jealous over Demi, and Dominic has next to no experience with women except for Bianca, his One True Love. He's just curious, I tell myself. "But maybe we can use this," I say, thinking aloud. "Sounds like he's given you far more access than he should have, if you could listen in to those kinds of conversations. Did you get the chance to look for exits?"

"Yes, but I don't know what I was looking at," Demi replies. "I think they mostly use translocation pads. You know, teleporting?"

Dom doesn't know, so we take a moment to explain.

"And there were two giant space suits," she continues, "but even if we got into them, I wouldn't how to get outside."

Dominic relays the conversation to Jerrold, who is sitting just outside the adjoining walls. Although according to Demi, the walls aren't *actually* adjoining. It just feels like they are.

141

"At least we know more than we did yesterday," Demi ventures. Her tone is somewhat flat compared to how it was earlier. Perhaps the overheard conversation threw her. "But I have a lot of questions. Like, what's a son of Atem?"

I shrug just as Dom says brightly, "Oh, I know that one. They're clones."

Demi's eyes bug, and we both turn to stare at Dominic. "Come again?" I ask.

"Clones of Atem," he explains as if it's an everyday thing. "It was on my activity time video today. Wasn't it on yours?"

"No! Mine was about the landscape!" Although there had been mention of Mighty Atem or Awesome Atem or something, there'd been a lot of information to process.

Dom glances over his shoulder for a few moments, then turns back to us. "Dad says his was about the Great Disaster where the Gate turned the alien planet into Swiss chess, or something."

He glances over his shoulder again. "Oh. *Cheese*, Dad says. Whatever that is."

"Right." That sounds like an interesting topic. "So this Atem…"

"He's a hero to the aliens, the founder of their city or something, and he was immune to the virus," Dominic explains. "Every year a new clone is created from his original DNA, trying to recreate that immunity. The clones are called the sons of Atem." He shrugs. "But in the pictures, all the clones looked a bit different from each other, and none of them are immune, right? So I guess it's not working."

"Kris says he's immune," Demi says. Her eyes are wide. "If he's a clone of someone who was immune, that's actually possible."

"He said this directly to you?" I ask.

"Hmm. Not directly," she demurs. "But it makes sense, right? He could be immune to syn?"

"Yeah, I guess so." I shrug, although my mind is ticking over. Perhaps there *is* a chance the formula could work. Or perhaps not, if it's been a thousand years and they're still pumping out Atem clones.

Demi continues, "And these training programmes you've been doing. Ah, activity time. Do you hear the speech in English?"

Dominic and I both stare at Demi. "Sure," I reply. But the incongruity of it strikes me, and I realise what she's getting at. "They must be intentionally translating the language for us. But Dom, you said they've only just started speaking with you – maybe they've only just created a decent English translator as well. And now it's like…they're educating us."

"All different topics," Demi agrees, frowning thoughtfully. "Like a crash course on their culture. I wonder why."

It's clearly not because they're nice people. If Demi's heard right, the one half-decent alien is also half-insane.

Then suddenly she lifts her head, looking over one shoulder. "I have to go."

Demi

I've been waiting for someone to show up and pull me away from my conversation. I'm so aware that anyone could be eavesdropping if they cared enough to, since I did it to the others. But it's not Kris who comes to get me; it's Petra. She's just as giant in person as I remembered, and her expression isn't especially friendly.

Eh. Could be worse. It could be that Jood bastard standing in front of me.

"Come, child," she says from a safe two-metre distance. "You need to go."

I glance back at my new friends, and the last thing I want to do is leave them. Does she know I was listening on her conversation in the greenhouse? Besides, Kris said not to share my abilities with anyone, and that the translator was secret. That was why I didn't mention it when Liam commented that proper translation to English could be a new development. I know it *is* a new development, because Kris told me so.

Petra stares at me for a long moment, her green eyes bright in her shiny face. "Is your translator not working?"

Oh, that's right. She was there when Kris was talking to me, so it's not so secret after all. "It works," I reply, feeling my cheeks heat. "Is there a problem?"

She frowns. "Of course not. It's time for first meal, and you can't eat it in a hallway."

I would have been totally fine eating in a hallway if it meant staying with the others, but I don't argue. Instead I follow her back along the moving pathway to what might be Kris's suite again, or perhaps an identical-looking one. Then I'm left at a tiny table in a small side room as a tray of what smells like food appears in front of me, like a series of small, colourful bricks. Petra leaves, and I stare at the food for a while before launching in.

The food bricks taste as odd as they look, with completely unfamiliar flavours, although they're not all bad. A bit bland, maybe...and at least it's not breadish.

I don't get to see the others again for a while. After lunch, I'm directed to a 'cleansing chamber' which seems to replace my clothing without removing any of it, and which blasts me with tingling air. I squeak in surprise while Petra tells me not to fuss. She's like the impatient aunt I never wanted.

After the post-meal cleansing, there's my own activity time. It involves walking on a treadmill that moves in every direction, while the walls around me turn into video screens. I'm treated to what might be the same video Jerrold mentioned: a detailed description of the Great Disaster.

It starts on a planet covered in massive cities. They're clearly made by the same people whose buildings we've been using down in the Wilds, but they're clean and solid and they go on forever. There are people everywhere too. They're all Perfected, except not so shiny, and with actual hair that moves as they do. Wonders never cease. In fact, they look a lot like big, strange humans.

Hmm. My parallel universe theory doesn't seem so far-fetched.

Anyway, the video's pleasant audio gives me play-by-play description of events as they happen. In summary:

Here is the mighty Perfected empire, wonderful in every way but short on certain resources. More views of those alien cities that don't look entirely alien.

Here's the Perfected discovering a way to get more resources through a massive translocator that works along with a 'spatial tear' – whatever that is. An image of the Gate appears, the very same one I was almost eaten by scavs under.

Oops! The Gate's set wrong, and here's the Perfected accidentally ripping huge chunks of materials from their own planet's past, permanently damaging their atmosphere and weather systems, and releasing a terrible virus to ravage the population!

Argh. Now that one's hard to watch. The walls around me display a civilisation collapsing in a matter of moments as colossal sinkholes appear, swallowing entire cities, and a thick mist seeps out to cover the land. Vegetation withers as people flee into spaceships that head off towards the tiny lunar colony.

They lost ninety percent of the population in the first thirty days after the Gate was first used. Many more succumbed to the syn virus in the months afterwards, while others died from hunger, riots, and sicknesses that would have been treatable in better conditions. Even the lunar colony was decimated – lack of food, violence, and the merciless syn virus the survivors unknowingly carried with them.

The last few Perfected shut themselves away and implemented severe cleanliness laws. Safety laws. Behavioural laws. They renamed the colony Rule-of-Law, and there were severe penalties for anyone who broke even one.

They were their people's last hope. And of those survivors, just one showed an immunity to the virus.

Atem.

I stop walking and stand on my treadmill, numbly listening to the pleasant, neutral voice telling me about unspeakable disasters.

The Great Disaster. And it all came back to the Gate, one terrible mistake, and a people who unwittingly destroyed their own planet.

Nice job, guys.

"You've finished your activity time," the voice tells me pleasantly. "Please move into the cleansing chamber."

I'm not even sweating, but I do as I'm asked. I can pick my

battles.

"I'm going back to talk to my friends," I say after I've been pronounced clean yet again. "Can you direct me?" Petra's nowhere to be seen, so I'm testing the limits of what seems to be artificial intelligence.

"Time for a rest," the voice says as if I haven't spoken. A low bench appears from a nearby wall, lightly padded and just big enough for me to lie down.

OK, that's enough. "I'm not tired," I tell it. I head towards the door.

It slides shut. "Time for a rest," the voice says again in exactly the same tone.

Ah well, it has been a busy day. I guess I could lie down for a bit. Treat it like a siesta.

It's a good time to think, too. I lie on the mouldable foam and try to make sense of what's happened, but it all feels like chaos from the very moment I found that spider in my sleeping bag.

I wish I hadn't reacted so badly. I wish I'd shaken it out and carried on with my day. I would have complained about the rough conditions of the camping trip, not even knowing what I was missing. Freaking Wilds, alien abduction, alien apocalypse...

Hmm. That last one sounds like the name of a movie.

And now I'm here as a sort-of-guest, sort-of-captive. I feel like I've got the chance to make a difference, like maybe I can get the four of us out of here, and maybe it'll be the best decision.

Or maybe I should wait for Kris, because we humans have no idea what we're doing, right? And if he really is a good guy, then he'll help us. That has to be better than running from scavs and boggarts, wearing rags, and eating breadish.

But if he is deluded after all, then it'll be a wasted opportunity, I remind myself as I stare at the perfectly clean ceiling. And while I'd *love* to believe that Kris is going to be my hero, even his own champion Petra didn't seem that convinced.

My hands clench into fists at my sides as despair twists my gut, and I take a deep breath, closing my eyes.

No. I'm choosing to believe that Kris is good for his word, because if I don't have that hope…I've got nothing.

"Time to get up," the auto-voice informs me. Then the bed platform slides into the wall, neatly tipping me onto the slightly padded floor.

"Argh!"

Liam

The day is regimented. There's a second activity time, too short to get my heart pumping or to see the planet properly, and another small but tasty meal. It's probably the equivalent of prison gruel, but I'm just desperate for anything that's not unsalted meat or breadish.

Then there's an unnecessary clean and a rest, followed by more exercise, another clean…

The video in activity time number three tells me about how the aliens treat their sick. As soon as someone's got the virus, they're removed from their people, as is anything that touched them. They're taken here, and they can choose two options.

One, to stay awake, take experimental tests, and talk to their families through technology as their bodies decay. Or two, to sleep until a cure is found. The sickness spreads slower that way, apparently, although it still does spread. And if they stay sleeping, they don't have to feel the pain of slowly dying.

Apparently most of them choose to sleep. Voluntary coma over experiencing the 'taint'. Damn. As for me, I'd rather live and interact, squeeze every moment out of my life till it's gone. Although maybe if it hurt too much, I'd choose sleep as well. Hopefully I never have to make that decision.

Demi hasn't come back. I figure she's probably OK, or else they've decided she's tainted after all, and she's been put in some other chamber.

But we do get more visitors. Unfamiliar aliens, male and female, all oversized and with those shiny, sharply carved features. All walking past our chambers/zoo enclosures, all studying us with visible derision or disinterest. Like we're not people. My chamber light flashes red a dozen times, as if they keep testing me throughout the day. Testing the cure we were given, I mean. But it keeps failing.

I hate it here. I hate being so helpless, so restricted. And I hate how they look at us, or don't look at us. I try to talk to some of them even though Dominic tells me not to bother. I eventually figure that no one's going to talk back, but at least I'm not dropped on my face again. My scav cuts are just scabbing over from my last fall, which is surprising in itself. Usually those cuts never heal enough to scab properly.

Talking to the aliens seems to make them move on faster. By unspoken agreement, we don't discuss anything important when the aliens are around.

"Lot of visitors today," Dom comments. He watches them with narrowed eyes, his scarred arms crossed in front of him against our adjoining wall.

"This isn't normal?"

He shakes his head. "Usually only one every day or two. The new priate shows up more, but he usually tries to talk."

"Which one was he?"

"He wasn't here."

Huh. Still no Demi either.

The visitors finally go, and I start moving around my chamber, looking for weak points, trying to figure out how I even got in here. Unless I was teleported – ah, *translocated* into here, in which case I'd need to smash my way out.

Stupid technologically advanced aliens.

"I hate this," I mutter for the tenth time today. "Not being with you, Dom, just being trapped."

He doesn't respond, and when I glance at our adjoining wall, I can't see him at all. I walk over to it, pressing my face against the surface like he always does. The wall seems to turn transparent, and I can see right into an empty chamber.

Either he's blending in with the non-existent wallpaper, or he's gone.

"Dominic?" I call. But of course he doesn't reappear. The doorless, windowless chamber is completely empty.

They must have taken him away for more tests, the bastards. It's the only thing that could have happened. I curse under my breath, pacing back and forth, filled with helpless fury. I can't think of a way to help him, but there's got to be *something* I can do.

But then I see a figure out of the corner of my eye. It's a lady alien standing on the outside of my chamber. She's taller than any human I've ever seen, with blueish hair and eyes as green as a cat's. She stands there for long minutes as the light flashes red, and her expression is…different. Worried, I'd say. Intent.

Then she steps forward. "Human," she says. "We have a problem."

Demi

I spend my spare time making my way around the suite, looking for a remote or key or useful guide labelled 'translocator', but find nothing I can understand.

I'm *so* bored that I don't even feel anxious, in spite of all the things that could worry me. I can't leave, either. I can move around the suite, but the oval door leading to the outside hall won't open for me.

That seems at odds with what Kris told me earlier about staying in the Lystra block, which implies more freedom than I've currently got. But perhaps Petra didn't get the memo when she brought me here.

Some hours pass – maybe it could be mid-afternoon, if days are counted the same here –then suddenly the outside door opens and Kris steps inside.

I launch myself away from the desk/shelf thing where he'd got my translator earpieces and try to look casual. *No, I wasn't just rummaging through all your drawers.*

I move towards him, intending to ask him to take me back to the screens where I can speak to my friends. But then I see his face. He looks weary, lined, with shadows under his bright eyes.

I guess even genetically perfect clones can get tired.

"Hard day?" I ask.

Kris smiles a little. "Something like that. I see you managed not to go through any airlocks while I was gone. Well done."

"Uh…thanks. How was your…ah, meeting?"

Kris's smile falters. "It went as expected." He moves over to the desk-shelf I just fled from and sits down in front of it, then begins rummaging around. "But let's not speak of that now. I have something you may find interesting." A moment later he holds out a small white stick.

I stare at it, and he adds, "This gives manual access to translocators and quarantine chambers. Of course, we only use it in emergencies when individual access is broken or overridden."

It's a sort of remote control, I realise. This is basically what I've been looking for all day, in between forced naps and exercise time. And now he's holding it out, right in my face. For a moment I visualise myself snatching it, pressing buttons madly…and ending up spinning in space outside Halfway Point.

I swallow, feeling my eyes widen. "How does it work?"

Kris points at various bumps on its surface. "Because it is for emergencies, it is preset for certain locations. This one takes you straight to Halfway Point's main landing pad," – now he points to a raised round ball – "and this one opens any chamber."

"Are you…are you offering it to me?"

"Of course not," he replies briskly, moving the remote away and sitting it on the nearby desk. "It would be irresponsible for me to give such a thing to a young person with little experience of this place. But I would like you to be prepared in case of emergencies."

That's the third time he's said 'emergencies', and I take the hint. "Are we going to have a problem?" I ask carefully.

"I expect we will soon enough. I am not popular with some of High Priates, and they do not fail to tell me so."

No kidding. I've overheard two conversations in twenty-four hours, and both were votes of no confidence. I look down at the tiny remote control, then up at the seated alien. Even sitting, he's looking me in the eye. But his silver eyes are droopy, and deep lines are carved beside his mouth.

"Kris," I say slowly. "I overheard something today. About you. Some people close to you...they don't want you in this job."

He just looks at me, his expression unchanged.

I carry on, filling the silence. "They don't like me, either. And they don't think you can do what you said you can do. Cure syn, I mean, and reverse the Great Disaster."

"Don't they?"

"No."

Kris leans forward. "And what do you think, Dee-mee?"

I squirm and my gaze slides towards the floor. "I..." *I think you're the only person trying. And you're the only one who's treated me like I'm a person too. And it's not like I have any other options.*

But I've taken too long to answer. He sits upright, a sad smile on his face. "It doesn't matter what you think, or what they think. It matters what I do, and who I am. Now I have to go away for a while, and things may look very bad. But remember, when there is life, there is hope, and I always keep my promises."

Oh God. That sounds ominous. I lick my lips, trying to formulate a response.

But then Kris turns his head towards the outer door as if he's waiting for something. I turn with him...

…And then the door flies open. Perfected flood in, wearing striped blue and white that reminds me of circus tents, and carrying alien doodackies that remind me far more of death rays.

I leap back behind Kris, my heart in my throat. Where did they come from? What's with the stripes? Why didn't we get one of those automated warnings? And why are they all so damn enormous?!

They're huge, all of them filling the space and looming over us like malevolent circus performers in a way that doesn't seem funny at all in spite of their bizarre clothing, and I'm on the edge of laughing hysterically or bursting into tears. I manage not to do either, but Kris doesn't react at all. Not one bit.

And then another Perfected steps in. This one's wearing long purple robes and a distinct sneer on his purple-eyed face.

"Krys'tof-Atem," he says in a familiar, unpleasant voice. "I have come to advise you under the authority of the High Council of Priates that you have broken the law. Now I see you've done it twice over with that tainted *thing…* in here."

He's looking at me. He's calling *me* a thing – and I recognise his voice now. He's the horrible one from the conversation I overheard on that first day, from when I was hiding in the ventilation passage. And now I see his awful sneering face, I hate him just as much as I did then. It's a landmark feeling for me: I've never fallen into hate with someone so quickly and so intensely, and along with that hatred is a solid dose of fear.

Kris glances at me intently. "No need to get rough, Sy'lis," he says mildly as he brushes one hand over the desk/shelf behind him. I see the remote slip into his hand. "I will come quietly."

Everyone takes a step towards him…and then he hurls the

remote in my direction. It skids across the floor and comes to a halt at my feet. I dart down and pick it up, gripping it awkwardly in both hands, since it's far larger than it looked in his oversized alien hands.

Suddenly I've got the whole room's attention. Two of the stripe-wearing guards are on Kris, pressing what might be weapons against his neck and chest, and one of them stands a body-length away from me as if afraid to catch my human germs.

Behind him, purple-eyed Syliss sneers. "Stupid creature. Do you even know what that is?"

I take in the scene in an instant. I'm not going to be able to reach Kris, and I'm not going to get him away from the guards. But no one's touching me.

I hold up the remote, then press one finger deliberately over the bump Kris had pointed out earlier – the preset translocator to Halfway Point.

I hold Syliss's gaze and push down hard. Here's hoping it worrr-

Chapter 11

Liam

There's an alien woman outside my chamber telling me we have a problem. I know we have a problem – I'm stuck in a cell. But is that the same problem she thinks we have?

She continues in a deadpan voice, "I have been ordered by Priate Krys'tof-Atem to return you and the other humans to the planet at once, disregarding any injuries or health issues you will face in such an environment, and disregarding that the greyce formula you were given two days ago has not been proven successful. I am legally required to follow his orders."

I blink at her. Could I really be so lucky? "You're going to send me home? Back to the Wilds?" She sounds so enthusiastic about it, too.

The alien waves a hand dismissively. "If I follow orders, which of course I will. But the chamber translocators have stopped working. I have just returned the other two males to the, ah, 'Wilds', but you will need to walk through the facility to the main translocation pad."

Excitement and confusion swirl inside me as I realise that Jerrold and Dominic are already gone. "So…?"

"On foot," she adds impatiently. "Can you do that?"

"Yes!" I burst out. What's with these giants thinking we can only survive the slightest exercise? "Yes! Anytime!"

"Good. Now follow my instructions, because you may not

156

get a second chance."

Her figure blurs then disappears, and it occurs to me that she might be lying, and maybe I'll be walking to a lab for some nasty experiment instead. Because how could I be so lucky? Literally yesterday some bastard was telling me I'd die here, and now I'm leaving?

But then there's a hissing sound and the entire wall in front of me slides upwards. On the other side is a hovering sphere the size of a baseball. It's dull grey with a smattering of blinking green and blue lights, and behind it is a plain white wall.

The woman's voice comes from somewhere around the sphere. *"Well? Come on out, human, unless you have somewhere better to be."*

I decide the risk is worth the reward. So I step out of the chamber, waiting for sirens to go off and for me to be shoved back inside. But instead I find myself standing in an aisle on a shiny white floor in my stiff white sock-booties, outside a box that's been my prison for the last few days.

I glance around. Just across from me is another identical box. Then next to that, with a slight gap, is another box. And another, and another. The whole room is full of them, and it seems to go on forever.

"Come along!"

While I've been staring, the sphere has zoomed off some distance down the aisle. It pauses as if waiting for me, then picks up speed again once I move towards it. It reminds me of the drone technology that was being developed when I was last on Earth – except far better, of course. Surely the woman must be operating it, watching me through some kind of camera.

"Are you even in the facility?" I ask. "Because it looked like you were talking to me through a clear barrier, but was it just a video screen?"

"The details are not relevant," the sphere tells me as it sharply turns a corner down another aisle. *"But yes. We are not in the same location. I am on Rule-of-Law, and as a tainted specimen, you are held on Halfway Point, safely away from the clean population."*

Jeez. I follow the sphere/drone through a high doorway which leads into an identical room, at a pace a little faster than I'm comfortable with. "I'll choose not to take offence at that, since I think you're doing me a favour. But what about the girl, Demi? You're sending her back too."

I say it as a statement, because it's unthinkable that they'd keep her here. Except they've had her aside from the very first day, like some kind of pet. My stomach twists at the idea.

There's no answer for a while, and the sphere speeds up enough that I move into a slow run through the second warehouse-sized room. "Hey," I call out to it. "Demi. What's happening with her?"

"I have been given no particular instructions regarding the girl."

Then the sphere stops abruptly just through a new doorway. Everything's cold, clean white in here – of course – and there are opaque boxes of all sizes, but I hardly pay attention to them. I stop short too. "Then respectfully, you'd better get some instructions, because I'm not going without her."

The sphere's lights blink, and there's a flash of orange under my feet. Then suddenly the whole room's lighting changes, casting everything in an odd pale green.

"Kzthaka," the woman hisses through the drone's speakers, and it sounds like a curse word. *"The main translocator isn't working either. It must have been shut off."*

I realise too late that my refusal to leave without Demi

158

would have been pointless, since I'm actually standing on the translocator.

I step off this orange patch of floor, unsure of what to do next. Around me are boxes of different shapes and sizes – some as large as shipping crates, others as small as toolboxes. I bend to pick up the nearest toolbox-sized shape, then drop it with a huff as its full weight hits me. It's as heavy as lead, but it falls open as I drop it, spilling its contents on the pale green ground.

"Junk," I murmur in surprise, bending to pick up a metallic piece that reminds me of a wrench crossed with a toilet plunger. It's all junk in this box, seeming to have come straight from the Wilds building wreckage.

At least they're recycling. And at least this plunger-wrench has some good heft to it. It would make a decent weapon, even.

"I *shut it off, Peh'tra, along with everything else in Halfway Point,*" a smug male voice says through the sphere. "*You are to stop what you're doing at once and return the creatures to their chambers.*"

I freeze. That doesn't sound good.

"*Under whose orders?*" the female voice snaps back. "*Priate Krys'tof-Atem told me to release them at once. Jud'or, you must turn the translocator back on.*"

Yeah, Joodor! Turn it back on!

There's a sneer – yes, you can hear a sneer – and he retorts, "*And High Priate Sy'lis told me to shut it off. So it stays off, along with everything else except the quarantine chambers. Now, where's that human?*"

"*Sy'lis!? Since when can he override the elected facility priate? The law states that the facility priate has all authority-*"

"*Since this morning when Sy'lis pushed through a new law allowing him to absorb the facility role into his own position, that's*" *when."* The male still sounds smug, but now exasperated too. *"Stop that, Peh'tra. Turn the visual back on."*

"I will not! This cannot be lawful!"

"I just told you it is!"

Still holding the plunger-wrench, I back away from the sphere, which doesn't move, just blinks red, blue and green as the voices alternate. I'm starting to regret my decision to stay put. I can't save Demi – I might be lucky to get away myself.

There's a scuffling sound through the sphere's speaker, then Joodor says in a slightly puffed tone, *"Ah, visual's back on. Aha! There it is."*

I grip onto the makeshift weapon tightly, holding it slightly behind me. The sphere still hovers in the air, blinking different colours, but somehow it seems to be pointed in my direction.

"You there! Tainted creature. I order you to return to your chamber at once!"

I stare at the sphere in disbelief. The female – Petra – was blunt but bearable. But this male, whoever he is, needs a lesson in manners. "I'm surprised you're asking," I say very politely. "And it's a rather long walk for my poor, tainted feet. Can't you just knock me out and send me back yourself?"

Of course it's a risk for me to ask him that, but I figure if he could force me back, he would've done it already.

There's a pause. *"Naturally,"* the male informs me. *"But there is a temporary suspension of all translocation services in the facility. I don't expect you to understand, but it means that no, I cannot render you unconscious in this moment. And you being out of your chamber means the facility will need to be decontaminated everywhere you've touched. It's most inconvenient."*

Basically, he can't get me right now. "Sure." Then I swing the plunger-wrench like a baseball bat. It hits the sphere full-on with a nice, meaty *thwack*, and the sphere goes spinning through the air and hits a nearby crate as big as my bedroom back home. Its round shape now has a distinctive dent on one side.

I'm panting, gripping my new weapon as I stare at the dented sphere, waiting for it to explode or send out lasers to if not render me unconscious, then at least make me regret my actions.

But the lights just blink, then dull. There's no more sound. I seem to have broken the thing.

And then, just because I can, I make a point of touching half a dozen crates with my bare hands. I consider spitting on the ground as well, just to make extra work for whoever will be cleaning the places I've 'tainted', but then decide against it. I'm not *actually* a barbarian, no matter what they call me.

Mild revenge: sorted. Now what?

Demi

I've pressed the translocator button. For a moment my whole body buzzes and orange light fills my vision. Then there's an awful feeling like a full-body sneeze, and suddenly I'm in a new location.

All the Perfected are gone. Instead I'm standing on an orange square of flooring, surrounded by familiar crates. But instead of the blinding white I've expected, everything looks strangely green and dim. Like the lighting has been changed to 'ominous' setting.

In spite of that, I'm definitely back at Halfway Point, in the very same location where Liam and I were first brought through from the planet.

The men. I have to get the men – then we'll be out of here as fast as I can figure out which button to push.

I step off the translocator pad, comparing the greenish environment to this morning's trip with the viewer. This particular room was on one side of the station, I remember, surrounded by massive rooms full of cell-chambers, although unfortunately I was unable to find the men's chambers once I lost them. It'll be trial and error, I guess.

I spot a door in the near distance and take off at a run.

"Demi!"

I know that voice. I screech to a halt, skidding a little on the smooth floor, then turn to see Liam step out from behind a small mountain of crates. He wears his head-to-toe quarantine outfit, and with his plastered hair and shiny skin, he still reminds me of a life-sized GI Joe. The green light makes him look unhealthy and even a little spooky, but I'm so pleased to see him that I almost cry.

"You're out!" I exclaim, running over to him. "Who let you out? Where are the others? I think we're in-"

"We're in trouble," Liam says.

"Of course we're in trouble," I mutter. "When are we ever *not* in trouble?" This whole place has been trouble from the moment I came through the Gate.

Except for running into Liam just now. That's lucky enough that it feels coordinated, which means it probably was. (Thanks, Kris.)

But Liam spills out his story, I share mine in the briefest terms, and next thing we're running back to the place where we were first brought. The main translocator leading back to the planet.

"It might not work," Liam warns me. "I told you how the lady alien had her access revoked by this really awful alien, Syliss. I could hear her arguing with one of the other aliens about it. They might have even shut down the whole facility."

Fear pangs through my gut. If that's true, then how can we possibly escape? "That Syliss is ruining *everything*," I mutter. "I just met him, and he really is awful. But the lady alien must be Petra, and maybe it was just her translocator access that was shut off. They wouldn't have known to cut mine till I escaped Rule-of-Law just now. We at least have to give it a try."

Liam nods brusquely, and the translocator pad comes back into sight. It's just a patch of colour on the open floor, about the size of my living room rug, and without any obvious controls. How does it even work?

I glance upwards, and above the marked area is a cluster of enormous spheres, each twice the size of a Swiss exercise ball and marked with swirling designs that remind me a little of those on the Gate. They're faintly lit up the same green as everything else, and appear fixed to the high ceiling.

"Just like the hover balls," I murmur. "Except huge." Still no instructions, of course. But I've got the master remote, and Kris did tell me how to use it. It seems like he saw this coming.

Liam and I step onto the pad. While it's big enough to fit both of us, I step close to him and he puts an arm around my shoulders. "To make sure we stay together," he says.

Sure. I put an arm around his waist, because he has a good point. Also, because it feels like a hug, and I need one of those around now. My face is close to where his pure white clothing hits his neck. He smells oddly sweet yet chemical, kind of like bleach mixed with custard, and it's not what I would associate with him at all. But that's alien shower gel for you.

"Brace yourself," I say. "Translocation isn't nice."

I fumble with the remote one-handed, then press my thumb hard against the button Kris showed me.

Nothing happens. Not the slightest tingle.

I try again, but the translocator is as dead as an unplugged toaster. Our environment doesn't change one jot, and neither do the massive spheres fixed above us.

"I don't think it's going to work," I whisper. "I think the whole thing's been shut down. So how do we start it up again?"

"We don't," Liam replies flatly, lowering his arm from around my shoulders. Hug over, I guess. "What's the backup option?"

I'm about to say that we don't have one, but then something comes to mind. "We could try the control room."

Liam

The control room. *Of course* there's a control room. And considering we're now stuck in a massive space facility surrounded by sleeping diseased aliens, complete with creepy, dim green lighting, we run for it.

I can run faster, but I let Demi lead the way since she saw the proper view of the facility. She seemed uncertain about the direction, but we're just going for it anyway. I try not to think on how low our chances are of getting out, or of even finding the control room. What if we can't get in? If we're recaptured, it won't be good.

I don't say any of that to Demi. Instead I focus on how Jerrold and Dominic got home – or how the alien female said they did, anyway. It seems likely based on everything else that happened, but I can't trust a non-human right now.

But we have to escape. If we hang around because we think they might still be here, and then we get recaptured, we'll be the biggest idiots in both worlds.

I tell myself that as we jog down narrow aisles filled with individual chambers, dozens and dozens of them in each warehouse-sized room. Most chambers appear empty, with yellow lights on their roofs and lighting up their insides. In other, orange-lit chambers I glimpse shadows of what looks like coffins.

Demi stops suddenly enough that I almost run into her back, then she turns a corner. I jog after her – a fast walk, really, since her legs are short – and then we're suddenly against a high wall.

"I think this is it," she says, indicating at the blank wall in front of us.

Then I see there's a faint square outline marked in the ubiquitous pale material, probably eight feet high. I suppose it could be a doorway. Why else would it be there?

Demi looks down at the narrow stick that functions as a remote. "Kris didn't tell me how to open doors, but he says *this* button opens chambers. So maybe…"

Whoosh. In the corner of my eye I see a chamber wall fly upwards and disappear into its own roof. The interior is empty and lit up yellow.

"Huh. Not that one," Demi says. "Now let's see…"

She studies the remote with narrowed eyes, and I turn back to examine the room we're in. It seems strange to me that there was only the one sphere drone that I broke earlier. Shouldn't there be others chasing us? From what Demi said earlier, the

Perfected use these for everything, including abducting people from the planet. Could the spheres have also been shut off when the rest of the power was? But the chambers are still going...

I step inside the open chamber, checking its ceiling for any weaknesses. If we get recaptured, I'll want to-

Whoosh. The wall/door slams down, and suddenly I'm lit up orange.

I suck in a breath, and my lips tighten. Not gonna panic. Demi's right outside; it'll be OK.

The orange light vanishes, but I can't see anything outside, either. From in here, the walls are completely opaque. I move to the door, which now looks the same as all the other walls, then press my face against the plain surface, tapping against it with my knuckles. "Demi. Demi. Let me out."

A moment later a faint shadow appears on the other side. There's a flash of orange light again. Lighter this time, and noticeably different from when I was in my usual chamber. There must be something wrong with the tester here, since in that other chamber the light was always red.

"Don't run the syn test," I snap, assuming she can hear me. "Open the door!"

The tester light flashes again, but this time it's almost yellow. Hmm. Maybe it's not the test after all. I wait, thinking the door must be about to open, but nothing happens. "The door, Demi!"

Oh God. What if she's locked me in here, or what if the aliens have shown up in the last twenty seconds? I begin to pound on the wall as a bright green light flares up to fill my vision.

"*Syn-free,*" the pleasant auto-voice says. "*Queueing results to send to the High Council once connection is restored.*"

I freeze. "What did you say?"

The auto-voice doesn't respond. But then the door/wall slides open again and Demi's standing there, the remote in her hand and a relieved expression on her face. "Sorry! I don't even know how I did that. But the control room's open."

Indeed, there's now a tidy open space behind her where there'd just been a wall. But I plant my feet. I'm shaking a little. "Syn-free," I say. "Did you hear the auto-voice say I'm syn-free?!"

"No…"

I turn away from the open control room door and run back into the chamber. "Do it again," I order her.

"Uh…OK…"

The door slams shut, and thirty seconds later the green light is flashing again. *"Syn-free. Queueing results to send to High Council once connection is restored."*

It worked. The crazy alien's cure has actually worked.

Demi

We're inside Halfway Point's control room, the door having closed behind us. Liam paces across the small space, visibly jittering. "Do you think it's true? That I'm healed from the scav sickness?"

"Sure looks like it," I reply, but my attention is fixed on the massive screens set around us, against three walls of the smallish room. Another screen splits the room in half, and on the other side is a collection of alien hazmat suits, helmets, and unidentifiable items. "Don't you think these kinda look like space suits?" Far too big for us, though. We'd rattle around in them like children wearing their parents' clothing.

"But if it's healed me, we need to get some for Bianca," Liam continues, still pacing. "Her knee is a wreck. She got gored by a boggart on her hip, would you believe, but the knee's where the worst wound is. Ten years ago almost, and it's just getting nasty now. Hell, it's a death sentence if we don't get her a dose. But how would we administer it?"

I look up from where I'm studying the remote, trying to line up its functions with this unfamiliar room. "Did you just say 'death sentence'?"

"Mm. The scav sickness always kills you eventually."

I stare at him, stunned, and my gaze fixes on those fine white scars across his eye area. "But *you've* got the scav sickness."

"Yeah. But maybe not any longer."

"But…" We'd talked about it when I first arrived, but there was so much happening that I forgot the details. He'd said something about antibiotics, and I'd just…forgotten the rest of it… "But you never said Bianca would definitely die from it," I persist, distracted from my task. "Are you saying that if we don't get her the cure, she *will* die from it?"

Liam nods. "But it could take a long time, and until just now, I didn't think a cure was possible. That's why we were trying to go back to home base anyway, without extra doses of the formula we were given. But now…I don't know what to do."

I don't know what to do either. "Kris has been arrested. I don't know how we're going to get hold of any more greyce formula without him. And the other aliens…"

"Want to lock us up and experiment on us till we die," Liam says. He runs a hand through his hair agitatedly, then looks frustrated when the plasticky mess just makes a squeaking sound. He throws his hands up. "We have to go. We don't have a choice right now."

We have to find a way to go, first. "I wish I could read Perfected," I murmur. Not that it would help with this too-simple universal remote, since there are no symbols on it at all.

I point it towards the nearest screen and mash a couple of random buttons. There's a whirring noise, then a hole opens in the wall behind Liam. Freezing air rushes in, and behind him I can see the planet far below: grey cloud swirling over its ragged surface, lit up by what looks like the rising sun.

I squeak, and Liam glances over his shoulder then leaps away. "Shut that damn thing! Do you want us drifting off into space?"

"Sorry!" I mash at the same buttons again, and next thing the hatch closes with a whir. I clear my throat. "We wouldn't actually drift off into space, you know. There was air coming in, and there's no air in space. Plus, we're far closer to the planet than the moon. This place isn't really halfway."

"Fine, then we'd fall miles and land so hard we end up like pancakes. Either way, let's not."

Fair enough. I press a different button, and suddenly the screens around us light up. "Success!"

But what are we looking at? There's a different view on each screen: one displays the planet below without its cloud cover, another displays a gleaming image of the silvery moon with its sparkling cities, and another shows a big room with long balconies lining its high walls. Little alien figures file into the stacked rows, each seeming as small as an action figure in this distant view. I squint to see if I can recognise anyone.

Beside me, Liam studies the screen with the planet view.

"Hey, look at the continents."

I turn away from the alien-filled scene to Liam's one. I can just make out the jagged shapes of land masses, but can't see anything interesting about them. "What about them?"

"They're pointy on top."

"What do you mean?"

"Back on Earth, you know how some of the continents are like upside-down triangles? I mean Africa and the Americas and even Australia, kind of – they have the bigger part on top and the pointier part down the bottom. But it looks like on this planet, it's the other way around." Liam tilts his head sideways, then leans over so far he's almost upside down. He swears. "Demi, are you seeing this?"

I just stare at him, and he continues, "Can you flip the image?"

Some random button-mashing later, I've managed to get quiet audio along with the screen view, but it's clear I can't flip any of them. So I curl over to echo his upside-down pose, and then I see it.

"It's Earth," I blurt out.

Or what's left of it.

Chapter 12

Demi

We stare at the viewing screen in silence, at the grey, ragged planet in front of us, and then Liam lets out a long, slow breath.

I know he's seeing what I see. The shapes of the continents aren't quite right – a bit skinny in places, and the north and south poles are almost non-existent – but there's no question of what planet this is.

"I said it could be an alternate universe," I say numbly. "I guess this is the...disaster version of Earth. And they've got their maps around the wrong way."

"There's no up and down," Liam says. "It's just the perspective of the people who made the maps, since they didn't want to be on the bottom."

You don't say.

"And why do you think it's an alternate universe?" he continues. "Wouldn't it be just as easy for it to be our Earth's distant future? Or distant past, for that matter, although it seems unlikely considering the damage to the planet. We could have time-travelled."

I hate to think it, but the time-travel option sounds more likely. Especially since... "The experiments."

Liam turns to look at me. "What?"

"The Perfect experiments on *us* so they can get their

formulas right, before they'll consider using their own people." It's all starting to make sense. "But that would be useless, unless we're practically the same species anyway. And…their name. Perfected. Why would they call themselves that if there wasn't an *im*perfect version to compare to?"

"Genetic modification." Liam groans. "Oversized people with weird features and colouring, but still people. What kind of future has humanity got to look forward to? This is a disaster."

It shouldn't be. It shouldn't make any difference to me whatsoever, because unless we can get a specific date, this world seems millennia away from our own version of Earth. Knowing it's probably our Earth's future shouldn't affect our current perilous situation, but somehow it does. It feels terrible.

We stare at the screen a while longer until the faint voices from the balcony-alien scene get my attention. Or maybe I can't call them aliens. Alien-ish humans?

"-filthy primitives pulled from their natural environment and thrust upon Rule-of-Law, using precious resources that should have gone to our own people…"

"They're talking about us!" And not being nice about it, either. And although I can't see who's speaking, the voice sounds kind of familiar.

Liam turns to watch the alien screen along with me. "What are they saying?"

"Um…it's not very flattering. Let me listen a bit longer." It's still the same distant view, but now there must be a hundred people in the scene. The layered levels have perfectly spaced balconies, each with a different shiny-faced alien in it, but quite a few balconies are empty. I'd say this place could fit double the number.

A different shiny-faced alien stands up in their balcony.

"It's hardly their natural environment, Sy'lis. You know that they're out of time, and they're refugees as much as we are."

Out of time? That sounds like a threat...or like Liam's time-travel theory is spot on. "It seems to be happening right now," I murmur, trying to listen and translate at the same time. "Syliss. That jerk – it's him again."

And now I see the first alien, down near the bottom left of the screen. He wears purple, and even in miniature I can see his squinty, unnaturally bright eyes in his sneering face. Ugh. He says, *"Feel pity for them if you like, Aloy'sius, but cleaning them up and dressing them in white doesn't remove their taint, nor does it adhere to the laws that keep us safe. Krys'tof-Atem* has *committed a crime, and that is why we are here, fellow councillors. No other reason."*

"It's Kris," I say as a feeling of dread comes over me. I've just identified Kris himself in the middle of the screen, at the bottom. He looks...weary, with his shoulders slumped and his expression flat. "I think this is a council session, or a court session, or something. And Syliss is trying to get Kris in trouble. Not sure what for."

"For the crime of bringing the taint into Rule-of-Law!"

"Oh. Me, I think." If I'm 'the taint'. Makes me sound quite mysterious and powerful, actually.

There's an outburst amongst those seated, then a rapid argument that my translators struggle to keep up with. "Now they're bitching about me being brought to their home, and someone else is saying I don't have the syn virus anyway and I'm actually human so should be treated as such – oh! That's support for our theory, Liam – now someone *else* is saying that Kris's systems are clearly wrong so how can they trust it..."

Huh. Now someone else comments nastily on Liam's facial

scars, as if they're a mark of shame rather than hardiness. Syliss clearly has his supporters, and they seem to be shouting louder than the others.

Liam seems to be listening intently, and I wonder if he can understand any of it. "Their language kinda reminds me of Italian," he says abruptly. "Or maybe Cantonese."

I shoot him a startled glance, since he's clearly missing all of this. Also, because those two languages have nothing in common beyond the letters A, N and T.

The aliens argue. They continue to insult us – not that Liam can tell – and they say the most dreadful things about Kris, who still sits quietly at the bottom of the screen.

Finally an elderly female stands, and the others quieten. Considering the chaos, that must be a real sign of respect. *"Enough,"* she says, her voice clear even though her face is deeply lined. *"I cannot see that Krys'tof-Atem has truly broken any law in attempting to rescue an ancient human child from a life of poverty and despair. At least not any law that existed when he first did it."*

Poverty and despair? A child? Well, I wouldn't put it quite like that...

Just then Syliss lifts his hand to his ear, as if he's being spoken directly to. His eyebrows shoot up, and he leaps to his feet. *"He* has *broken a different law,"* he says loudly. *"This very morning, Krys'tof-Atem gave his unproven greyce formula to every last tainted Perfected in Halfway Point. Now that, fellow councillors, is law-breaking."*

There's an incredible silence, and I suck in a breath.

Liam

I don't know how we've gone from desperately trying to fix the teleporter (aka translocator) to giving our full attention to a Perfected courtroom. I can't understand a word they're saying, but then Demi gasps in line with everyone else on screen.

"What?" I ask urgently. "What's happening?"

She bites her lip. "Good news and bad news," she says as the room bursts out into uproar again, this time louder than before. "Kris seems to have given all the sick Perfected the same formula he gave us. But he did it before it was proven to work."

I frown, because that wouldn't go down well on Earth either. Our Earth. "I'm guessing that's a problem."

"By their reactions, yeah."

I watch as a familiar male walks into a balcony at the bottom of the screen. He's right next to the male Demi already identified as Kris; apparently the one Perfected that actually wants to help us regular humans. His mouth hasn't moved this whole time.

Demi leans in, fiddling with the remote, then brightens as the image zooms in so faces are clearly recognisable. "That's Joodor! He's confirming that Kris gave the order for doses this morning. He says he couldn't stop it, which is why he went to the council."

To be fair, unproven medicine can be as bad as poison, but it doesn't seem to me like they've given this Kris a proper chance anyway. Who would give a medicine only a day to work before declaring it a failure? But that seems to be what the others have done.

And the formula *does* work, because it worked on me! It just takes a few days to do so. I'm still coming to terms with being healed, because something that good doesn't feel real yet.

Demi scowls. "Ugh. Now Joodor's saying all kinds of nasty things about Kris, and about us. What a rat."

Joodor the Rat leaves, and then a blue-haired female is pushed onto the same balcony. Her eyes are wide and her posture speaks of fear; her shoulders hunched. I recognise her as the one who tried to help me escape, but she looks different here. So small.

"That's Petra!" Demi exclaims. "I guess they got her."

"It's the moon," I say flatly. "Where was she going to go?"

Questions are blasted at the woman, and Demi quietens as she fixates on the scene. After a minute or two of silence, my attention wanders, and I start to look around the room. Maybe I can spot something we've missed.

Behind me Demi says, "And now Petra's turning on him too. Seriously? Can't poor Kris get some decent friends? She's saying she was just following orders and had no idea what Kris was up to. Well, *that's* obviously untrue."

Hmm. Here's the outline of that exit hatch Demi accidentally opened, the one I almost fell through to my death... Doorway back to the main room full of quarantine chambers... Screen with planet view... Screen with moon view; a little black shape glaringly obvious against its pale purity...

I pause, staring at the shape. Its shape reminds me of a boxy bumblebee, and it seems to be getting bigger.

"Now they've got Kris up there," Demi's saying behind me. "And he's *finally* got the chance to speak. But ugh – all they're asking is if he believes he's immune to syn! And he's saying that of course he is, and he made the cure with his own...blood. *Oh.* And now he's saying he wants to, um, 'reverse the Great Disaster' and resettle the planet, but no one seems to like that idea. They're accusing him of...destroying their society. Oh dear. I think he's in trouble, Liam."

I'm still staring at the shape in the moon screen, which is becoming increasingly obvious as a shuttle or spaceship of some kind. "We're in trouble too."

"Yes, obviously. But they're saying something about testing Kris. They just keep shouting 'test him, test him'! I wonder what that means-"

"We're about to have company," I cut in, pointing at the moon screen. "Something's coming towards us."

"Oh." Demi finally turns away from the Perfected-filled screen, and in the silence I hear them chanting something over and over. But she looks at the moon screen and frowns. "Crap."

Agreed.

"What do we do now?" she asks. "Try to hijack the shuttle, take a hostage?"

"With what? We don't even have a stick, and they'll knock us out from a distance!"

"If they could do that, wouldn't they have already done it?"

I'm pacing across the control room now, trying to run my fingers through my stupid plastic hair in what is clearly a nervous gesture. I forcibly move my hand down by my side. "They obviously can't use any more drones against us here, or even translocate straight here from Rule-of-Law at the moment, or yes, they would've already done it. That must be the system shut-down the Perfected talked about. But I think they'll have weapons we can't even compete against. Physically, *maybe* we could kick them in the groin and run for it. But I think our chances are terrible."

Demi visibly sags. "Then what do we do? We can't just let them recapture us. Not when Kris is...being tested, or whatever.

The others – they think of us like animals."

"I don't know," I say. "We've got no options." But then my gaze falls on the space/hazmat suits hanging on the wall nearby. "Or maybe we do – we could get into those. Maybe they won't be able to zap us through the suits."

"Zap us?"

I wave a hand. "You know. With alien weapons, like the ones you said those striped guards held on Kris."

Demi grimaces. "It can't hurt, can it? The suits, I mean. The weapons will probably hurt."

So after a little wrangling to find openings and access points, we get into the suits. The material's thick and rubbery, but light for its size. There's no obvious fastening, but once we put our feet into the oversized boots, everything seems to *shlllp!* suck in and zip right up to the neck. Demi looks like one of those rolly dogs with all its loose skin, the fabric having to cover far less distance than normal, and I imagine I look the same.

I pick up a helmet and sit it over my head. It locks into place with the suit, and a moment later its visor comes down to cover my face entirely.

Then the whole visor lights up on the inside. It's covered in scrolling text, shapes and symbols that make no sense to me as they move in front of my face.

"*Katsa dee kahmen.*" A familiar voice comes right into my ear. "*Deff tallip eksassion.*"

It's the same voice used within the chambers, but of course I don't understand a word it said.

"Translate?" I ask hopefully. "English, like in the chambers?"

"*Deff tallip eksassion.*"

Through the scrolling shapes I can see Demi wearing a

matching helmet. She's standing still and quiet, then suddenly she starts jumping up and down, gesturing to me.

A moment later I hear her voice in my helmet's speaker. "Cool, it's a computer! Is it working for you, Liam?"

"Not in English!"

"Damn." She puts her hands on her hips. "Give me a minute. I'm going to ask it something."

There's a faint *click* and I can't hear her anymore. I turn back to the video screen displaying the moon and the shuttle that's steadily growing closer, and to my horror it's more than just closer. It now fills half the screen, so close that it appears to be attached to the station.

"*Deff tallip eksassion,*" the auto-voice says again.

"I don't know what that means!"

There's that *click* again. "The shuttle's connecting to the station," Demi says tersely through my helmet's speaker. "Ah. Now it's connected. Three people onboard...stepping through the access point. They're on the other side of the facility, it says, but they'll be here in...um. Don't know that unit of time."

It feels like we're counting down till our own capture; standing here uselessly. I look around the room again, desperate to find something that'll work as a weapon. But you can't fight superior tech with just desperation, can you?

"Wait," Demi says suddenly. "The computer says these aren't just hazmat suits."

"So?!"

Her suited up figure turns awkwardly towards the wall, the same one with the exit hatch I almost fell through earlier. "So it turns out we're a *lot* closer to the planet than the moon. And the suits are designed for emergencies *outside* Halfway Point..."

"Where are you going with this?" I ask with a growing

179

sense of dread.

Demi turns away, fumbling with the remote. A moment later the hatch (AKA chasm of death) opens, revealing the grey-clouded surface of the planet far below. The sun's hit it, touching the clouds with gold, and it looks surprisingly lovely from up here. "The suits are used as escape pods, Liam. Out in open space."

"You're suggesting we throw ourselves out of this *space station*, into freefall, and see where we end up."

"More or less. Yes."

I glance at the open hatch again. Freezing air must be rushing in, but I can't feel it through the suit. Still, it's a hole with an unfathomable drop underneath. Every part of me shrivels at the mere idea of going through it.

"Demi." My voice comes out in a squeak. "Even if these suits *do* have built-in parachutes or rocket packs or something and we *don't* die, we have no idea where we'll end up! We could land on the wrong continent!"

"They're programmable," she replies stubbornly. (I can't see her expression, but by her tone I expect it's stubborn.) "I've told my computer to take us both to the Gate. It seemed to understand."

"So our suits are connected?"

"They are now. Mine controls yours."

That makes me *very* uncomfortable. I twitch a little, glancing once more at the gaping hatch. "OK, so it's an option."

"Also," Demi continues, "I've just been alerted that one of those three people who boarded Halfway Point is trying to take control of both our suits, but I think I've shut them out for now."

Ah. "Right," I say, far more calmly than I feel. "I guess

we've chosen our option."

I just don't like it.

Bad option. BAD OPTION!

I feel like I'm in a gigantic wind tunnel, like every limb is being massaged by massive jets of cold air. Only it's not really cold, not through the layers of the slightly too-loose suit which flaps rapidly against my skin.

But that's not the real problem. The problem is that we're in free fall, spinning through the upper atmosphere on our way to the planet down below. In space suits. With no guarantee of where we'll land...or *how* we'll land.

This is the worst idea I've ever agreed to.

"Isn't this amazing?" Demi's voice comes through my helmet's speaker. "It's like extreme sky diving!"

While I'm near-paralysed by fear, Demi seems energised. Strange, because I'd thought...well, that I'd be better at this sort of thing. Just goes to show you can't tell how you'll respond till you're actually in a situation.

I grit out a reply through clenched teeth. It's all I can do to keep my eyes open. When we first jumped – or she yanked me out, to be honest – we'd been holding hands in hopes of staying together. That hadn't lasted long. Now we're separated enough that I see her, but there's no way we could touch.

"Are you *sure* these things follow directions?" I manage to ask. "Are we *definitely* heading to the Gate?"

"It says we are! Let's just see where we end up!"

Now I do close my eyes, because I don't like that answer, and there's literally nothing I can do to change the outcome. We could end up miles apart, on the wrong continent, never to see another person again until the not-aliens come back to find us…

I'm cursing myself a thousand times over. It's easy to do since after my initial panic at falling, it's turned into a surprisingly smooth ride. Fall. I'm snug in my oversized suit, the fabric hardly rattling at all now, and I'm not even spinning anymore. Instead I'm facing downwards, and it feels like I'm falling gently despite our true speed.

It's all an illusion, of course. We're not falling gently at all, but instead as fast as gravity can pull us to the planet below.

I can't believe people actually sky dive *on purpose.*

Out of my clear helmet I can see actual landscape now: grey mountain ranges, plateaus and bodies of water, and these colossal pools of grey cloud that might cover water or…the pits.

I wonder if there really are parachutes on these suits. Nothing's released, and we don't seem to have slowed at all. I picture what it'd be like to hit the ground at this speed. There wouldn't be enough of us to bury, that's for sure. But I must have reached maximum panic for one day, because the idea just makes me feel resigned and a little depressed. I guess I won't be around long enough to care.

Splat. Damn it. What a way to go.

But at least it'll answer my questions about whether there's an afterlife. I hope so, since this regular life has been crappy enough that I'll feel ripped off if it's the only type of existe-

"*Dahfalla k'ratha. Ee ratha nee kennard,*" the auto-voice tells me.

I perk up. "Demi, my suit said something! What's happening?"

There's silence within my helmet.

"Demi?"

Still no response. "Ah…is it saying to release parachute?" I say hopefully. "Locate other suit? Locate landmark?"

"Ee ratha nee kennard."

Suddenly my helmet's full of foam, and my cheeks and lips are crushed into an awkward pout. I can't move an inch or do anything except look at the rapidly approaching ground. I'm rushing towards an expanse of greyish brown, right on the edge of a swirling expanse of white cloud, and I realise in dismay that I'm about to land right next to one of the pits.

I tense, my whole body bracing for an impact I can't avoid. Well, I guess I'm about to answer that afterlife question…

…But then I *miss* the ground, and shoot right past it into the cloud…into the pit. Grey fills my vision, and suddenly there's the strangest feeling like *'boiinngg'* and every molecule jolts to a stop. My heart skips a beat, and I let out an involuntary squeak.

But that seems to be it. I'm not moving any further. I don't seem to be falling at all, either. Maybe it wasn't a pit after all, but a low pool of fog that I'm still caught up in.

The auto-voice murmurs something unintelligible, and a moment later the crushing pressure releases from around my face and body. I slump down, but the ground under me seems soft and squishy, although becoming less so. I feel like I'm on a deflating air bed, or possibly stuck in a pool of gel.

So this is what a Perfected parachute feels like. I feel oddly apologetic towards whoever designed these things, since I cursed them in my mind so many times as I was falling. But I'm also annoyed because I was freaking terrified and didn't need to be. (Unnecessary terror is such a waste of energy. Really.)

Although did the suits really have to disconnect me from Demi *just* as we were landing?

A few moments later I wriggle my way free of what looks like a giant bouncy ball, partially deflated and stuck against a high rock wall, mostly hidden by the pervasive mist. The suit seems to have blown up into this protective barrier/ball which cushioned me from impact, but I can't escape from its protection without leaving the suit behind.

So it's just me in my bright white alien booties and tunic, completely unprepared for the cold. Amazingly, apart from the adrenaline shakes and a slightly swimming head, I seem to be unharmed.

Well. We missed the Gate, but I seem to have landed on a path of some kind. I could swear I went into a pit...

"Liam?"

Demi! I jump up in excitement, because my number two fear has just been dashed: being left alone for the rest of my life. (The number one fear is being splattered on the ground into a pancake ten feet wide.) I can't see her, but she sounds nearby. Those wonderful, terrible suits *have* landed us close to each other.

Not so useless after all.

"Here," I call as loudly as I dare. We're back in the Wilds – that means every second thing out here wants to eat us.

"Where's here?"

"Follow the sound of my voice," I call again, "but be careful. We're on the edge of a pit, or maybe even inside one." I climb to my feet, one hand on the nearest rock wall to steady myself. I can't see more than five feet of worn ground in any direction, and I'm wary of launching forward into what might be a colossal drop.

"Oh," Demi says a moment later, her voice sounding thin through the fog. *"There's a drop."*

Yes, I just said that. But better that she knows it too.

I move into a crouch, shuffling forward in an awkward

duck-walk as I pat the ground ahead of me. It soon becomes clear that I'm on a narrow ledge, with the ground dropping steeply away from me and a rock wall behind me.

"Watch yourself," I tell Demi, even though she's probably figured that out herself.

"You don't say."

Her voice sounds closer now, and we persist, shuffling towards the sound of each other's voices until I can make her out through the grey, pervasive fog. Dark hair still plastered to her head; bright yellow clothing, light brown skin.

My heart leaps at seeing her. There's been too much fear today. Too much separation.

"I'm so happy to see you," Demi calls across to me, her voice holding much of the same emotion I'm feeling. "I thought we were dead for sure, or at least lost."

"I second that." Another wash of relief comes over me, and I pick up my pace. But a moment later it's clear I celebrated too soon.

There's a ravine between us. A gaping gorge full of mist, only about ten feet wide, but too far to jump. It could be ten feet deep or a thousand.

"There's still a drop," Demi says redundantly.

You don't say. "It's OK," I tell her. "We just need to follow it along till it joins up. I'm sure I saw us go into a pit, so best-case scenario, it's the one near home base."

"It is that one. I saw the Gate as we came down. We were meant to land here."

"Meant to land at the Gate," I correct. "Rather than in the pit next to the Gate. But if we're near it, then best-case scenario we're on the same side as home base. The pit's as big as Australia."

Demi harrumphs. "Worst-case scenario?"

"We're weeks away?" I quip. Ha ha, *ha*. "But let's just get ourselves out and worry about it later."

Her lips flatten, and she gives a sharp nod. I take that as agreement, and try not to dwell on any more worst-case scenarios. Like, that we're deep in the pit, so deep we'll never get out. Or the moment we get out, the Perfected abduct us again, and get the others too. Or we get attacked by something and don't have any means of protecting ourselves...

My hands clench as I shuffle along, as if reaching for a spear, and I push the thoughts aside. I have to focus on what I can control: finding a way out.

The ravine looks to be narrowing in one direction, so we begin to move in unison, faster now but making sure to keep each other in sight. We walk along for a good twenty minutes, and every time I *think* it's getting narrower, it just widens again. We seem to be moving uphill, though. Maybe.

"Stupid space suits," Demi says a while later, panting a little at the exertion. "They could have landed us anywhere at all, and it had to be here!"

I go to say that I'm still happy to be alive, (and still planning on a celebratory hug with more glee than I ought), but even sucking in a breath makes my throat hurt. I put one hand over my mouth. "I think there's something wrong with this air."

It's the mist, we eventually decide. There's something in it: some kind of gas or chemical that definitely doesn't suit humans who need to breathe. It makes me feel like I've run a marathon when all I've done is shuffle along a rocky path. So we cover our mouths and focus on moving as fast as we can – the sooner we're out of here, the better. Besides, it's surely safer to be quiet.

I periodically check in every direction, looking for any kind of landmark, or even any kind of animal. Not that I want to run into a scav or boggart or any of the myriad oddities that live in this version of Earth, but it's not a good sign that this place is just…rock. It makes me wonder how deep we might have fallen.

But just as I think that, I see a deeper grey shadow on the rock wall behind Demi, across the ravine. I cock my head. Is it just her own shadow?

She hasn't noticed anything and keeps walking, her tunic pulled up a little to cover her nose and mouth. The grey shadow moves along with her, but its shape isn't right. It's as long as she is, wider, and its parts seem to move individually. And now I can hear a skittering sound, like rapid typing on a computer keyboard…or like something else.

"Demi," I say in a low, steady voice. "Move faster."

She freezes. "What?"

Shoot. That wasn't what she was supposed to do. "MOVE!" I shout, breaking my rule of silence. I can't see the thing properly but I KNOW she has to move.

My words propel her into motion, and she scuttles forward, looking around her with noticeable anxiety.

Then I see the moment she spots her 'shadow'.

Demi

We've been walking along these ledges for ages. I wonder if once it was one path that was somehow split down the centre, maybe in an earthquake. My head's kind of fuzzy, and I wonder if that's due to the mist or the shock of our colossal fall.

I can't believe we're *alive*. Jumping out of that hatch had to be the scariest thing I'd ever done, and if we hadn't been out of options, I don't think I could have managed it. The fall was strangely thrilling, though. And then the landing…

Thank goodness the suit gave some explanation as it went along, so I had an idea of what was about to happen. Unlike poor Liam…

But I keep thinking about Kris being tested, and what that might mean for him and for us. About this place being an awful lot like Earth's terrible future full of terrible semi-humans; about how grateful I am to be with Liam, even if the ravine separates us.

I couldn't bear to be alone right now.

"Demi," Liam says from across the gap. "Move faster."

I come to a halt. "What?"

"MOVE!" he roars.

I shuffle forward as if on autopilot, but then I follow his gaze to the vertical rock wall beside me.

It's moving. It has…legs. Lots of them, each as long as my arm. Grey legs on grey rock, and a fat grey body the size of my head, and what looks like a long lobster tail pressed against the rock. The tail curls away, revealing what looks an awful lot like a stinger.

It's a scorpion the size of a teenager, and it's right. Next. To. Me.

"EEEEEEEEEEEEE!!!"

I let out a primal, terrified scream and sprint down the path.

Chapter 13

Demi

Driven by panic, I run headlong into the mist. I can't see more than a few feet in front of me, but I can hear this monstrous *thing* keeping pace right behind me; can hear the *snicksnicksnick* of its claws against the rocky cliff beside my path.

Then abruptly the path reaches a dead end. I lurch to a halt in front of the pile of rocks and rubble, reach down and grab the biggest rock I can find, then turn and heave it towards the creature.

Smack. The rock hits it mid-body. I see a glimpse of it falling off the vertical rock wall and onto the path in a tangle of grey limbs, then it's just a body-length away from me, lying as if it's stunned. It looks more like a giant spider now, if spiders had tails.

That's worse!

My heart pounding, I scramble for another rock and hurl it at the thing. Then another, another, another… It's still moving, and I know that if it comes at me, I'll have no way to defend myself. We're here without coverings – without weapons!

"Demi." Something touches my wrist.

Liam's a moment away from getting a rock to the face, but I recognise him at the last moment and lower the rock with shaking hands. How did he get on the same side as me?

"You've killed it," he says, and his lips curl upwards. Is he actually *smiling* right now? "Look, Demi."

I look. Instead of a giant spider-scorpion, there's just a pile of rocks. I can see a pointy shape that might be an insectoid foot, sticking out from the side. It's not moving, but I don't trust it to stay that way. I'm panting and shaking, but I don't let go of the rock I'm holding. "That…that…"

Liam whistles low. "That must be what Jerrold meant when he talked about land lobsters. I've never seen one before."

"Land lobster? That's a gentle name for such a monstrosity!" I mentally apologise to the memory of the spider that started all of this – the one I'd found in my sleeping bag. Really, it had been only a few inches wide. Nothing in comparison.

"Mm. Apparently they're good eating, if you can get through the carapace. Tastes like lobster." He grins at me. "Shall we drag that one home for dinner?"

I stare at the leg with its thick chitinous shell…and I actually consider it. "I'm not touching it," I warn. "But if you can make it look like shredded lobster, you're on." Beggars can't be choosers.

Liam moves towards the pile of rocks that now reminds me of a travel grave. "You're lucky," he says. "Never thought I'd run into one of these without a weapon, but I guess fifty stones does the job."

Lucky. I study our surroundings and realise that his own parallel path comes to a dead-end at the same place mine does. He must've jumped across when I was stoning the land lobster.

I turn back him to comment on it, but then I see the rock pile covering the beast shift suddenly.

We both freeze. "Um…" I squeak.

Then it shifts again, sending stones cascading off the body

and the side of the path. The drop is so high that I can't even hear the rocks land.

"It's alive!"

The land lobster/hell beast is *definitely* alive. It seems a little stunned, moving slowly as it pulls itself from the pile of rocks I'd covered it with. I leap up onto the rockpile blocking the end of the ravine, ready to climb for my life, but then Liam says, "Look, it's leaving."

Indeed, the beast presumably decides we're not worth the trouble, because it shuffles its way right over the edge of the cliff. All the panic-energy deflates from me as it becomes clear that the beast isn't coming back. Those things must have *amazing* grip, and I know there was nothing like that alive in our own home time. The same people who came up with parrot-monkey scavs must have decided to resurrect some ancient arachnid or crustacean. Idiots.

They were probably the same people who created the Perfected. As I said, idiots.

"I was going to kick it over anyway," Liam says.

I laugh, because I'm happy to be alive. "You sound disappointed."

He turns and smiles at me, one corner of his mouth crooking upwards. "Maybe a bit. But let's get going before that thing comes back with all its friends."

Agreed!

We're walking side by side up what turns out to be a distinct path, also going distinctly upwards. I'm keeping as close to Liam as I can manage, and he doesn't seem to mind. He even takes my arm to help me around rock piles, and I don't mind that either. Human contact feels good, even though our varnished skin squeaks with even minor contact.

My limbs ache from the exercise, but the Perfected kiddie shoes are comfortable enough, and it's not any worse than my original team trek through Mount Freedom National Park. The air seems to improve as we go, and we relax into quiet conversation.

"You said you saw the Gate, but we'd be lucky to be really close," Liam says. "First thing we do once we're out is find shelter and weapons. Then, we can find home base. See if the others have made it yet."

I glance sideways at his tight expression. See if they made it out at all, he means. "If Petra says she sent them back by translocator, then I'm sure she did. She might have cast all the blame on Kris at the trial," – the coward – "but apart from that, she seemed to be on his side, and he was on ours. The translators he gave me have been invaluable." I raise a hand to one ear, grimacing a little since I'd forgotten I was even wearing it. "Maybe I should take them out. They could have some kind of tracker in them."

Liam freezes. "Damn. We better get rid of those."

But when we stop and try to remove the translators, the little shapes seem to be stuck fast in my ear canals. "Ow!"

"It's no good," Liam says regretfully, moving away from me. "They're not going anywhere, and I don't want to hurt you."

I don't want to hurt me, either.

"Besides," he continues, "they could just as easily have put something in our clothes – even injected into our skin, and how would we know? Their tech is better than anything we've come up with back home, and *those* chips are small enough to hide."

I rub my bare arms nervously. "I hope Kris gets away from that testing soon. He can help us out, or even Petra if she's brave enough. I suppose it's better to keep the translators so he can find us more easily."

Liam gives me a sharp look. "You're expecting the aliens to come help us? You *want* them to?"

"Just Kris," I say defensively. "Who else is going to open the Gate? You? You've been here for what – five years, and you haven't worked it out yet? And you weren't even the first one here."

Liam pauses, then steps away from me. "We should keep moving."

I follow him. "How long *have* you been here? I can't believe I haven't asked this till now, but I guess it's been busy." To say the least.

He doesn't answer at first, seeming to focus on the path. Then he replies evenly, "Eight years."

I skip a step. "That's...a long time. I didn't realise you'd been here quite that long." Or maybe I'd suspected it had been near that long, but I'd purposely refused to think on it. It sounded far worse when he stated it bluntly like that.

"We didn't exactly get the chance to talk about it."

Not entirely true. He could have told me when we were walking together, before we were taken. But the knowledge of *eight years* makes me feel strange inside. "So...Jesse was born here. You must have been here when he was born."

Liam nods.

"And...if the Gate opens quarterly, then you've had...thirty-two chances to go through it," I say carefully. "But you're still here."

"I told you, it's hard to operate-"

"And how long has Dominic been here?" I persist. "Jerrold? How long, Liam?"

Liam

This is the conversation I never wanted to have. I didn't have much time to think about it, but I'd had enough to decide that I'd keep it from her as long as I could. Same as the others did for me.

Honesty isn't always the best policy – not when the truth can be so upsetting that it prompts you to make terrible decisions.

But I can't lie to her. Not outright, not again. Not here in this isolated path where we could be ambushed by land lobsters at any time.

She deserves to know the truth.

I let out a long, heavy sigh. "Dominic was born here too, Demi. Just like Jesse. Jerrold came through the Gate with his wife when he was a young man. He was...the first, or maybe the second – but there wasn't much left of the first person, since they only found remains outside the Gate."

She gasps a little behind me, and I slow down, waiting for her to catch up. But I can't look at her. "But...why would they stay here for so long?" she murmurs. "It's not a good life, and they need antibiotics for the scav sickness-"

"They couldn't get the Gate to work," I cut in. I'm trying to be careful with her, but I've just got to say it. "It doesn't work in reverse to let people back through to Earth, Demi. Nothing they did worked, and they tried for *years*."

"But you said it opened quarterly..."

"*Nothing*," I repeat emphatically. "Nothing works. And...it's not any different quarterly. I...I just said that so you wouldn't get upset."

There's silence, and when I don't even hear her shuffling

steps, I stop and turn around. Demi has come to a halt behind me, and her pretty face wears an expression of betrayal. She stares at me for long, long moments. Then when she speaks, her voice is tiny. "Upset because you don't know how to go home? Because you thought we were...stuck here?"

I shrug in confirmation. "As far as we know, once you're through the Gate, you're here to stay. But of course...we didn't know about the Perfected." For all that's worth. They might have cured us of the scav sickness – I *hope* they have – but I expect nothing more from them. I don't say that now, though. She's angry enough.

"So you lied to me," Demi says, her volume rising. "You told me to just wait three months and I might be able to go home, but as far as you knew, it was impossible! You thought I was trapped here forever with the lot of you. Is that right?"

"Uh...yes. More or less." I don't like how she's said 'you thought', as if there's any alternative. As if it's my opinion rather than hard-won, painful certainty. "But please, keep it down. We don't want to attract any attention."

She huffs in a sharp breath through her nose, her lips still in a tight line of displeasure that I can *feel*. Then she continues in a low, hissing whisper. "Let's leave aside the fact that you lied to me from the moment we met, shall we? Liam, you and your *friends* didn't even notice that the moon was inhabited! Kris said the Gate is damaged, but he's working on fixing it. *They* are going to fix it, because he promised he could heal syn, and he did that too!

"So he'll finish his testing, come find us, and fix the Gate. Then we'll go home, because there is no way in hell that I'm living out the rest of my days in an abandoned compound with five other people, eating burnt meat and rough grains!"

Damn. And she still doesn't know what breadish is, either. *And* she really thinks the Perfected can send us home... Could she be right?

A pang of hope rises up in me so sharply that it steals my breath. But I quickly squash it down, which is almost as painful.

I can't hope. Not now. Not after I've finally come to terms with my situation – that if we're lucky enough to get back to home base, the best I can expect is to die away from our Earth, trapped by that bloody Gate and living off a wild, high-protein diet. Because if I allow myself to have hope now, and then it's dashed... I think it will destroy me.

"That'd be real nice if the Perfected can send us home," I whisper back, intending to sound sarcastic, but my voice comes out ragged. I gesture to our current position, stuck on the side of a terrifying drop. "And even assuming they're kind enough to let your friend Kris out after whatever he's done to annoy them, which I doubt, you're being harsh on me. On *us*. Yes, I lied so you wouldn't get upset! And I was looking for Jerrold, who I thought was...dead, and I couldn't have a panicking newbie on top of that. Do you know what happened when *I* found out the truth about the Gate?"

I don't give her a chance to respond, continuing, "The others kept me believing we could work it for five years. *Five years*, testing the Gate and trying out different methods and believing, believing there was *some way* we'd make it work! And when I found out the truth, that they'd only been humouring me so I wouldn't lose hope, I was so upset that I punched Dominic and ran off into the Wilds by myself. He came after me, and we got into a screaming match that drew a pack of scavs. They wrecked my eye, and we both almost died. Until yesterday I thought Dominic had! And it was only my guilt that kept me going. I didn't...I don't want to leave Jesse alone when the others are gone. I *can't*."

I turn away from her, my shoulders slumped and my arms wrapped around myself, unable to look her in the eye. "I'm sorry I lied, but I don't know what else I could have done."

Demi doesn't reply for long enough that I wonder if she won't. Then finally she says in a dull voice, "Any more terrible secrets?"

Breadish springs to mind, and I pause. To reveal, or not to reveal? Ah, better to get it off my chest while she's mad at me about the other lies. "There is one thing, but it's really not that bad."

"*Please*, just tell me. I can't stand any more surprises."

I glance at her, and her expression is sincere. And while I know the breadish 'secret' is nothing compared to the Gate being one-way, it's still hard to admit. "It's about breadish. It's, ah, not made from grains. It's actually made from a sort of...um...locust."

Her expression doesn't change, and encouraged, I add, "It's nutritionally sound enough that it keeps us alive when there's nothing else to eat. It's made in machines in the walls that breed the locusts super-fast and then...process them."

Demi's face is completely straight. "So when I said I found a bug's leg in my food the other day, the truthful answer would have been that it's *all* bugs."

"Er...yes."

Silence.

Silence.

Silence...

Then Demi cringes and lets out a long, low, horrified shriek, scrunching her eyes shut.

I cringe back, looking around us frantically. "Sshh! We need to be quiet-"

"I don't care!" she hisses. "Liam – I do not want to talk to you again, OK? I need some...some space!"

I look down at the path we're stuck on, with its rocky wall on one side and the ravine split leading to a massive drop on the other. "But we need to travel together-"

"I don't care!"

Then she stomps on up ahead...maybe treading a little quieter than she could, but it doesn't seem like it.

I get the hint: breadish being bugs *was* a terrible secret after all.

I sigh, pick up a couple of rocks to serve as weapons, then head off after her.

Demi

Ugh.

UGH!

I can't stop shuddering when I think of what I've eaten. On top of everything else, it's too much to handle. But I can't escape Liam, and I shouldn't try to, not when we're in such danger and I've already made more noise than I should have. Finally I calm down enough for my logical self to override my emotions.

Plenty of cultures eat locusts, grasshoppers, even ants and scorpions, logical Demi points out as we trudge along, Liam's footsteps sounding behind me. *It's not a big deal. At least it's not cannibalism.*

Fine, so it wasn't cannibalism – which would be a line I could never forgive myself for crossing, even accidentally – but *bugs?* Bugs are for...scavs, and long-bearded prophets, and people from other cultures much more creative than mine.

But I suppose it's not *that* bad. Better than starving. But the thing about him thinking the Gate was one-way, and just telling me it wasn't so I wouldn't get upset...

My shoulders tense, and I shoot a glare over my shoulder before I manage to get myself under control. I hate being lied to, just hate it.

But the circumstances weren't normal, logical Demi points out, so I should probably let that go. It's true that when I first came through the Gate, Liam was desperately trying to find Jerrold, and if he'd said it was one way I'd have panicked for sure. I probably would've tried to run off into the wilderness – anywhere away from the crazy guy with the mismatched eyes and the trash-chic outfit.

Logical Demi makes sense, but is often overwhelmed by emotional Demi. Right now both are battling inside my head, but I'm able to think clearly of what needs to happen next.

We need to get to familiar ground. We need to find Kris, we need to get a dose of greyce for Bianca and Jesse, and we need to arrange a way for the Gate to be reopened. Or Kris will need to, anyway. Once he's got away from horrible Syliss and whatever the 'testing' is.

Except that at home base, you'll have to live off breadish, logical Demi points out unhelpfully.

Urgh. I shudder again and add to my mental list that we

need a new way of getting food. What's this world's version of chickens? Or we can arrange for the nicer Perfected to ship us proper food regularly, even if it comes in squishy blocks. I can mentally prepare myself for living here for months, maybe even…years…if I know there's the hope of going home eventually.

Because Liam was right about the importance of hope, even though his methods were screwy. Without it, we've got nothing.

Part 3:
The Gate

Chapter 14

Demi

We take several hours to reach the top of the pit. It's deadly dry in this whole area, without a hint of greenery, and I'm so thirsty my mouth feels like it's coated in sand. Even though I've decided to forgive Liam, we don't talk. It's too hard.

Luckily, the mist becomes thinner and it's easier to breathe. And while we spot other suspiciously moving patches of stone, we don't have any other close encounters with land lobsters – or anything living.

I don't look over the edge of the path. Not even once. Not till we haul ourselves up the last stretch of path, and the flatness ahead proves to be real land, not just another stretch of path. Then I finally look over my shoulder.

Whoa. The cloud has thinned enough that I can see down…and down, and down…and for a moment, my head spins at the sheer drop.

I feel Liam's arm tight around my wrist, and he pulls me away sharply. "Don't fall in, please," he says, and his voice is hoarse. "I'd rather not go back to get you."

It's a joke, of course. If I fell in there, I wouldn't be lucky enough to find a path. I'd probably find the bottom after a long, long drop. For a moment I meet his mismatched eyes, then he looks away, letting go of my wrist. My skin tingles where he touched me, and I step well away from the edge.

"You're still mad at me, then?" he asks.

What...? Oh. I'd forgotten about that. "Too thirsty to be mad," I croak. "Let's find water."

We manage to find some not ten minutes' walk away – or Liam does, rather. He also finds a couple of sharp sticks to use as makeshift spears, and stands over me with them as I bend down to sip from the muddy puddle that passes as a stream. It tastes like the leaves that fill it, and might give me giardia if I'm unlucky, but it's still delicious, and I drink till that sandy feeling is gone from my mouth. I even try to wash the shiny layers off my skin, with little success.

I take watch as Liam goes to drink. It occurs to me that we must stand out like sore thumbs here in our bright white facility finest. I could fix that with a quick roll in the mud, but I can't face doing so. Not when I could be wearing these clothes for some time.

"I'm not angry at you anymore, by the way," I say quietly to Liam's bent back.

He looks up at me, a cupped hand half-raised to his mouth. "Really? Could've fooled me."

OK, now *he's* mad that I'm mad. Good stuff. "I am annoyed about the whole situation," I explain. "It's rubbish, and I hate being lied to. But given the circumstances...I can't blame you. I probably would've done the same thing."

Liam gazes at me for a long moment, perhaps trying to judge my sincerity. Then he nods. "I'm glad. It'll be easier if we can all get on."

"Yeah." I drag the end of my stick through the water downstream of Liam, watching as the mud swirls up with each movement. "Lucky we don't need to worry about that anymore, about having hope, I mean. Once Kris works out how to fix the

Gate, we'll be fine. We just need to get by till then."

There's another long silence, and Liam moves into a crouch, looking up at me with a flat expression. "So you really trust this Kris, huh?"

"He promised he'd do it," I say, not for the first time. "And he managed the cure, so he can do this too."

Another silence, then he stands. "Alright."

Liam isn't convinced. That's obvious. But he didn't spend time with Kris like I did; instead he was stuck on a wall in a quarantine cell.

So I don't argue, because I need to hang onto my hope too. And Liam doesn't push. Instead, after a good long rest, we begin to walk again, moving around the edge of the pit in the direction of home base. While I can't see the Gate yet, Liam recognises the landscape.

We make quiet conversation as we go along. Nothing more about our future (or lack of one), but instead we talk about every detail of the last few days, even those we've already discussed. Anything to take our minds off our hunger and aching feet, and the danger of our surroundings.

Then when those topics are exhausted, Liam tells me about his life back on Earth – *our* Earth – and he sounds remarkably normal compared to my first impressions of him. In turn, I tell him about my job, my family, and my also remarkably normal life. Up till now, of course.

"You weren't married? Dating anyone?" Liam asks.

I shake my head. "I was dating a coworker till a few months ago, but…it didn't work out."

He gives me a sidelong glance. "You weren't in love with him?"

Now that's a personal question, but it seems silly to get

offended considering everything we've gone through. "I don't know," I admit. "I thought I was, but then I found out…something, and I broke it off. Connor didn't fight me on it, and he's dating someone else now." I frown. "I think I could have loved him, if we'd stayed together. But as it was, my pride was mostly hurt rather than my heart broken. Especially since we still work together. I was hoping he'd leave first." I let out a short laugh. "I guess he wins that one."

"If we ever get back through the Gate, I can help you to make him jealous," Liam teases. "You can show up again at your workplace with a survivalist at your side, complete with cyborg eye." He taps at his scarred temple, and for the first time I connect the silver of that iris with Kris's own.

"As long as you haven't grown back that survivalist beard," I retort, but I make sure to smile.

If we ever get back, he said. But it's *when*, not *if*.

The grey day becomes even greyer, heralding the approaching evening, and we stumble across another puddle/creek. This one's a bit fresher than the last, and we drink as much as we can before searching for shelter. It's too late to make it back before dark, and there'll be no ducking out for a drink in the night.

Luckily there are abandoned buildings scattered all around, and Liam knows this area well. We're only a couple of hours away from home base, he says. So we find another building to stay in. This one makes me uncomfortable because it's clearly damaged, with gaps in its walls where perhaps once there was some kind of panelling. Anything could get inside – and clearly has, in the past. It's empty except for the faint musty smell of old animal scat.

Liam visibly perks up at seeing the broken sections, though.

"We can make armour out of these old wall panels," he says, pulling away large, rectangular chunks of plastic. "See if you can get anything to curl, or to have a sharp point. These sticks aren't good for much."

I almost smile at how we're already making spears out of rubbish, because of course we are. I think briefly of Rule-of-Law with all its bright, terrifying cleanliness and convenient everything, and how they consider us filthy primitives. For a moment I wish *they* could find themselves down here, with nothing but their hands and desperation to keep them going. Then who'd be the filthy primitives?

I watch Liam carefully as he tries to make a fire for a long, *long* time, but eventually gives up in disgust. "We'll have to rough it," he says ruefully. "It's hard to make a fire from scratch. Usually I carry around a piece of reflective metal, but that's gone now."

So much for my plan to become a wilderness expert. Not that I'm planning to stay long-term, because I still expect Kris to make his way here eventually and open the Gate. But in the meantime, I don't want to be deadweight.

Then we find a section of the building with a closing door and no gaps. It's dead dark in here, but not as cold as it might be. We bunk down early, because there's nothing to eat, and the sooner we sleep, the sooner we can get up again. And while I might usually be hyper-aware that I'm alone in a dark space with a man, right now I'm just hungry. Hungry, and cold enough to huddle next to Liam without caring that I'm spooning a near-stranger.

"This is a closet, isn't it?" I say.

"Yep. Probably."

Who cares? It's *warm.*

Liam

I'm lying awake on a rock-hard floor, with the not-at-all hard Demi huddled up against my back. My eyes are wide open, not that she can see in this darkness.

Act normal, I tell myself urgently. I literally haven't been this close to an attractive woman in eight years. (Barring Bianca, but she's no Demi. Sorry.) But it's cool. I'm cool.

Really.

Demi shuffles behind me and sighs heavily. And because I'm awake, and I'm acting cool – really! – I say, "What's up?"

Argh. Yes, I actually said that.

There's a pause, then she laughs. I feel the puff of air on my neck. "Everything," she replies in a low voice. "It's *everything.* But I was just thinking that it could be worse."

Yeah, it sure could. "How so?"

"Well…we could still be in the pit, breathing in that toxic air and trying to avoid land scorpions-"

"Lobsters."

"Land lobsters. Sure. And…you could be a creep."

I freeze. "Uh…"

I feel a cold hand pat me awkwardly on the arm. "It's OK, Liam. You're *not* being a creep. You're being decent even though we hardly know each other. It's the only thing that makes this nightmare bearable."

"You're welcome…?"

Demi huffs out another soft laugh. "I'm not usually so blunt either. It's just…"

"Everything."

"Everything, yeah. And…it's good not to be alone."

I'm glad she can't see my expression, because she has no idea how much I agree with that statement. "Yeah," I agree quietly. "It *is* good not to be alone."

Then she ruins that statement by adding, "I'm not hitting on you! I just…need a friend, and I hope I can be one to you as well."

I can't help but laugh, even though my heart sinks. "Friend-zoned when I'm the last man on Earth," I joke. "Oh…except for Jerrold, I suppose, because Dominic's taken. But I do get that I'm not your type." The words come out awkwardly, but it's no worse than anything else we've discussed over the last few days.

There's a silence.

"Why do you say that?" she asks.

Seriously?! I partly roll over, turning as if I could see her over my shoulder. In the near-pitch darkness I can just make out what might be the line of her cheekbone or her varnished hair. "You've made it more than clear that you wouldn't consider me. And I am *almost* the last regular man on the planet. So fine, I can deal with that." I can hear that I sound huffy in spite of my words, and I'm aware that I'm ruining my 'decent' status. "I mean, it's not as if we're spoiled for choice."

There's a long, resounding silence. "You're right," Demi says finally. "We don't have much choice. I get that for you, I seem like the last woman on the planet, and it's either me or no one. And I get that you're interested for that reason, and I understand.

"But if we were back on our Earth, would we even bother going out for a drink? Because while I don't want to be alone, I don't want to be someone's last choice either." She pauses. "And while I don't know where you got this idea that you're not my type, I think you deserve better too."

"You called me a wildman," I point out.

"Oh."

"And I said that Elizabeth died in childbirth so best not to get pregnant, and you laughed and said it wouldn't be a problem." I'm trying to see her expression in the darkness, but it may as well be a blank mask. "I'm trying not to be difficult about this – but we've got to be honest. You *did* say that."

She giggles. Actually freaking giggles. "But you *were* a wildman," she counters. "You looked about forty. And then they shaved you clean and sprayed you down, and now you look like a skinny, shiny twenty-five. If you could find something in the middle between wild and plastic, I think you'd be just my type."

My heart lifts. Is she just saying that? She sounds sincere… "But the…childbirth thing," I persist.

Demi's laughter is gone. "Liam," she says quietly. "I can't have children. That's why I broke up with Connor – my last boyfriend – because I'd just found out, and he wanted kids. So while I'm still not hitting on you – not AT ALL – that wasn't a dig. OK?"

"Oh." I fall quiet, feeling like a jerk and maybe a creep too. Finally I say, "And I'm not hitting on you either-" (it's a lie – I would if I thought she was interested) "…but it's probably a good thing that you can't. Have kids, I mean. No matter what else happens on this side of the Gate, it's not worth taking the risk."

"I'll keep that in mind," she says dryly. "Now shall we go to sleep?"

"Sure."

We lapse into silence, and I do try to sleep. It'll be a big day tomorrow. But then I remember how she said if I could find something between wild and plastic, I'd be just her type…and I smile.

The next morning we're trudging along with our new, roughly made armour and weapons. Mine is a stick with a piece of sharp plastic-metal stuff shoved in one end. It won't hold up for much, but it's something.

My stomach is rumbling audibly, competing only with the sound of Demi's stomach and our soft, crunching footsteps. I half want a boggart to come storming out of the bushes – self-delivered breakfast – but it would be no good. We have no way of cooking it out here, and I'm not convinced my rough spear would even hold up.

The Gate slowly looms larger as we walk, and I know we'll have to pass it to reach home base. We've talked about taking the long way back, a winding route to avoid being caught by the Perfected again, but it seems pointless. If Demi's translator earpieces are also trackers, or if we've been alien-microchipped, they'll find us regardless. So we head straight back, making sure to keep to the shelter of the trees. Scavs are still a real threat in this area.

As for Demi, she grows quieter the closer we get. I'm caught in my own thoughts too. Jerrold…Dominic. Are they both back at home base? Or did they get dropped in a terrible location like we did, and are still trying to get out? I'm desperately hoping it's the first option, because if they're missing in the Wilds once again…

Well. We won't be able to help, that's for sure. We have to

get back to Bianca and Jesse as fast as we can. Unlike us, they've got food, but Bianca can't keep up with Jesse, not with her injury. She can't provide for him beyond breadish, and she can't catch him if he decides to take off.

Or if the Perfected decide to pick them up instead. No way will I be able to stop them – and the thought makes me despair.

Freaking alien humans. Alien to us, anyway. While we learned a lot up there, I almost wish I hadn't known. It doesn't feel good, not being at the top of the food chain.

That thought makes me pick up my pace until Demi calls for me to slow down. So I move at a pace that's slightly too slow for the length of my legs, but I can tell Demi's stumbling to keep up. The Gate is looming up ahead – perhaps only twenty minutes or so away now – and today the mist is clear enough that I can see it in its entirety. It's stark against the pale grey sky, without any sign of scavs or two-legged visitors.

But then when we get closer, I see it's not entirely empty. At the base of the Gate, set firmly against one side of the archway, is a small boxy shape. It's made of some opaque, white, plasticky stuff, and it looks to be straight from a Perfected lab, sitting all on its own and out of place against the barren surroundings.

We both stop and stare.

Demi

The boxlike case is about knee-high and square, and it's clearly from *up there*. After a brief pause, I rush forward. Liam grabs at my arm before I can touch it. "Careful! What if it's a trap?"

"What if it's not?" But I do stop to study it. Its clear lid reveals a series of little parcels and boxes, packed in tightly together. "Could that be food?"

Liam seems to like that idea, as he doesn't stop me when I reach down again. But as soon as my hand touches it, there's a flash of green light and the lid pops open. Then Kris's voice comes from somewhere around the box: *"For you and your friends, Dee-mee. Six vegetable supplement packets. Two doses of greyce formula for the bitch and the puppy, ha-ha. One special dose of something else experimental, but I hope we won't need that yet. But if you don't see me, put it at the base of the Gate with your translator pieces."*

Kris sounds clear enough that I actually stop to look around for him. I've pulled my hand away in fright, but when I go to touch the case again, the same message repeats.

"What did it say?" Liam asks eagerly.

Thank goodness for the translators I'm still wearing. I repeat the message as well as I can. "That's great about the formula! But the translation isn't perfect, because I don't understand the bit about a bitch and puppy...?"

Liam lets out a long, slow breath. "Dominic was trying to hide that Bianca and Jesse were still down here, but I guess using code words didn't fool anyone, since the box includes doses of greyce formula for both of them." He smiles at me crookedly. "That's a relief, but we'll have to explain to Dom that it's not a good idea to call your girl a bitch."

"He doesn't already know that?!"

"Dom is..." Liam pauses. "...He's the most innocent person I've ever met. His parents didn't see any point in teaching him about the ugly ways people can behave, because they thought he'd never need to know."

"Except that he just spent three years as a lab rat," I point out.

Liam's smile falls. "Except for that."

I manage to open the case by holding my hands against either side of it and ignoring the message that plays yet again. Inside is a collection of tidily arranged tubes and smaller boxes. They have markings on them, spirals and ye olde alien-in-a-cornfield symbols which are actually the Perfected's written language, but of course I can't read them. "We'll have to guess which ones are medicine and which are vegetable supplements," I murmur. It's not at all clear.

But finding the case has galvanised me, and I can't shake my smile. "Kris must've arranged this when he got Petra to send us back. I'm so glad he's sent food! I wonder if he's finished his testing yet?"

"He knows where we are," Liam says, sounding unsure if he's happy about this.

"He already knew we came through the Gate," I point out. "There's nothing sinister in that. He just means he can find us when he fixes it."

Liam sucks in a breath as if to speak again, then closes his mouth.

I don't care what he thinks. Kris planned ahead enough to leave us this surprise, so he'll have planned for other things too.

It's surely just a matter of time.

The rest of our trip back to home base with the case is uneventful. Nothing attacks us, and we don't see any hovering spheres or even a single scav. And when we reach the doorway set in the rock wall, the same one Liam had brought me to a couple of days ago, I find myself overwhelmed with relief.

Amazingly it does almost feel like home. It's not, obviously, but at least here we're in control of our own lives.

Liam pauses outside the door.

"What's the matter?"

"Jerrold and Dom," he says softly. "I guess we'll find out if they made it. And if Jesse and Bianca are OK, for that matter."

Argh. Good point. Imagine finding them again only to lose them *again*, or to lose one of the others. I hardly know them, but even I can't face that idea.

We head inside, but we haven't yet walked down the tunnels for even ten minutes before we're greeted by Jesse. He sees us from the end of the corridor we're in, and he turns and shouts with both hands cupped by his mouth, "THEY'RE HERE! THEY'RE HERE!"

Whoever Jesse is shouting to is out of sight around the corner, but he doesn't wait for a reply. Instead he sprints towards us and throws his arms around Liam's waist. Then there's the sound of pounding footsteps, and Dominic comes charging around the corner in much the same way, followed more sedately by Jerrold and a heavily limping Bianca.

Then there's a welcome back celebration that I get caught up in. Everyone's hugging everyone, and I get hugged too, even though I'm practically a stranger. And I find my eyes are stinging with tears. Instead of four survivors, there are six.

Six regular humans in the whole world. The tears...they aren't just happy ones.

Liam

I'm buoyant with relief; floating with it. Jerrold and Dom are both here – both of them – and Jesse and Bianca are still in one piece.

Everyone's made it. Everyone's here. *We* made it too. In spite of terrible odds, my whole world has held together.

I collapse onto a bench with sudden exhaustion, as if I've been running on anxiety this last day or so. Dominic, back-from-the-dead Dom, sits beside me and puts his arm around my shoulders as if I'm his brother. To him, I am.

Jesse is huddled up against Jerrold, and a few minutes later he awkwardly comes to sit between Dominic and I, although he's definitely leaning into me. He watches his father with wide, dark eyes, as if he isn't sure what to make of him.

Poor kid. Jesse was only three when Dominic went missing, so Dom's been gone for half of his life. And he sure had more hair last time Jesse would've seen him.

Although I do notice that Jerrold's plasticky hair-helmet is partially crumpled, with a section of it standing up in a distinct, off-balanced rooster comb kind of way. He and his little family are hanging onto each other in a way that speaks of desperate gratitude, and his eyes are red, as if he's been crying.

Demi's sitting nearby, within the huddle but not quite part of it, and her expression is a little blank and glassy.

"Are you hungry?" I ask her. Unless she's been hiding a chocolate bar in her pocket, neither of us have eaten in some time.

She startles. "I'm freak- um, yes. I'm hungry."

"We've got breadish!" Jesse tells her brightly. "We ate all the meat while you and Liam were lost."

We were stolen rather than lost, really.

But Demi's expression turns rueful. "Oh, yum. Crushed bugs. Liam, why don't we try those vege supplements Kris sent us?" Then she brightens, sitting straight up in her seat. "Ohmigosh! I can't believe we forgot – Kris sent us doses of the cure for Bianca and Jesse too!"

Bianca leans forward, her expression filled with hope. "There's a cure...?" Her voice cracks.

The other two men exchange uncertain glances. "It's unproven," Jerrold says hesitantly. "Wasn't that the whole trouble? Something about red lights..."

Ah, of course he's missed how I was green-lighted just yesterday, three days after being given the greyce formula. He's missed a whole lot more than that. I'll need to tell them all about the upside-down planet with Earth's continents, and about the fact we seem to have time-travelled. But the formula's a good start.

But Demi pipes in excitedly. "It does work! It's just slow to start – by Perfected standards, anyway, which are *insane*. I accidentally shut Liam in another quarantine chamber while we were escaping, and the tester light was green. And look, his cuts are finally healing!" She turns to me, tapping at her face with a wide smile. "Aren't they, Liam?"

Suddenly I'm the centre of attention as the others crowd around me. Bianca prods gently at the injury around my eye. "They do look better," she says, sounding surprised. "Does the wound hurt?"

"It doesn't," I admit. "Not at all." That's the first time in three years it hasn't hurt, and I didn't realise until this moment.

Matching expressions of desperate hope come over the

other adults' faces, and Bianca slumps down to her seat, trembling. "My knee..." Her voice cracks. "It's *so* bad, and the infection is spreading down my leg. If this formula works..."

If it works, then her slow death sentence has been revoked. All of ours will have been, even Jesse's, who we think must've been exposed to the virus in the womb, although he hasn't shown any sign of sickness.

"It does," Demi says with more certainty than I feel she should have. She bends down to rummage through the clear box we found at the Gate, and Jesse, Bianca and Jerrold lean in to watch.

But Dominic stays beside me, an expression of anxiety on his still-shiny face. He murmurs, "I want this to work. We *need* it to work. But how did they know we needed two more doses, Liam?"

Ah. "What Demi didn't mention is that Kris said the two doses were for the bitch and the puppy. Then he laughed."

Dominic's eyebrows shoot up. "Oh. I guess...the aliens are smarter than I thought." His face falls again. "Then they know we're all here. Jesse and Bianca too."

If he's thinking like I am, that means Jesse and Bianca aren't safe from them. Aliens or not. And that's something else we need to talk about, the sooner, the better.

"I want to see the aliens," Jesse chirps from beside me, proving that his listening skills are both great and awful.

Argh. *No.*

"They'll cut off all your hair," Dominic tells him in a dramatic voice. "They'll stick you to a wall and spike you full of tubes until you can't move. And they'll cover you in glue so you're all shiny and squeaky, see?" He holds out a shiny arm, which indeed does squeak when he runs a finger over it.

Jesse crinkles his nose but doesn't look convinced. "I like my hair," he says in a small voice. "Maybe I won't see the aliens."

Not if I have anything to do with it. (Also, they're not really aliens, but let's not be picky.)

I turn to where the others are hunched over the contents of the box. There are half a dozen silvery parcels arrayed across the ground, each the size of a box of chocolates, but they look far less edible. "How are we going with finding the greyce formula?"

Demi holds up a tiny gold vial, no bigger than her pinky finger. "We think this is the cure, but I can't get the container to open."

"Better figure it out," Jerrold says. "Bianca needs this yesterday."

Jesse picks up a matching one, pulling it close to his face. Then suddenly he drops it. "Ow! It bit me!"

"Let's see?"

He pouts, holding out his finger to display a drop of shining gold on the tip. But even as I see it, the liquid vanishes into his brown skin. His mouth falls into an O of surprise. "It's gone!"

Bianca puts her arm around Jesse protectively. "Have we really just given untested alien medicine to my child?!"

"Not on purpose," Demi mutters. "But it didn't respond to me. Maybe it knows I've already been dosed."

"I can't believe I'm doing this," Bianca groans. "But if Jesse's had it, I will too." Her eyes narrow on Demi. "But if we die, I'm blaming you, OK?"

"OK," Demi squeaks.

But when Bianca touches the second vial and has much the same result, she takes it staunchly. "Wish I could have put it straight on my knee," she mutters. "How long is this supposed to take to work?"

"Three days for us," I say. "If it did work."

She huffs out a sigh and leans into Dominic, who wraps his arms around her. "I guess it can't get any worse."

I don't tell her that she's wrong, because things can always get worse. Better not to extinguish her hope till absolutely necessary.

Jesse moves to study the silvery parcels with Demi, and I lean in to talk to the other three adults. "So we've got a problem," I say in a low voice. "It looks like the Perfected know we're here. All of us. And unlike the one who's all friendly with Demi and gave us these doses, the others want to keep us locked away, like Dominic has been. We need to decide if we run for it, and if so, where to."

The explanation was mainly for Bianca. Her eyes widen and she grips on tighter to Dominic. "They know we're here? In home base? I thought that box was at the Gate." She gestures to the open container.

"We don't *know* if they know we're here exactly," I hedge. "But what if there's a tracker on the container? On *us*? How would we even know? And Demi's still wearing those translators, which we couldn't get out before."

"If we've got the trackers, there's not much point leaving unless we find and remove them," Jerrold says dully. "What're we looking for? A new scar?"

Dominic holds out his arms, criss-crossed with pale scars. "How would we tell? And where would we *go* that they can't find us if they were to look? We can't take the breadish machines with us. How would we eat, or even check the Gate?"

We sit in silence, and finally I sigh. "At least we can check for trackers. Dom, will you look me over?"

I take off my shirt and move to a nearby area where we've set up a privacy screen. I check my front while he looks at my back; looking for any new scars, lumps or discolouration. The hairlessness does help, while the varnish seems to hinder, but I don't find anything different at all. Neither does Dominic.

But better safe than sorry. We quickly check over Jerrold and Dom too, finding nothing out of the ordinary. And I tell you, scanning another guy's shiny backside for random lumps isn't how I'd hoped to spend my day.

I come back into the main area, and Demi looks up at me from beside the fire. "Am I missing something?" she asks.

Yes. Would you please come behind this screen and take off all your clothes? "Ah…we're checking for trackers, but we haven't found anything."

She wrinkles her nose. "I suppose you need to check me too. But either the trackers would be so small we couldn't find them, or they're just in our clothing or these things here." She taps at a massive shape which has sprung out of nowhere. It's about a metre high and twice as wide, appears to be made of cellophane, and has something small and purple inside.

I step forward. "What's that?"

"Vegetables!" Jesse shouts joyfully. (I know he's only joyful because he's never eaten a vegetable in his life.) There's a sound like *'sproing'* and suddenly another of the silvery parcels expands into a matching frame, pushing him sideways. "Oof!"

"Careful," Demi says, grabbing his arm and sitting him upright. "Ooh, what's this? Corn, maybe?" She smiles up at me. "The vegetable supplement packets are actually miniature greenhouses, and the trays are already full of plants. Amazing, right?"

Amazing's right. We set up the others in short order, in the brightest, warmest spot we can find. Although judging by the light within the frames, they seem to provide their own sunshine. Incredible. But there's just one issue – the plants are all tiny seedlings.

"Might be a while before this'll be dinner," I say wryly to Demi.

She sighs heavily and her shoulders slump. She smiles, but it doesn't reach her eyes. "Breadish, then?"

Chapter 15

Demi

I'm doing it. I'm really choosing to push past my automatic revulsion and think on how I need to eat because I'm starving, and it doesn't matter if this is a bunch of ground-up locusts mixed with some kind of emulsifier.

I chomp down on the tiny chunk of breadish, fixing my mind on the conversation rather than what I'm consuming. The conversation is just as unpalatable, though.

"So do we leave?" Jerrold's saying in a low voice. "Strip off everything they've provided us, including this damned glue coating, and drop it in the pit? Then run for one of the safehouses?"

"We'd have to seal up the new place properly before we can live in it," Liam says. "And come back regularly for the breadish. Personally, I'd rather just get rid of the extras and stay here. It feels safer."

"Personally, I'd rather not be naked, and all my own clothing is back on Rule-of-Law," I cut in. "And are you so convinced we need to hide right away? Guys, Kris is literally our only hope of getting back to our own time. Why would we make it hard for him to find us?"

Suddenly I've got everyone's attention.

"You wouldn't have to be naked," Dominic says brightly. "We have stuff here."

"Sure, that's the one thing you heard," Bianca scolds him,

but her tone is amused. She's sitting in his lap, one arm around his neck, like she doesn't want to be anywhere else. But then she thought he was dead till last night – the men having been translocated straight to the base of the Gate. (Nice for some.) "He means boggart skins," she tells me. "Or we could punch some arm holes in that sleeping bag of yours, and you could wear it like a tunic."

My lip curls, since that doesn't sound like much of an improvement on a hairy boggart skin.

"Never mind the clothing," Jerrold cuts in. "Did you say, 'getting back to our own *time*'?!"

Liam and I exchange a glance, and I realise that we haven't shared some of the most important information.

So we share it. We tell them about the similarity between the planet's surface and our Earth, and about all the things I heard the Perfected say that confirm our theory.

"So the Gate doesn't lead to a different world," Jerrold says thoughtfully, "just our own future. Well, isn't that the darndest thing."

He doesn't sound upset. No one does, actually.

"I always wondered," Bianca says suddenly. "With the moon being so similar, and all. And now we know."

"But that doesn't really matter," I continue, "because it doesn't change our situation whatsoever. But like I said, Kris can help us get home. He said he would, and he promised he'd cure us too, and he's done that. So we should stay near the Gate, check it regularly."

The others look to Liam. "What do you think?" Jerrold asks him. "You stayed on a bit longer than we did."

Liam glances at me, and I can see the doubt in his expression. "Hard to say when Demi's the only one who spent time with him," he says slowly, "and only a couple of days at that. We would've checked the Gate anyway. So I suppose we could throw a rock through it each time, see if anything changes."

Bianca's shoulders visibly slump. "So this Kris guy can't fix it?"

"He can," I say, and my voice trembles. "We *need* him to. What else are we going to do? Resign ourselves to living here forever?" I wave my arms at our surroundings, and I see doubtful glances between the other adults.

Jesse just looks blank. "Are we going somewhere?"

"No," Dominic says soothingly. "We're staying here, at home."

I glare at him. "You don't know that!"

"Alright, alright," Liam cuts in. "We *don't* know that, and I for one won't miss the chance to go back, if there *is* even the smallest chance. So we keep our hopes realistic, *and* we check the Gate like usual. OK?"

It's probably the best I'm going to get from them, but I'm still agitated and shaken that the others are so disbelieving. But they've resigned themselves to living here, haven't they? I chomp angrily at my breadish, then cringe as there's a noticeable *crunch*. There's something stiff and thready in my mouth, like a bug's leg…

Ugh. I'm about to gag, and I take a deep breath through my nose. In…out. *Swallow.* "You lot can do what you want. But I won't be getting rid of my clothes, or these little greenhouses, and I definitely won't be getting rid of my translators just in case they happen to be trackers. They've done us so much good, and I bet we'll need them again."

I've memorised Kris's message, along with his final

statement to put the translators at the base of the Gate along with the special item, if I don't see him. I'll be keeping them for that reason alone.

"That's what I'm afraid of," Jerrold says in a low voice, but I hear him clearly.

"Well, I haven't eaten a vegetable in a decade, so I'll happily keep the greenhouses," Bianca says firmly. "Now who's up for some boggart jerky? We've got some left from that last lot, Liam."

Jesse gives her a wounded look – he had mentioned earlier that the meat was all gone – and she ruffles his hair. "I hid some of it so it would last longer. This one would've eaten it all in a day, if he could."

The subject has been decisively changed, and I sit back as the others bustle around as if we haven't just had a terrible argument. But I see the hushed conversation and glances in my direction, and I feel sullen and stubborn and somehow weepy.

I haven't even mentioned the last thing in Kris's care package, since the others seem to have forgotten it. The 'experimental' something that he hoped we wouldn't need.

It's a little silvery rectangular shape rather like a smartphone case, no bigger than my palm and covered in scrolling Perfected symbols. I put it straight into my pocket, and it's staying there. I can't risk the others remembering it and taking it away.

No matter what they say, they *have* given up hope, and they're just humouring me. It's like they're scared of hoping for anything more, and they've accepted this terrible life. And now it's extra terrible, because they have sort-of-alien abductions to be afraid of as well, and nowhere to go.

But *I'm* not giving up until I'm forced to. I crunch down on an especially gritty mouthful, then shudder. In spite of my empty, aching belly, it takes everything I have not to spit it all onto the floor. With great effort I manage to swallow, then wash it down with a gulp of musty water from the broken pipe that serves as a tap.

That's enough. I can't manage any more, so I stand. "I'm gonna try to wash this stuff out of my hair," I say to no one in particular. "What serves as a shower around here? A bath?"

"I'll show you the facilities," Dominic says, leaping to his feet. "But you won't get the glue out. Bianca scrubbed me for an hour this morning, and it didn't make a difference." He shrugs. "You get used to it."

"I'll try anyway," I say, because I need something to do. I need to occupy my mind.

It suddenly occurs to me that all my specially bought outdoor clothing, including my expensive and uncomfortable hiking boots, was vaporised up in the Perfected labs. I'll probably resent it more once these lab shoes wear through, but I suppose it's not my biggest problem right now.

Dominic's still wearing the lab clothing too, but he's paired it with some kind of fabric wrapped around his legs and feet, serving as trousers. It's an odd look, although no stranger than how Liam was dressed when I first met him.

Now that I'm meeting Dominic face to face, he's rather more boyish than I expected. He's only an inch or two taller than me, lean and energetic – but isn't everyone here lean? His skin is pale and clear under the lights of home base, and his blue eyes are wide and eager in a way that makes me wonder if he's going to hit on me the moment we're out of sight, Bianca or not.

The guy is remarkably cheerful for someone who's been a prisoner for years – but then maybe it's his newfound freedom that gives him his joy.

"Here you go," he announces some distance down a nearby hallway, pointing to yet another door. "We wash in the sink." He beams, showing exactly where Jesse got his wide smile.

It turns out to be just another room like the other bathroom I used earlier, but with a narrow sink made of blueish metal, worn from use. I figure out how to turn on the water, but when I go to close the door, Dominic's still standing there.

"We can't go back," he says.

I frown. "What? Back to the main room?"

"Back to the cells," he says impatiently. "Back into captivity. If they get me again – I'll die. I feel like I'll die. And I'll do anything to stop them getting my family. If they get us... it'll be terrible."

I've got nothing to say to that, because he's right. It would be terrible, especially if we're all treated like he was. I know I was a special case, and I'm still not even sure why. I can't even promise him that we won't be found, because the Perfected have technology that goes through walls. If they want to find us, they will, trackers or not.

"I made a mistake with Liam, did he tell you?" Dominic continues earnestly. "When he arrived, we told him that the Gate could open and take us home, that we just needed to work out how to do it. And he believed us. And when he found out we'd lied, he was so betrayed, and we fought... After I was taken away, I thought he'd died because of me. And I swore if I could ever make it back, I'd never lie again. Not even if Dad and Bianca say it's for someone's own good."

"Where are you going with this?" I ask. But I think I already know.

"This Kris person," Dominic says. "You seem so convinced

he's going to come through for you. And I hope he does! But…I don't think he will. Liam says he's being tested. That's what the others are doing to him, right? Because they're angry at how he favoured us humans?"

Suddenly I can hardly breathe. "Yes, that's what the translator said-"

He sticks out his arm, holding it right in front of my face. "This is testing! This is what it looks like. And even if he *can* work the Gate, you think he's coming back from that?"

The scars. He's talking about the scars. For a moment I can't breathe, imagining what kind of damage would cover Kris in the same markings.

"I don't want to upset you," Dominic continues more quietly, lowering his arm to his side. "And I'm sure Bianca will tell me off for this. But if we give you false hope…that's far worse than just telling you the truth in the first place."

"Your version of truth," I say, forcing out the words between numb lips. "Your view of life. I'm sorry things have been so bad for you, Dominic. But you've always lived here, and you don't know what you're missing back on our Earth. I won't accept this life till I've got no other choice."

Dominic studies my face for a moment, then gives a short nod. "Enjoy your bath."

He turns away, and I push the door shut with its damaged sliding mechanism. Then I lean back against it, closing my eyes for a few moments.

He's wrong about Kris and the Gate. They all are. I refuse to believe otherwise. And with that decided, I move to the small sink for my 'bath'.

But it turns out Dominic is right about the hair varnish, at least. I manage to pry my hair from the tight spiral it's plastered in, but the glue isn't going anywhere, from there or from my shiny skin. Eventually I give up and let it settle back into the same shape on top of my head.

Sigh. I guess I'll be plastic a little bit longer.

Maybe back on our Earth, once I'm home, I'll try turpentine.

We don't go back to the Gate. Instead we spend the rest of the day in furious conversation alternating with tears and hugs (that's the others, not me) and finally I bow out and take myself to bed, AKA a spot on the floor. The sooner I sleep, the sooner I can get up again. Liam has agreed to take me back to the Gate in the morning, even though he said there probably won't be anything there.

I pointed out that someone has to check the Gate every day, right? That set off an argument about the 'aliens' grabbing us again – because Dominic's light-heartedness appears to be surface level – and I ended it by pointing out that they could grab us all from anywhere, at any time. Their technology means walls aren't an issue, and it's only because they think we're filthy primitives (I quote) that we're likely to be left alone. If anything, we'd be wise to flee from this whole area, but then we'd be leaving the Gate, and I won't do that.

Kris will be coming for us.

I keep telling myself that as I get up the next morning, as I choke down a handful of breadish, and as I check the line of pop-up greenhouses.

Incredibly, the seedlings have grown several inches overnight, and I see the beginnings of tiny fruit on some of the plants. The set up must include some way to pollinate the plants, because back home, you'd need insects or else to

229

pollinate by hand.

Liam hauls himself up. He's got a short beard coming through underneath the shiny layer of varnish, and it suits him. He quietly gets ready, but then before we go to leave, he gently taps Dominic on the shoulder. Dominic's eyes pop open, and Liam gestures towards me, then the door.

I guess we shouldn't head off without warning. Not after what happened last time.

We pile ourselves with what serves as armour in this place, and I pause, then grab my sleeping bag. I turn it inside out and wrap it around my head and shoulders like a cloak, with the grey side out and red side in. It gets cold around here.

Then we set off.

We make our way down the hallways in silence, then through the door, locking it behind us. We retrace the barren path that's becoming familiar to me, until the Gate appears in the distance, the top of it visible even from here. There's a light mist this morning, and it holds a distinct chemical tang to it, unlike other mornings. It reminds me of what was inside the pit, and I lift my tunic collar so it covers my nose and mouth.

As we get closer, Liam puts a hand to my arm. "Scavs," he murmurs.

I grip my makeshift spear tighter – it's the exact same piece of junk I used last time. "I don't see anything."

"They're not moving. They're huddled on the ground, see?" He frowns. "There's something red under the Gate."

I squint in the direction he's pointing. I can just make out lots of tiny shapes, either grey-brown or brighter blue and green against the pale mist. There's a plain red splotch directly underneath the Gate's massive frame that reminds me of my sleeping bag, except…I'm wearing my sleeping bag.

"It must be for us," I say decisively. "Kris must have sent something today too."

"There are scavs-"

"They're not moving, look! Don't scavs normally move?"

He frowns. "Yeah, but…"

"They must be knocked out, or dead," I cut in. "It'll be fine."

"Demi!"

I ignore him and creep steadily forward, making sure that all my important bits are covered in case there's something behind me. (Besides him, I mean.)

But when I get closer, I see that the red thing isn't an object at all.

It's a person.

Liam

Demi lets out a cry and goes racing forward faster than I realised she could move, straight into the scene of fallen scavs and whatever that thing is. I run after her even as my mind is making sense of what's in front of me.

The red thing is person-shaped, sprawled out directly underneath the Gate. It looks like someone had a bucket of crimson paint spilled over them. Demi rushes up to them and stops at a distance, then she lets out a sob. A moment later I catch up with her, and we stare down at the body.

It's big, of course, and I'd known it must be one of the Perfected for that reason alone. It just as easily could have been a regular human who'd come through the Gate by accident and had run into the scavs – but not with these proportions. I can see glimpses of white amongst the red of the clothing, and a patch or two of silver hair or brown skin. It's definitely male. His eyes are partially open, revealing silvery irises.

"Kris," Demi whimpers.

Oh hell. It's that one she was so attached to. The one she was relying on to reopen the Gate.

Demi kneels down and picks up his hand, feeling for his pulse. But then she drops it in revulsion, leaving her own fingers stained crimson. "He's cut," she breathes, her eyes wide and staring. "He's all cut."

"He must've been attacked by scavs," I murmur. "He must've fought them off." I look around us, my spear at the ready. There must be two dozen scavs scattered around, but not a single one is moving. That's almost the entire horde that lives in this area. They aren't bloodied, though. They look…asleep.

This scene reminds me horribly of the last time we found a dead man under the Gate, almost seven years ago. That was when we'd found out definitively that human blood wouldn't reopen the Gate – not even a life's worth.

Demi shakes her head. "No. No, these aren't animal scratches. *Look.*"

I crouch beside her as she pulls out her makeshift water flask and pours a little water on that same hand she just dropped. The red runs away in a pink flow, and now I can see the cuts. They're thin and distinct and neatly spaced from each other, as if he ran into a fine wire fence.

"They look like Dominic's cuts," she continues, her voice trembling. "They *tested* Kris, Liam. For…for his immunity to the virus. Remember?"

Ohhh.

It seems like he didn't pass that cruel test. But who would

have? They've cut him from head to toe. The amount of blood he must have lost...whether he could catch the virus would have been irrelevant.

In the corner of my eye I see a small grey shape move – one of the fallen scavs is stirring. I curse. "The scavs aren't dead! They're just asleep."

And we're surrounded by them.

Demi

"We've got to go," Liam says urgently. "Or we'll be mobbed."

I ignore him and focus on washing the blood off Kris's arm. If it wasn't for his silver eyes, so similar to Liam's false eye, I wouldn't have even recognised him.

At least the cuts have stopped bleeding. Maybe he'll be OK once I've cleaned him up. I don't check for a pulse again. I didn't feel one before, but that's alright. Better to clean him up now. This fabric hasn't soaked up the blood at all. In fact, it's coming up bright white in all the places I've cleaned.

"Demi! He's *dead*. We have to go."

I resist Liam's pulling arm and hunch down over Kris's body. Liam's wrong, because Kris can't be dead. He said he would open the Gate. He said he would send us home.

He's not dead.

Liam mutters and stomps away. He's doing something behind me – what, I'm not sure – but I focus on Kris.

"The priates really are beasts," I murmur to him. "Complete animals. Who would do this to their own people? And...I'm sorry you got in trouble because of us."

A drop of water falls onto his chest, running away to reveal a patch of brilliant white. It was a tear, I realise. Clearly an effective clean-up method.

Mm. He's cold too, so I take off my sleeping bag and wrap it around him, grey side up. I don't cover his face, because surely he'll need to see. It can't be too comfortable with his eyes partly open like that – when he's not blinking – but I don't close them.

It would make him look dead, and well…no.

Just no.

"We gave the greyce formula to the other two," I whisper to him. "And I've got your experimental thingy. I don't know how to use it, though. You can explain when you wake up."

Kris doesn't respond. His face looks more normal now the blood's gone, although the cuts mark his cheeks and forehead with distinct red stripes. Under the natural sunlight his skin is an odd yellow, like someone who has jaundice.

That's OK too, I decide. It'll be the shortage of blood, no doubt. His body just needs to make more.

Some time later, Liam comes up beside me. "I dealt with the scavs," he says grimly. "They're all in the pit."

That's good. "We can use my sleeping bag as a travois," I tell him. "To carry Kris back to home base, so he can recover."

There's a silence.

"Demi," Liam says softly. "He's not going to recover. He's not breathing, see?" When I don't answer, he adds, "People can't lose that much blood. Not even futuristic super-people like the Perfected."

I hunch my shoulders. I'm hearing what he's saying, but it *hurts*. "But the Gate…"

"He was going to try to open it for us," Liam continues gently. "But there's no guarantee it would have worked. And he didn't deserve this – what they did to him. But we can honour what he did and give him a proper burial. We can *live*...because he gave us all the cure. And even if it's an imperfect life, at least it's a life."

His words land like lead, each one weighing me down. I feel numb and heavy and slow as I stare at Kris lying in front of me. The blood and water have filled up all the carvings that span the distance between the Gate's two pillars. Now it looks like a design marked in dark red and grey, spread on either side of where Kris is wrapped in my sleeping bag. His eyes are still open, which is creepy.

He doesn't look asleep. He looks dead.

That's because he is dead, inner Demi adds sympathetically. *I guess we won't be going home after all.*

Sh*t.

And all my hope, all my frantic, determined believing that kept me out of despair – it all dies with him.

Chapter 16

Liam

Poor guy. I can't guess why all the scavs were unconscious around Kris – maybe the Perfected did something to them when they dropped him down here. But it can't have been a painless death. Kind of like poor Sigge all those years ago.

Still, I take the chance to finish them all off and toss them well into the pit. It feels a little cruel, killing them while they're sleeping, but they wouldn't have given us the same mercy.

Scavs are *brutal* – and now they're gone. That's something, considering the horde in this area has been a hazard ever since I arrived. Now a former hazard.

Demi is still huddled over Kris's wrapped body, but she doesn't stop me when I reach down to close his eyes. I can see her expression has changed. It's now dull and empty.

"It's hard to dig around here," I tell her quietly. I know that from experience. "But we need to deal with the body."

It would be easier to toss him into the pit as well, but he doesn't deserve that. We settle for dragging him to the nearest structure: a small, stone-built shed that I think must have been something to do with the Gate itself. Now it stinks of scav, since it appears that horde lived in it, but they're gone now, and it's solid. We leave him covered in the sleeping bag, then force the massive door shut. It's so solid that I expect it never could be opened naturally, as if it was made to withstand earthquakes.

Now it's a crypt.

"We'll tell the others not to come in here," I say. "And we'll make a memorial for him. Come back and set up a headstone, maybe."

Demi doesn't respond.

She doesn't talk as I direct her back to home base, and I cast one final glance at the mess under the Gate. There's an almost perfect outline of where the body had been, and the violent red of the blood hasn't yet faded. I also know from experience that within a few days the blood will be dried up and gone. Something about the atmosphere of this place – or maybe something eats it.

Demi doesn't speak as we get back and tell the others what we've found. We discuss plans for leaving, but decide to keep quiet, to stay in here with the doors shut and see what happens. It's no easy feat rebuilding, and as she said earlier, the Perfected think of us as filthy primitives. Something they don't want in their clean, shiny, 'safe' society.

Except even we don't kill our own people.

Two days later, Demi has retreated into herself. She eats when she's reminded to, but she doesn't say much. Mostly she just sits around or sleeps. The contrast to her usual self is shocking.

I know why. It's because even though I told her earlier that she'd probably never go home, she didn't really believe it. She'd kept her hope in Kris bringing some miraculous breakthrough, because she didn't want to accept the alternative of staying here in the Wilds. Now it's clear that he won't be doing anything, her hope has gone.

I never let myself hope in him in the first place. I know well that it's not worth the pain on the other side, when hope dies and disappointment kicks in.

"Remember Sigge?" Dominic says to me quietly. "He went all quiet too, before he…"

Oh yes, I remember Sigge. We all do, except for Jesse, who wasn't yet conceived when Sigge…left.

A while later I sit down next to Demi, who's curled up with a rough boggart-skin blanket. Her eyes are half-shut, but I know she's awake. I hold out one of the plasticky bottles that serves as drinking ware. "Hey. Have some water."

"Not thirsty," she says dully.

I persist. "You haven't drunk anything since this morning. There's no point you getting sick. Come on."

She doesn't answer.

"Demi."

Suddenly her face scrunches up and she ducks her head forward, shaking. I realise a moment later that she's crying.

Argh. It's been so long since I've comforted anyone crying, let alone a woman, that I pause in panic for several seconds. Then I gently put my free hand on her back. *Pat, pat.* That's right, isn't it?

Demi cries for what feels like half an hour while I sit with her in silence. My back-pats turn into an arm around the shoulders, and the others occasionally come by long enough to ensure we're both still alive, then leave me to it.

Yay. But I suppose she had to react sooner or later. The numb stage was never going to last.

"Kris is dead," she says finally, her voice thick. "He was supposed to take us home, but he died instead. And I *trusted* him…" And then she dissolves into sobs again.

"You did trust him," I agree, keeping my tone even. "And maybe he even would have come through-"

"He would have!"

My lips tighten, then I sigh. "If he was the person you thought he was, I'm sure he would have tried. But nothing's guaranteed, especially not here."

Demi's quiet for a bit, and when I look down at her, she's scowling fiercely into her knees. "Why are you so convinced Kris was no good? I've heard you all, what you were saying. You wouldn't even give him a chance!"

I'm dumbstruck by her sudden anger, and over such a pointless topic, too. But then I realise what she's doing. She's devastated and feels helpless, so she's trying to take control in any way she can. Even a stupid way.

So I consider my words. "I *would* have given him a chance. But I need more than a few days to decide if someone's a friend or foe, especially under the circumstances. You trusted him very quickly, Demi. You'd literally just met him."

"You expected me to trust you when I'd just met you," she shoots back. "What's the difference?"

Huh. Good point. "You were about to be attacked by scavs. And my people weren't trying to keep you in a cell."

There's a silence. Then Demi huffs, "Well, my experience wasn't yours, and I chose to trust him, OK? You have to trust someone. And now...I've got no one!"

'No one' has just sat here for the last forty minutes being cried on. I say carefully, "You're right. You *do* have to trust someone, and you can trust us-"

"I want Kris!"

"You were scared!" I explode. "You were terrified of being stuck here away from your normal life, and you wanted someone to save you, so you decided it was him. *That's* why you're so shattered now that he's gone. But your trust wasn't built on evidence! You didn't know him, you didn't know if he

239

could follow through *at all* or if he was just like us, telling you what you needed to hear so you wouldn't freak out. He wasn't a saviour."

She's gone quiet, but now I've started speaking, I can't stop. "In real life, no one saves you, Demi. No one can get you back to your old life. You have to…you have to decide to be here in this one, and make the best of it."

She doesn't respond for so long that I think she's fallen asleep. Then finally she whispers, "But what if I can't?"

If she can't decide to stay here in this one? Then we might have another Sigge on our hands. And I'm definitely not telling her *that* story.

So we make sure Demi's not left alone, not for one moment. People deep in despair can make terrible decisions. Bianca makes sure to follow her even to the bathroom. Amazingly, Bianca is moving more easily now, and the terrible greenish infection on her knee has almost vanished.

The greyce formula worked. Apologies to Kris's memory for doubting his cure, although I'm still unconvinced he could have ever reopened the Gate. But thanks to the formula, for the first time since I discovered the truth about this place, I finally have hope for a decent life.

So do the others. It doesn't matter that we've decided to stay underground indefinitely; no one having checked the Gate since we found Kris's body. Even under these restrictions, Bianca, Dominic, Jerrold and Jesse are noticeably happy and hopeful. Bianca smiles more easily, and the shadows under her eyes seem to be fading along with her knee wound.

Jesse's original caution around Dominic is gone, and the two of them play madcap games around home base, dashing around the carefully stacked and sorted piles of junk while their family looks on, smiling.

I'm still twitchy. Partly from watching Demi fall into the depths of despair (not the Pit of Despair) and partly because I keep expecting to see a hovering sphere come through a wall, ready to snatch us back into our gleaming prison cells. I think part of Dominic's mania is from that same fear.

But I'm just as helpless on that matter as Demi is on Kris's death. So I focus on what I can control – watching over Demi, listening to Dom's endless chatter, playing with Jesse, and admiring our rapidly growing fresh vegetables.

And who would've thought I could be so excited by those? I'd prefer a cheeseburger, but I'll take what I can get.

I stir early the next morning. The fire has dwindled to embers, but the room is just light enough that I can see a figure moving out of the main room and towards a doorway.

I'm instantly awake. I can see by the shape and size that it's Demi, and she's not heading to the bathroom. She vanishes from sight, and I leap out of the pile of cloth that serves as my bed, chasing after her.

I catch up to her in the hallway near the Gate exit. She stops and looks up at me dully. "What do you want? Are you my designated stalker for today?"

"It's early," I say, feeling a little defensive. "Where are you going?"

She shrugs. "I need a moment to think."

"It'll be dark outside. Wait an hour and we'll go in the light."

"What part of 'I need a moment to think' implies I need your help?"

Her tone carries some of her usual spirit, but I don't give in. "Actually, it implies you're about to hurl yourself into the Pit of

Despair. And while I understand that – I remember feeling the same way – that feeling doesn't last. I know it's hard now, but it *will* get easier. Life can have good moments even when it's really not what we would have chosen for ourselves. We have to choose to live it as well as we can."

It's the same spiel that Jerrold and Bianca gave me after Dom went missing, and after I knew there was no chance of returning home. It didn't mean much at the time, but I guess it sank in after all.

Demi stares at me, then raises one eyebrow. "I'm not going to hurl myself into the Pit of Despair, because with my luck I'd just break a leg then get eaten by one of those land lobster things. I've got something from Kris, and I want to give it back."

She holds up her free hand to reveal a glossy little shape, like a glass teardrop or a gob of dried glue. "It was in the case with the greenhouses and greyce formula. Kris's message said it was experimental, and…that I should leave it at the Gate with my translator pieces, if he…doesn't come back." Her lips tighten and tremble. "So…I'm going to put it there like he told me to. And if it doesn't do anything, then I want to leave it with him…with the body."

I'm astounded. I'd forgotten the extra piece even existed, along with its odd instruction, but Demi clearly hadn't, and her request is reasonable. "Oh. Well, at least let's take our armour. There might be one or two scavs still hanging around."

"Or a land lobster that's crawled out of the pit."

"Ah, we can only hope. They've got to be tastier than breadish."

Demi lets out a startled sound that's almost a laugh.

I'll take it.

Demi

After days of not feeling much at all – not daring to think about my situation for fear it would overwhelm me – I woke up with one determined thought. I'm going to do something with the last object from the case. He gave me instructions, and even if following them turns out badly, I'm going to do it.

And I want to give Kris some kind of memorial. I've never seen anyone in that kind of condition, and I hate that my first thought was for myself. *Now I can't go home.* I didn't even think about him: this decent sort-of-human man who'd tried to help us and had died a nasty death.

I want to do something respectful for him, and I don't even mind that Liam comes along. Probably better, really. Life might feel grim and pointless, but I don't want to be eaten by boggarts on my way out.

I let Liam set us both up with our usual trash armour and weapons, although of course my sleeping bag is still with Kris's body. My lab shoes are supplemented with impromptu foot wraps, and by the time we make it out the door, the sky is noticeably lightening. We make our way back up the path to the Gate once again. It's about twenty minutes at the slow pace I'm leading, and by the time we arrive, the sun is peeping over the horizon. It's always grey around here, but there's a strip of lighter greyish-white revealing the sun's location as it rises.

Good. If it had been a glorious, tropical-type dawn, I would have felt even crankier. Unlike in the movies, the weather doesn't usually alter to fit my mood. (But then my current mood would be steady downpour.)

Today the Gate itself is free of both mist and scavs, and I can

243

see the dark stain at its base even from a distance. Close up, it's clear that the pooled blood hasn't really dried. It's become a semi-congealed puddle, marked into the deep carvings of the stone base. I poke at it with the base of my makeshift spear, and it leaves a reddish-brown mark on the plastic: it's still wet.

Yuck.

But there's an odd feeling in the air; a kind of buzzing tingle. It reminds me of when I first came through, and it makes me twitch. "So much for blood opening the Gate," I mutter.

"Blood brought us through," Liam says quietly. It's the first he's spoken since we left home base. "But even an entire body's worth doesn't reopen it for the other way back. There's something missing – some kind of key or button or something we don't know about. Maybe the Gate is broken. Who knows."

"Clearly."

He pauses. "Did anyone tell you about Sigge?"

He pronounces the name 'Sig-ya', but I know who he's talking about. "I've heard snatches of information from the others, but no one's told me the whole story, if that's what you mean. I figure the guy killed himself, right?"

"Well, sort of. I don't know if he meant to, but that's what happened."

Then Liam tells me about how Bianca arrived through the Gate a couple of years before he had, along with her boyfriend, Sigge. They were backpackers who'd met while travelling and had proceeded to travel together here as well. Just like with Jerrold and his first wife, once one person mysteriously vanished, the next person went looking for them. Except for Liam and I, of course. No one saw us disappear.

But it seems that Sigge and Bianca had been determined to make the Gate work. Sigge in particular would spend most of his days testing out different techniques to get 'the buzz'; as they described that tingling feeling you'd get from the Gate, or that we're feeling right now. In hindsight it reminds me of translocation, but then of course the technology was made by the same people.

But Sigge had finally decided the Gate wasn't going to open without extreme action. Apparently he'd said to Bianca that it must be the quantity of blood it needed, not the type. He'd gone quiet for a few days, and then he hadn't come back from one day's excursion. This was around a year after Liam had arrived.

So Liam had gone along with Bianca and Dominic to look for Sigge. They'd found him under the Gate, in the same place Kris had been, and he was dead. It seemed he'd been testing the quantity over quality idea, and he'd bled out. And there were scavs everywhere, Liam explained, and it wasn't a good scene.

So even when a human gave up every last bit of blood they could, right to death, it wouldn't reopen the Gate.

I listen quietly to what is surely a terrible memory for Liam, but he's only filling the gaps of what I've already considered. There was a tragedy here; there was some kind of backstory for Bianca and Dominic; and we'll never get the Gate to reopen on our own. We've got the wrong type of blood for a return. The wrong ingredients. Kris had talked about some kind of genetic key held in his ancestor Atem's blood – but he'd poured himself out over this very location, with nothing to show for it.

Well. I don't think he did *that* on purpose either.

"And then Bianca got together with Dominic, I suppose," I muse. "I wondered about that age gap." Bianca looks at least ten years older than Dom – not that it matters. But hearing this story, it sounds like a grieving woman leapt into a relationship with an infatuated younger man. Considering the circumstances, I can't blame her. They're lucky to have each other. "Rude question, but are we sure that Jesse is actually Dominic's? The time frame…"

"He was born two years after Sigge died," Liam says. "But it wouldn't matter. We're all family here. We're all we've got."

I'm silent for a moment, because the reminder that I've been added to that 'we' makes my gut twist. I've been doing OK because I refuse to think properly about my circumstances. Keep a distance.

But he's right that Jesse's parentage wouldn't matter. It's not like there are any spare grandparents around, demanding a DNA test so they can get to know their grandson. And Sigge's parents will never find out what happened to their own son.

Neither will mine, if they even know I'm missing yet.

My throat burns, indicating unshed tears, as I pull out the small glassy object I've been carrying around these past few days. I've had a good look at it, but it still seems to be just a glassy, gluey glob. I'm not sure what I'm supposed to do with it, so finally I just set it down on the red-brown base of the Gate. I'm waiting for it to explode into action – to do something – but it just sits there, bright and shiny against its ugly backdrop.

Typical. Is anything ever easy in this place?

Liam shuffles his feet. "I'm going to check on the crypt."

I see him go out of the corner of my eye, but I stay watching the glob in frustration a few more moments before realising I've missed half the instructions. Put them *with the translator pieces*. But last time we tried to remove them, they wouldn't come out.

Even as I think that, my translators tingle inside my ear canals, and I scratch at them irritably. A moment later, something falls out into my hand.

I stare down in shock at the marble-sized glob. I can now see that it's almost identical to the 'special something' I've been carrying, as if they're part of a set. This close I can make out sparkling shapes within the larger form, but nothing recognisable. Maybe they were set to loosen at the right location, or if enough time passed.

But how would Kris know that he wasn't going to make it?

A moment later I've got the other translator piece out; both tiny objects sitting in my palm. They glow slightly in the morning light; a faint gold that seems to intensify as I watch it.

"Liam, do you see this?"

He's walking over from the little stone building that served as Kris's crypt. It's just out of sight from the main Gate, and he's holding something in one hand. "Uh...they're glowing."

"They *are* glowing!" It's not just my imagination! I duck forward to the base of the Gate, then set them down on either side of the 'special something'. "Right. They're under the Gate, just like he asked."

Liam's watching them narrow-eyed. "Maybe we should give them some space. What if they explode?" *Kris wouldn't do that,* I want to say. But then Kris wasn't meant to die, either. So I move with him as he backs away some distance, then we stop and study the scene. The huge Gate with a faint cluster of lights at its base, growing brighter by the second.

"They probably won't explode," I say, mostly with hope rather than certainty. "But I hope we don't need the translators again. If we don't get abducted, then we won't."

Liam looks unconvinced, and I don't blame him. To me, the chances of getting taken again are fairly high, but I can't bring myself to care.

Then he says, "So...the crypt. It's, ah, empty."

"What?"

"The door's open," he explains, pointing to the small blocky shape whose door is just out of sight. "There was nothing inside except your sleeping bag. No mess, either." He holds out a familiar grey and red shape marred with patches of darker brown.

It's dried blood, but I don't even care. I take the bundled-up sleeping bag even as my heart sinks. It's obvious what's happened – the Perfected have come back and picked up the body. They didn't even need to open the door, although clearly they did it anyway. "They couldn't even leave him two freaking days?" I explode. "They'd better be giving him a good funeral instead of experimenting on him some more!"

A sudden, loud crackling noise echoes across the space, and we both jump.

"The translators," Liam says, pointing. "Their colour's changed."

Indeed, the lights now shine orange, and they're glowing more brightly. But I can hear static, like the sound of a poor-quality radio, and it seems to be coming from the translators I've just put down. "Do you hear that?"

"Yeah… You probably shouldn't touch them," Liam says, but he doesn't sound very concerned.

"Just a quick check." I shuffle back to the Gate quickly – as if moving fast makes it safer – then duck down to check if I can make anything out.

Nope. Without the translator pieces in my ear, I can't make out anything except that it's repeating something in Kris's language. 'Flee for your lives'? Or 'don't worry, help is coming'?

I carefully pick one up, trying not to crush it, then hold it to my ear again.

Attach to the other pieces. Attach to the other pieces. Attach to the other-

What other pieces?

I stare at the translator piece in confusion for a few moments before understanding dawns. "Oh. Duh."

I set both translator pieces carefully down next to the glob which is still sitting directly under the Gate. The glob is no longer shiny-clear, but instead seems to have soaked up some of the dark red-brown mess it's sitting in, right up into its centre. This time I push both translator pieces in so they're pressed hard against the central item.

But the moment the glowing translator pieces touch the glob, they latch on with an audible *click*, connecting as smoothly as Lego pieces back home. Then the whole cluster turns a deep, glowing red. The sort you'd usually see on a warning light.

"Um..." I stand up and stumble backwards as the Gate's buzzing intensifies, filling the air. It feels like the first time I came through the Gate, but it's so much worse. It makes my skin tingle, irritates my ears and seems to drill right into my head.

What's going on?

Liam

I'm watching Demi as she crouches over the tiny glowing devices at the base of the Gate. She's practically kneeling in the still wet blood and water from two days earlier, and I can only conclude that the mist here stops it from drying out completely. There's only a little today, creeping along the edge of the nearby pit.

The sun's above the horizon, but the devices' lights still show clearly against the surrounding darkness.

I should probably tell her to be careful, or offer to step in myself. But I don't. She was given the translators and instructions, not me, and...I'm curious. It's all probably going to come to nothing, but...

Like I said. Curious.

But now there's a humming noise coming from near the Gate, like when you're too close to a power station on regular Earth. I feel it buzz against me, irritating and then overwhelming, and although I can't see past Demi properly, it's clear that the objects are glowing brighter and brighter...

Demi stands up and stumbles back towards me, and the strongest feeling hits me that *something* bad is about to happen imminently.

"GET BACK!" I shout.

Then the world explodes in brilliant white light.

Chapter 17

It's an earthquake. It has to be, since I'm flying backwards, tumbling arse over face across the hard ground until I sprawl to a stop. My ears are ringing, and I've surely broken something. The rocky ground is rumbling and shifting underneath me, but I can't move a muscle.

I don't know how much time passes – full of noise and light and pounding pain in my head. But finally the world comes to a standstill again, and I find I'm lying face down in damp mud. My legs are twisted, my arms akimbo, and I just focus on breathing for some time.

I can still feel all my body parts – whew. I blink. Yep: I can still see. My ribs ache, but it's nothing compared to my head. I must have hit it when I fell…was thrown.

Demi.

Where's Demi?!

I manage to sit up, but my head must still be spinning, because the landscape around me makes no sense. Where I'm expecting to see a flattish slope leading up to the monolithic Gate, instead there's a small mountain of boulders and broken stone. At its top I can see part of the Gate – but it looks as though it's fallen over.

I can only see one straight side. The rest of it disappears into the mist of the pit to my left. Although there's little mist up here, within the pit it's thicker than usual, running up to the pit's top and barely trickling over. It's oddly silent here too, without even the usual sounds of birds, animals or wind that are so common during the early morning.

"Demi?" I call softly, then louder. "DEMI?"

I can't see her anywhere, and she was closer to the Gate than me. I check in every direction, as if she might have been thrown even further. I clamber up the steep, awkward new hill that leads to the fallen Gate, but there's no sign of her. I even check inside the stone hut-place where we'd left poor Kris, but it's rubble. There's clearly no one inside or anywhere near it.

I swallow and look to the place I hadn't checked. Demi could have been thrown in any direction, but she'd been right by the Gate. And the Gate ended up in the pit…

My heart is sinking, and I can't finish that thought. Better to think that the Perfected took her while I was knocked out, since they seem to have a real habit of messing with me while I'm unconscious. But I can't face *that* thought either, because how will I ever get her back?

And even as I think that, I see a faint shape appear from the mist. It's round and grey, rather like a floating soccer ball, and it's coming straight towards me.

Uh oh. Looks like my abduction theory might be right. I hope it is, because it's better than the alternative.

I pick up my spear in shaking hands and point it at the thing. "Bring her back," I order. "Bring Demi back now. You're *not* doing this again!"

But if they did, how would I stop them?

And then behind the sphere, a much larger shape looms out of the mist.

Demi

I open my eyes to find I'm hovering in whiteness. There's cloud all around me, and a bright light.

Am I…am I in heaven?

Next moment, a chemical smell assails me, and I become horribly aware of the aches and pains all over my body. Nope, not in heaven, because being dead would surely hurt less.

A moment later I remember what just happened. The explosion – or whatever it was – from under the Gate. I can faintly hear voices, and when I look down, there's a ring of tiny grey spheres under my belly and my arms.

"The aliens," I say, and my voice is muffled by whatever is around me. "Ugh. I mean – the Perfected. Hello?"

I'm afraid they'll leave me here – wherever 'here' is – but a moment later a face materialises in the cloud, followed by a big, bulky body. I see a smile on sharply carved Perfected features and clothing the colour of the mist…and they're upside down.

A hand touches my arm and I'm flipped the right way up, but I don't feel my feet rest on anything. I seem to be hanging in the air. I look down, but I can't even see my own feet in this mist.

I can see *him* though. It's another Atem clone, this one with the same silvery eyes as my Kris. He beams down at me, because with him this close, my eyes are level with his mid-chest. I feel like a child looking up at an extra-large adult. This close I can also see the strange texture to his skin. Top to bottom, every inch of exposed skin is covered in pale criss-cross patterning, just like Dominic's arms.

The testing...and these scars are the marks of a survivor.

"Dee-mee," Kris says. "Are you well?"

I burst into tears.

Liam

The large shape turns out to be a space shuttle rising up out of the misty pit. About the size of a bus, but flatter and wider, and looking somehow exactly like I expected, yet entirely different. Its triple bands of lights break through the mist and get me right in the eyes.

And then the shuttle lands, and a door appears in the side. I can't see the interior, but it looks dark and ominous.

Uh uh. That's enough alien stereotypes for today. I feel my eye start to twitch, and I grip tighter to my makeshift spear. What's the bet that Demi's inside that shuttle?

I scream in fury and frustration and charge for the sphere where it hovers in front of the doorway, my spear raised. It neatly moves aside, and I find myself drastically overshooting and almost running straight onto the ship.

It's been a hard day.

I screech to a halt and go for the sphere again, and this time it raises up well out of my reach, then zooms into the ship's open door. A few moments later, a figure appears in the doorway. They're lit up from behind; tall, bulky and with an unnaturally round head...

Stereotype number three. Great.

"Leave us alone!" I spit at the Perfected. "We're not animals! We're people! Give me back Demi, give us some more damned vegetables, and then go away! We don't want you here!"

The Perfected cocks their head to the side, and a moment later the round face mask turns transparent. It's a familiar face – the female who'd almost rescued me a few days earlier. Her almost-human face wears an expression of distaste. *"Vegetables, really? Must you be such a barbarian?"*

The voice is familiar too, since it's the same auto-voice usually used in our cells back in Halfway Point. Petra, right? But her tone makes me calm right down, and I shuffle, embarrassed. I hadn't realised how much I appreciated those vegetables till now...but, well, there's not enough of them. "Well, have you got Demi or not?"

I'm fully tense, desperate to hear the answer. Because if they don't have Demi, then she's probably under those rocks...or in the pit.

A faint *crunch* sounds from my left, and I turn to see a second massive figure rising up out of the misty pit. This one isn't wearing a suit, just a regular Perfected tunic, and his arms and head are shockingly bare compared to his colleague. I get a glimpse of rough-looking skin and bright silvery eyes, and then Demi rises up out of the pit like an angel.

Her arms are outstretched on either side of her, her stained sleeping bag is hooked around her shoulders and waving in the wind from the hovering shuttle, and she seems to be propped up by a dozen smaller spheres, neatly holding up each limb. She's covered in pale dust, and she's beaming like she's just been pardoned from death row.

"Demi," I croak, suddenly weak with relief. "I thought you-"

"Kris."

I pause. "What?"

Demi floats to land on the ground next to me, and I see she's crying through that smile. Tear tracks run through the pale dust covering her cheeks, and she's jittering in place. "Kris! Kris! Kris!"

She throws her arms around my waist, and for the second time in twenty-four hours, sobs into my shoulder. I put my arms around her, baffled, but ready to appreciate the moment. She knows I'm not Kris, right?

Then I look up at the male Perfected, the one who'd been in the pit with her.

He stands next to Petra, who's come out from the ship but still wears her suit. Now I see that he has a wedge of silvery hair that matches his eyes…and that he's covered in scars, head to toe. Perfect, fine white lines across every inch of exposed skin, even the delicate spaces around his eyes. But they're all healed; every last one.

"You can't be Kris," I say in disbelief. All these damn Perfected look the same, right? "Kris is dead."

"I'll have to disagree with your statement, although I trust you aren't disappointed," the male says in careful English. He reaches down and takes Petra's hand like they're alien sweethearts or something. "As for me, I was grateful to be placed in the supply hut rather than tossed into the pit along with the flock of *Mona Volandor*. While our medic-chambers can heal many things, they cannot heal a smashed skull."

I'm stunned into silence. It's really him. That damned annoying Perfected who made the greyce cure and somehow convinced Demi to trust him implicitly after a mere two days acquaintance.

I open my mouth to say something, but I've got nothing. I close it again.

Demi lifts her head from my neck. She wears an almost savage expression, eyes too wide, mouth in a grimace. "He's here!" she says in a hoarse, fierce whisper. "Here! Kris!"

Wow. She's more hysterical now he's alive than when we thought he was dead.

Petra mutters something to Kris that doesn't translate, and he nods sharply. "I apologise for the haste," he says to us. "But our time is limited. The Gate is still rebalancing, and you must go through before it finishes doing so."

I blink at him. "What?"

"Rebalancing," he repeats gently. "Reversing its direction had a rather more powerful effect than we anticipated, but this will not happen more than once."

"What?"

The two Perfected exchange a glance, and Kris frowns at me. "Did Dee-mee not tell you what I had promised her? That I would-"

"SEND US HOME!" Demi screeches in my face. She's holding my collar in both fists, and her dark eyes are wide and mad-looking. "The Gate's open again! LET'S GO HOME, LIAM!"

Demi

I'm acting like a crazy person. I know I am, but I can't help it. I've spent the last two days in the depths of despair, feeling like I could just give up and die, and now in five minutes I've got everything back. Everything I had been desperately hoping for, even as those around me thought I was a fool.

But Liam's still staring at me with such a blank expression that I know he's in just as much shock. I grab his jaw and turn his head sideways, facing towards the collapsed Gate. "Look, dust is coming through! The Gate is open!"

Not just a little dust, either. Clouds of it, pouring through the broken gate and disappearing…somewhere.

"What…how…?"

"We found the key," Kris says helpfully. "It was genetic as expected, locked into the blood of the Atems. But it took some testing to determine exactly how to use it. Fortunately, I'd expected some resistance from Syliss and certain other priates, which is why I gave you copies of my most important work, tucked into your translator pieces and the extra special item." He smiles, warping the mesh of fine scars across his golden-brown skin. "We thought it better that you didn't know. If you hadn't brought those pieces this morning, we would have come to find you."

His language is a little different than I'm used to, his words more careful. I realise that since I don't wear translators any longer, and he can't rely on Halfway Point and Rule-of-Law's built-in translators, he must actually be speaking in English. He's doing really well.

I glance down and also notice that he's holding Petra's hand. Petra, who'd cast all blame on him when she'd spoken at the trial. But by the way they're standing, things hadn't been how they looked. I wonder if they planned all of this, right down to his apparent death at the foot of the Gate. And now both of them are dishevelled, appearing more human in this light, but they look…happy.

"Time short, Krys'tof," Petra says in slow English, and although she's looking at Kris, I know the message is for Liam and me.

Her English isn't half as good as his without a translator, but I can't criticise. I haven't picked up a single word of their language.

Kris nods, his smile vanishing. "I would love to tell you everything, little Dee-mee, but time is short. You must fetch the rest of your people now, or you may lose your chance." He gestures at the spheres which have detached from my arms and now hover in a tidy collection at his feet. "Unfortunately all translocators still aren't functioning, here and on Rule-of-Law. This gives us time to take action at the Gate, but it also means you must run."

Liam and I stare at each other, then back at Kris.

"Run," Kris says again.

Liam suddenly jolts upright. "If this is a trick…" But he doesn't wait for a response. "I'll be right back," he says to me, then turns and bolts towards home base.

I watch him go, then turn back to the two Perfected. "I thought you died," I say again. My cheeks are still wet with tears. How can it hurt so much to be happy? "I thought you bled out and left us here."

Kris comes to crouch beside me, putting us at the same level, and I can't stop staring at the marks on his skin. "This is not the way I would have preferred," he says simply. "But I knew what my people could be like, and we planned for every eventuality, including this one." He quirks his mouth into a smile. "Well. Not *quite* this one. We planned to carefully draw a small vial of my blood and mix it with our copies of the other items in a controlled, restrained way."

A small vial of blood? "Instead, you just about lost all of it," I say numbly.

He shrugs a shoulder, turning to smile at Petra. "But not quite. As I said, medic-chambers can heal even clinical death if the conditions are right. And even as my enemies left me here at the Gate, my Peh'tra followed behind with a medic-chamber."

His Petra? Cute.

Kris continues, "And now we've found the key to reversing the Great Disaster, we can reclaim these lands for our people. Those who will come here, that is, because it can be impossible to change some minds. But your people do not belong in this era, little Dee-mee. You must return to your own time in the past, while the eras are still rebalancing."

Eras, he said. "So it is time-travel, then," I murmur. I'm not surprised at all, since it's in line with what we were already thinking, and it doesn't matter one jot. "How does the Gate work?"

He gestures towards the fallen shape. "Simply walk through the remnants of the archway. I suspect that once you are close enough, it will pull you in to where you belong. It wants every last molecule back in its rightful place, you see, and it will only take what should not be here."

Like me. "That sounds easy enough." Although it'll be a few minutes before the others arrive, even at full-sprint. But something else is bothering me, guilt pricking at me. "Um...I have to confess something, Kris. I'm actually not a child."

He frowns as if confused.

"I'm twenty-eight," I continue awkwardly. "You did a lot for me, kept me safe because of some Perfected laws about children and so forth, but I'm an adult. I've been one for many years."

Kris's mouth curves into a slow smile. "Ah, little Dee-mee," he says affectionately. "We determined your biological age the first time you were translocated. But by Perfected laws, you are very much a child. We mark adulthood at forty years. I myself am one-hundred-thirty-five."

My eyes bug. "Oh. But...Liam and Dominic aren't forty, either." Even if Liam looked it originally.

"But they were tainted by the time I found them, little Dee-mee, and I could not stretch the laws so far even for them." He pats me on the cheek like you would a toddler. (I don't take offence.) "But here they come, see?"

I turn, but his eyes must be far better than mine since they don't come into sight for some time. Then I see them staggering up the hill, clearly having moved faster than they're used to. Bianca leans heavily on Dominic and Liam, and Jerrold's got a tight grip on Jesse's small wrist. Could this be Jesse's first time out of home base? Even from here, I see their wide eyes and stunned expressions, and I wonder if they even believe Liam's story.

But they came. They're here, all of them.

The Gate better work after all of this, or I'm going to feel really stupid.

Liam

I make the usual careful fifteen-minute walk back to home base in less than five, and I'm panting and breathless by the time I get back to home base's main area. It's cold in here, but unusually, everyone's already up, huddled around the small fire in the room's centre.

They look up in alarm to see me.

"What's happening?" Bianca bursts out. "Where's Demi?"

Of course, this must look terrible. "Fine," I manage between huffing breaths. "It's the Gate. It's open."

There's stunned silence.

"But…the earthquake," Jerrold says, gesturing at the room around him. "Are you saying that was the Gate?"

There was an earthquake? For the first time I realise that the neat stacks of goods (junk) are scattered around, and our usual disorderly space has descended into chaos. Of *course* the rumblings would have affected this whole area.

But everyone seems alright, so I nod frantically. "Yes. The Gate. Both sides are rebalancing, Kris says, so we have to go RIGHT NOW so we don't miss out." I gesture dramatically at the hall leading back towards the Gate. "Come on!"

"Isn't Kris the dead one?" Dominic asks. No one's moving. Instead they're all poised as if I'm crazy, or as if the information's far too shocking to process.

I put my hands on my hips and focus on breathing, trying to calm my pounding heart and my adrenaline-fueled panic. "OK. So Kris isn't dead, although he's got scars to beat yours, Dom. We ran into him at the Gate when we accidentally set it off – and I swear, I'll tell you everything once there's time. But not now. We have to run, alright? Run NOW."

The others exchange glances, and I see when the tide of opinion turns.

"This better not be a bloody alien trick," Jerrold says grimly.

"I'm sure it's not," I reply. "But can we risk losing this chance?"

It's clear that we can't, and finally, *finally* everyone starts to move.

The return trip to the Gate is slower. I'm tired, Bianca's knee is still healing so Dom and I help her along, Jesse's a kid so has shorter steps, and Jerrold is just old. (Sorry, Jerrold.) And as we walk-run to the Gate, I try to keep an eye out for scavs or hover-balls, while recounting today's adventure in as much detail as I can.

Jerrold keeps muttering "This better not be a bloody alien trick" until Jesse copies him perfectly. Then we fall silent, focusing on breathing and keeping up our pace.

It *better* not be an alien trick. I don't think it is, but what's the best we've got now? Hiding underground and living solely off bugs? It's worth the risk.

"You know you've got a big bump on your head," Dominic points out randomly. He taps at his temple. "Just here."

I reach up with my spare hand to find a sizeable egg just under my hairline. "Ow. Must be from flying rubble when the Gate fell. I hadn't even noticed." No, I was too busy worrying about Demi being dead, then about a second alien abduction, and then about getting back to the Gate ASAP since it looks to be actually working again, which I never thought would happen...

"Is that Demi up there?" Bianca asks. She's squinting up the long path ahead to where the Gate used to be. Now through the thinning fog we can just make out its fallen shape, plus three figures, and the space shuttle behind them. "Wow. The aliens are huge."

From here, Demi looks like a child next to them. But wasn't that the point?

The others' pace slows, and I can almost hear what they're thinking. Are we really all going to walk right up to the people who held Dominic captive for three years, giving them the chance to take all of us in one fell swoop?

But then I see the moment Demi notices us. She stares for a moment, then waves her arms in a 'hurry up' motion. Then I see her turn back to the nearest Perfected – Kris – but I can't hear what she's saying.

A moment later she moves towards the fallen Gate, clambering up on top of the rubble around its base. In its new form, the gap underneath is just tall enough for Demi to duck under. She pauses, silhouetted against its outline as she looks back at us, and then…vanishes.

Chapter 18

Demi

I wave frantically at the cluster of humans making their way up the path, but they're too slow. They're walking, not running, and Kris's warning keeps echoing in my ears. He doesn't know how long the Gate will take to rebalance. It could be ten minutes, could be ten hours – and ten minutes has already passed.

Standing this close to the Gate is starting to have an effect on me. I can feel vibrations through my body, like the buzzing sensation before a regular translocator works. But then the Gate is a colossal translocator, isn't it?

As the tingles increase to little jolts across my skin, I give myself a shake. "Let's see if this thing works, shall we?" I look up at Kris. "Thank you. There's no way I can say it enough, but…thank you."

He smiles kindly down at me, reminding me of a kindly (genetically modified) grandparent. "You are most welcome."

And then I turn to climb the little hill of rubble leading to the remnants of the Gate's archway. The buzzing/tingling gets worse the closer I move. Now it makes my whole body shake, and feels as if tiny fingers are snatching at every inch of my skin.

But everything in me wants to move forward anyway, and I put my head down and keep climbing until I'm just short of the archway.

Even with the terrible damage done by the rebalancing, the Gate's carved patterns are still distinctly noticeable. The blood-water combo has darkened to pitch black, clearly delineated against the pale dust from the fallen rocks which seems to be spraying through. My sleeping bag/cloak moves as if in a breeze, but it's being pulled towards the gap, not away.

I've got to go through. It *wants* me to – to go back to where I belong.

I wrap the sleeping bag tightly around me and take a moment to glance over my shoulder. The others are closer, but are still moving too slowly, and I can only just make out their faces from here.

But it's not my problem. They have to make their own decisions, and if they miss this chance because of some stupid hesitation then-

Liam

One moment Demi's there at the base of the Gate; the next, she's gone.

"It works," Jerrold breathes from beside me. "It actually works."

I can hear the absolute shock in his tone, and I don't blame him. It feels impossible that after having given up on going home, we've finally got the chance to go. "Come on, everyone! We have to make sure we're not left behind."

Two minutes later we're at the base of the Gate, standing on the humming rubble. The scarred Perfected, Demi's friend, watches us solemnly.

"So we just step up to it, do we?" I ask. It's more to comfort everyone else than myself, since I can guess how this thing works.

"The eras are rebalancing," Kris says in halting English. "The Gate will take what does not belong here, and will draw back what does belong. You must go through to your own time."

Well, obviously. I turn and reach out a hand to Bianca, who's closest. "Come on!"

But Jerrold holds up a hand. He wears an expression of absolute horror. "Dom and Jesse were born here," he says hollowly. "The alien said the Gate only takes what doesn't belong. My boys...they've never been through the Gate like we have."

Horror crawls over me, making me numb from head to toe, and I see the realisation echoed in the other adults' expressions. Dominic and Jesse *were* born here. And from what Kris just said, only things that came from our Earth will go back. Anything else...the Gate rejects.

They can't come.

Bianca gasps. "We won't go without them. We'll stay here."

There are a few seconds of silence, and Dominic stares at his feet. Then he looks up at me. "You should go, Liam. Go home. We'll be OK." He forces a smile. "This is all we know."

Jerrold is ducking his head, but his expression is crumpled as if he's close to tears. "Mm. Go on, Liam. Have a beer for me, will you?"

Jerrold was always talking about how he'd hated beer, but oddly it was one of the things he missed from our Earth. He reaches forward and rumples my hair as if I'm a child. It crinkles audibly under his hand, since it's still half-varnished.

I stare at him. Is this going to be how we say goodbye? Am I really just going to leave them behind after all these years? Bianca grabs me in a hug, and a moment later Dominic and Jesse do the same.

"I'll always remember you as my best friend," Dominic says, his tone thick with tears.

Remember me, as if our friendship is already in the past. "But my silver eye is from here," I point out numbly. "So shall I stay behind too?"

"Hell no!" Jerrold exclaims. "Just wear an eyepatch."

Wear an eyepatch, while drinking a beer. Alone, because all my survivor family will be back here.

I'm going. I'm really going…without them?

Hell no.

I grab Dominic by the shoulders – not hard since he's still hugging me – then spin him around till his back's to the Gate. Then…I give him a sharp push.

I get a glimpse of his startled expression, then there's another flash of orangish light and he vanishes.

Oh, thank you to whoever's out there watching over us. We don't have to leave anyone behind.

Without waiting, I grab the next closest person – Jesse – and step towards the Gate. It feels awful – that horrible buzzing like we're surrounded by a million angry bees, rattling my aching head. I look back briefly at Jerrold and Bianca, just long enough to meet their eyes…then I drag Jesse through.

Demi

Going home through the Gate feels worse than leaving. Maybe it's because I don't pass out this time, but I feel as though my atoms are all taken apart and then put together so rapidly that I collapse, retching. It's dry, though, since I haven't eaten properly in some time.

A few moments later, when my head stops spinning, I start to notice what's around me. Flashing lights. The hum of voices. Warm, humid air, and dry, dusty soil under my hands and knees.

For a moment of terror I think that the Gate didn't work after all, but then I look up and meet the eyes of an unfamiliar human woman. She's soft-featured and remarkably ordinary in her grey-green collared shirt. She's also staring at me as if I've grown a second head. "Where did you come from?" she asks.

I blink at her. "That depends. Where am I now?" But even as I speak, I'm recognising my surroundings. The steep, blueish-green peaks of Mount Freedom National Park are behind her, and forest that stretches on for ages. We're standing on a rocky, solid platform with a dusting of loose gravel. Under my feet are the deep, familiar carvings of the Gate's base, half obscured by that loose gravel. But when I'd first come through, I was under a rocky shelf in a ravine…

"Shelly! Get back behind the tape!" someone shouts from behind me.

I turn slowly to see a youngish man in a National Park polo shirt, standing behind several strips of plastic tape proclaiming

'DANGER!' A familiar, low wooden barrier sits under the tape. "You too, miss," he says severely. "You shouldn't be out here at all, let alone without, erm, proper clothing."

Clothing? I suddenly realise I can feel a breeze in an unexpected place. I look down to see that while the Gate allowed me through, my Rule-of-Law clothing didn't come with me. I'm wearing nothing but my stained, well-used sleeping bag, which is still wrapped around my shoulders like a cloak. It's not covering everything important though.

I squeak in dismay and spin around so my back is to the others as I try to cover myself. Oh, God. This is like a nightmare I had once, and it's really happening. "Argh! Sorry..,"

"I didn't even see her walk up," the strange woman, AKA Shelly says. "She must've sneaked up behind me."

She says the last part somewhat accusingly, and I don't know how to defend myself. *I didn't sneak up on you; I just came back from a sort-of alien abduction, OK?* But instead I wrap my sleeping bag tightly around my torso and tuck it in firmly, then turn back around. "I didn't sneak up," I tell them. "I came through an interdimensional gate."

Shelly and the man stare at me open-mouthed. Then the man murmurs in an aside that I hear clearly. "Dehydrated, confused. But where *did* she come from?"

Just then a second man comes up behind the tape, followed by another woman in a white T-shirt. They both wear backpacks, shorts and walking shoes, and they're staring at me with startled expressions.

I wave. "Hi." Boy, have they got a surprise coming when the others appear. I've just realised that while I have my sleeping bag, the others probably haven't been clothed in Earth-wear for years.

"Hold on a second," one of the newcomers says. "Demetria Wallace?"

"Yes...?"

"We've been looking for you for days!" he exclaims. He picks up what looks like a transistor radio – since there's no cell reception out here – and says, "We've found her. Repeat, we've found the missing person."

Before I know it I'm hustled over the 'DANGER' tape and the low, useless barrier, and suddenly people are clustering around me, taking my temperature and offering me water and swapping my ratty, Kris-bloodstained sleeping bag for a silver-lined emergency blanket.

They ask me questions about where I've been, but since they reacted so badly to my original comment about the Gate, I don't know how to respond. They conclude I'm confused, dehydrated and malnourished. They'd be right – but *they* should try surviving on breadish and weird piggy creatures and see how well they do.

And I've been missing less than a week. Hallelujah.

"We thought you might have been caught in the landslide," someone informs me. "We were about to give up the search for our own safety, at least until the land settled."

"Landslide?" I echo stupidly, since I have no idea what to say. I'd been so focused on getting home that I hadn't really considered what I'd do once I was there...or that I might be caught in the act of coming back through the Gate.

"There was a colossal landslide," Shelly explains. "Just an hour ago. There used to be a valley here, but now it's a plateau, see? It happened incredibly fast, but you can hear it's still going."

"We could have all been killed," one of the others says

emphatically.

My gaze follows her gesturing arm, and I realise what's wrong with my surroundings. Well, what *else* is wrong.

When I was last here, this was a rocky platform/look-out point over a deep valley full of trees, with those blue-green mountains right behind them.

But now, that valley is completely gone. The base of the mountains is almost entirely flat, with natural-looking gentle hills and dips making their way to a lower area in the far distance. I can hear the faint rumblings of earth moving or stones falling.

The Gate is still rebalancing, which means it's still open. But where are the others?

Even as I'm thinking that, Dominic suddenly appears from thin air. Literally from thin air. One moment there's the empty rocky platform where the ravine used to be, with the 'landslide' beyond it. Next moment, there's a semi- naked bald man sprawled on his hands and knees, vomiting profusely.

Ugh. At least it wasn't just me that reacted that way.

There's a stunned gasp from around me, and I realise at least three of the four here saw him appear. I stand up, wrapping my emergency blanket around me with dignity, then pick up my battered sleeping bag. "Excuse me," I say. "Dominic's going to need help."

He does need help. As do Liam and Jesse, then Jerrold and Bianca who arrive mere moments later. They're all disoriented and dirty and ill from the travel, and they look like they've dug themselves out of the landslide behind them. I must look the same.

"My eye," Liam's saying. He's got one hand slapped over that part of his face. "My eye."

It's gone, we see as he finally lowers his hand. There's a neat hollow where his silver eye had been. It's not even bleeding.

"I told you, you should wear an eyepatch," Jerrold says from behind him. "You'll look very dashing, like a pirate. But damn, where are our clothes?"

He's right. They're all wearing only scraps – Bianca and Jesse having just enough ragged layers that I imagine those clothes must have come through the Gate in the first place. If only I'd made a point of changing out of my Rule-of-Law clothes!

But there's nothing to be done now. I walk up to Liam as the search and rescue team flies into action with more emergency blankets, and one man gives his own T-shirt to Jesse. I keep my gaze fixed on Liam's face. "I thought you weren't coming," I say a little accusingly.

"We almost didn't." He touches his eye socket again, grimacing. "We were worried that Dominic and Jesse wouldn't make it since they were born on the other side. My eye is a small loss in comparison."

"Does it hurt?"

"Not really. Feels…strange, though, worse than a missing tooth." He scoffs. "I wouldn't recommend it."

I study his face, trying to work out why he looks so different – besides the obvious missing eye. He's also left the hair and skin varnish behind, I realise, and it leaves him looking rumpled, rough and strangely appealing in spite of his new injury. But then perhaps the state of undress is contributing to that appeal. "Are you…sorry you came?"

Someone shoves a mug into my hands, and I step back as they push Liam onto a travel chair and wrap him more tightly in a silver-lined blanket. He doesn't seem to notice. "Sorry?" he echoes, and his mouth curves into a grin. "Sorry? We made it! I can't believe we actually made it. I think I'd give an arm and both legs to be back here. Forget one measly eye."

He grins, and I laugh in joy and relief. Then I sip the contents of the mug, which turns out to be tepid hot chocolate. It tastes like heaven.

It occurs to me suddenly that Liam's not the only one who's had Perfected medical work done on him. Dominic's covered in silvery scars, and I had that lung disaster that was healed in only a day. It almost feels like a dream, it was so surreal, but it happened. I clutch at my chest and try to work out if it hurts, or if my breathing has been affected. Have I left something vital back on the other side?

Nope, I decide thirty seconds later. (Panic resolved!) Scar tissue seems to be fine to bring through, judging by my own condition. I'm fine. Cold, embarrassed, confused, but…fine.

I glance at Dominic and amend my opinion slightly. He's rubbing at the top of one ear that's shorter than it had been this morning, and I can see he's missing the tips of a couple of fingers. Ouch. He doesn't seem upset though.

Meanwhile, others are joining us. It seems our timing was perfect – people had been searching for me ever since I disappeared, although of course they never would've found me. Then after the apparent landslide – possibly caused by an earthquake, I'm told – the teams had been called in for their own safety.

I don't bother correcting their assumption about the landslide, because how could they possibly understand that two different time periods had been rebalancing and healing after damage done by the black-hole type Gate? It sounds crazy.

But my plan to keep my mouth shut proves to be pointless.

The others seem to be answering every question honestly, and it brings more questions from our rescuers, but it's too late to take back.

Yes, we all think we've been through an interdimensional gate to the future. We'll just have to ride it out.

And while I'm so, so glad to be found…heck, this is embarrassing. It's even more so when some of the other searchers reach us, and I realise that Connor is among their number. He wears a few days' worth of stubble, and his glasses are smudged. He takes them off when he sees me, cleans them, then puts them on again as if he hadn't seen correctly the first time.

"Demi?"

"Hey, Connor." I can feel my cheeks heating, and I wrap the blanket more tightly around me. I know there's plenty to see underneath. "How are you?"

"Me!? What about *you?*" He rushes towards me and hugs me tightly before being scolded by one of the others. He backs away, but he's still leaning in close. "Where have you been!?"

He's been helping to look for me. That makes me feel warm inside. Not because I still want to date him, but because it feels good to be missed. It feels good that I matter enough that people would look for me, even spend days looking for me. (Although with the nudity thing, I'm kind of glad my parents are on the other side of the country.)

I blink away sudden tears. "Well…" I don't want to deal with this question again, especially from someone I know. And Connor doesn't even know that several of the people here actually saw us arrive from thin air. "First there was a spider, then I dropped my sleeping bag in a ravine…and it went from there."

"A spider."

"Yes."

"No," he says, moving towards me again. "There's a spider on you. Don't worry, I'll-"

But I've spotted the leggy little creature where it sits on my blanket-covered knee, and I flick it off onto the ground. It pauses for a moment, stunned, before scuttling away to hide under a rock. "Sorted. There are a lot of them around here, right?"

Connor's struck silent. "I guess this week in the wilderness changed you, huh?"

More like, a regular spider is nothing compared to a man-sized land lobster. I shrug. "I guess it has."

He looks past me to where the others are still being treated. "And who are all these people? They look...rough."

"It's a long story," I begin. I glance over at the others, hoping to catch Liam's eye again, but his eye is being patched up – no pun intended. Jerrold and Bianca's attention is on a shaggy black and white dog that someone has brought along. One of the rescue team is showing a fascinated Jesse how to pat it, while Dominic watches bug-eyed from behind Jesse's shoulder. Perhaps Dominic's fantasy of 'dog' – a loyal, cuddly blanket – is a bit toothier and more slobbery in reality.

"I've got plenty of time," Connor says a little defiantly. His voice lowers. "I didn't realise how much I still cared for you until you were gone. Anything you need, Demi. I'll get it for you."

Liam's one good eye meets mine, and I smile at him. He smiles back briefly before closing his eye. Either he's in need of a good rest, or he doesn't want to talk right now. Probably both.

Ah, well.

"Demi?"

I look back to Connor. "Sorry, what?"

He sighs. "Never mind. We'll talk later, when you're feeling better."

But then the first of the search and rescue quad bikes arrives, and we're shuttled off down the track, back towards civilisation.

The landslide has stopped, we're informed. Which means the Gate has closed – the two sides have rebalanced. We're safe at last.

Home at last.

Chapter 19

Demi

'd been so desperate to get home that I didn't think about what returning would entail. What a *mess* it would be – explaining to people where you've been for the last week, who these people are that are with you, and why you showed up half-naked, of all things.

Then after all the initial palaver when we're given clothing, food and medical checks, Liam's recognised as someone else who went missing in this area. Then Bianca's recognised. Jerrold has to venture his own details since no one remembers him without being reminded. It was too long ago that he and his wife vanished in this area.

It's awkward. Awkward, and messy, and somewhat embarrassing to admit the truth of where we've been, and to be looked at like we're crazy. I don't blame people. I would have assumed I was crazy too – or that we'd actually been kidnapped by some bizarre nudist cult that lived in the mountains, which I think is the default explanation.

But we're all shuffled to the nearest ranger's station where there's more food, medical attention and strange conversations. I'm given someone's cell phone to call my hysterical, grateful parents and my workplace. (Who also seems grateful, although much less hysterical.) I tearfully tell them that I fell into a ravine and got lost, but now I'm OK, and that'll I give them more details once I'm home.

We'll need some time to get our stories straight.

The others don't ask to use the phone. Jerrold because there were no cell phones when he left, and Bianca and Liam because there'll be no quick conversations for them. As far as their families know, they're dead. As for Jesse and Dominic, till an hour ago, they didn't even exist here. No ID; no one to miss them.

Then the original search and rescue team (with dog) is swapped for another group of unfamiliar people, and we're taken to a quieter, larger, still somewhat remote building. There, we're probed for full details of our travels, and we give them. I'm a bit hesitant at this point, but when the others don't hold back, I figure I may as well do the same. And then these quietly dressed, quietly spoken people quietly explain to us that they believe what we've said, but it would be better for us to keep quiet on our travels. And what can they do to help us stay that way?

Homes. Money. ID. All the others need to start over. Even Liam's been away just long enough to be declared dead, and that takes a lot of work to reverse. Never mind the work needed to contact family members and friends – to find out who's still around, and where they might be. The longer the survivors have been away, the harder it is.

Not for me though. Seven days missing is just long enough to seriously worry people, but not quite long enough to assume death. In short, I can go home anytime. I do ask for one thing though – a scan of my lungs. But unlike poor Liam and his lost eye, my damaged lungs had been healed with their own tissue, and it all came with me. If they hadn't pointed out all the scar tissue on the scan, it would have been like that injury never happened.

Like all of it never happened.

I'm given the go-ahead to leave three days after my return through the Gate: three days after the enormous 'earthquake' that levelled parts of Mount Freedom Park. I call around for someone to pick me up. My workmate Tara ends up being closest, and not long later, her car pulls up outside our current accommodation.

She greets me with a hug and a squeal. "Girl, we thought you died! Tell you what, we will *not* be going hiking with you again."

Tara's been given the official story, which is that I was shaking a spider out of my sleeping bag when I tripped and fell off a cliff into the valley. I hit my head and wandered for days before being found by search teams, coincidentally at the same time as that colossal earthquake.

That particular story makes me sound like a klutz, which is only somewhat true. It doesn't do any favours for my street cred, and it doesn't explain why other long-missing folk reappeared around the same time. But the truth is worse.

"I'll pass on the hiking myself," I reply wryly. "Sorry about ruining everyone's trip."

Tara's lips purse. "Sorry about telling you to get rid of your own spider," she says quietly. "We're just glad to have you back safe and sound."

I smile, because I'm glad too. And what else is there to say?

"Are you ready to go home?"

I look back over my shoulder. From here I can hear the sounds of the TV that currently holds Dominic and Jesse in thrall. Bianca's in fervent conversation with someone over a landline in a side room. I can just hear fragments of her speech, hear the tears in her tone. Happy tears, though. It's probably the sister she mentioned yesterday, the one that our 'helpers' located.

And through a window I can just make out Liam's back where he sits on a bench at the far side of the building, facing out towards the lush vista of the national park. Jerrold's silvery head is next to his. They appear to be deep in conversation, so I won't interrupt them.

I already said my goodbyes this morning; gave my phone number. I need some time away, some time back to normal to figure out how I feel about all of this, about them.

So I turn back to Tara and smile again. "I'm ready," I say. "Take me home."

Liam

We hear the vehicle pull away down the gravel road. Jerrold looks over his shoulder for a few moments, then turns back to face the massive expanse of lush forest. "The girl's gone."

The girl being Demi, of course. I was the only one who'd spent enough time with her to see her as a real person, a real member of the group. To the others, she'd appeared briefly, got obsessed over aliens and reopening the Gate, and left again.

I grunt acknowledgement, thinking that it wasn't as if she'd wanted to be here anyway. But she didn't need to seem so happy to leave. While she left her contact details, I don't know if she'll ever follow up. I might never see her again.

Even though we're mostly strangers, that would be a shame. So few others will ever understand our story.

I'm reminded of a conversation we had in the Wilds. She

said that she understood why I was interested in her, but she didn't want to be someone's only choice. I figure that went both days. And…well, now we're not. Now we've got the whole world.

"Strange," Jerrold muses. "I never thought I'd be here, back among people. Never thought I'd sit outside, enjoying the sunshine and not being afraid of what's out here with us."

We're not quite outside. Instead we're sitting on a balcony mostly hedged in by glass. The view's fantastic, although a determined scav could easily reach us here. (No scavs. No scavs!) Jerrold sits on my right side, since I'm now entirely blind out of my left. No eyeball, and so forth, but someone's provided an eyepatch. I feel like an anemic pirate. A clumsy one too, since my depth perception's now terrible.

"Have you heard back about your family?" I ask. I was given details this morning about my own. My parents are separated and live on different continents. They found my mother pretty quickly, although they're still looking for my dad. I haven't called the number yet. I wonder if she's read the news – if we're even on it. *Missing mountain-biker found after eight years.*

Jerrold's quiet for a while, and my gut twists, convinced he's had bad news. But then he says, "My brother's still around. Lives an hour north of here."

"Oh. That's…great."

He shakes his head, a funny little smile curving his mouth. "Who would've thought. Family still alive, and just down the road. But would you believe, I just want to sit quietly in a cabin somewhere and…read a book. Or maybe watch one of those new television shows. I don't want to have to explain where I've been all these years."

I sigh. "I'm with you there. I *will* tell the important people the truth, even though it's going to be hard. My family wouldn't understand why I'd just leave for so many years, and it's not fair to expect us to lie about it."

Jerrold sighs. "Do you think they'll believe you?"

I make a wavering gesture with one hand. "Maybe? I think they'll be happy I'm back, and baffled that I left in the first place."

I was so woefully unprepared for returning, I almost want to just hide away for another six months until I get my head around this, and prepare a good explanation. Except add a laptop to my essentials list. I'd love to see where the internet's at.

And because of how things played out, we never got the chance to agree on a story. Ie, did we tell the unvarnished truth, or did we try for something that would be more convincing and make us seem less crazy?

In the end, it was the truth. And the polite men and women in plain suits asked us to politely keep that truth hidden; to avoid the media and anything else that would spread our awkward story amongst the masses.

Of course, it would've helped if half a dozen people hadn't seen us arrive out of nowhere, and if Dominic hadn't said, 'I've never seen so many people before', and if Jesse hadn't mentioned his family being stolen by aliens, and if Bianca hadn't cried and said how we'd all been trapped in another version of Earth and had to live off bugs.

I lean forward and take another handful of crisps. *Crunch crunch.* Something about the texture seems so familiar and pleasant, and I savour the salty flavour. Food that we didn't have to kill, and that isn't made of locusts. Yum.

"It's a hard road," I say finally. "But we won't be alone. And worst-case, we can just go and hide in the woods somewhere." I grin at him, and he shakes his head.

This guy may as well be my second father, and I'm not going anywhere. With or without Demi, no matter what happens, we won't be alone.

Three months later

Demi

There's a hum of conversation in the small café, and I sit quietly at my corner table, watching passers-by through the large glass windows. The café's name is written backwards from my point of view, but I look straight past it.

I can see a dark-haired guy getting out of a small, boxy blue car just outside. The driver is a young redhead, and I admire how her auburn curls shine in the sunlight. The guy – Liam – leans in and says something to her, and she smiles.

Huh. He didn't wait long to find a girl, did he? And I'm happy for him, I tell myself. He was forcibly single for eight long years, and if he likes redheads, he likes redheads. I don't care. We're just friends, OK? Friends who meet for a meal every weekend without fail.

I hadn't been sure if I'd ever seek out the survivors again. But I'd decided to give it a go, to see what they were like in a normal environment. To see if I could help them acclimatise to twenty-first century life.

So I picked up my phone and called the new number I'd been given, then arranged to make the two-hour drive back to this little town at the edge of the national park. And it turns out that Liam and I actually do get on really well. Shared trauma will do that to you, and the fact he's quite funny and interesting and fairly nice, too.

But I still hadn't been expecting the redhead.

You're scowling, inner Demi tells me. *Your face hurts, see?*

Dang, so it does. Just then, Liam looks up and sees me watching, and gives a jaunty wave. I wave back, smiling ruefully at being caught watching. But I can't help myself – he looks so different now, and every time I see him from a distance, I get a little jolt of surprise.

Part of it is the eyepatch, of course. But it's also the way he's filled out, no longer looking on the edge of starvation; the way his fair skin has a healthy glow, and that his hair and clothes are clean and modern. He looks…good.

Liam makes his way inside, and I notice how he gives everyone a wide berth. His movements are careful and steady. Few other people would know it, but that's because he's still adjusting to life surrounded by thousands of other people.

Noise, busyness, colour. People *everywhere* – or so he says. This is a small town right on the edge of the national park, and its population is only 2,500. Still, he finds it difficult – and he's doing far better than the others, who've barely visited the town centre since arriving, declaring it overwhelming.

"Hey." I gesture at the seat opposite, where I've already poured a glass of water. The small laminated menu sits in the empty space. "You hungry?"

"Always." Liam sits, rubbing his hands together in evident excitement. "Mm. I'll have the Eggs Benedict on wholegrain toast."

I look at him in exasperation. "You had that last week. You don't want to try something new?" I don't mention that the wholegrain bread looks horribly like breadish to me, so I doubt I'll ever eat it again.

Liam shakes his head. "I tried a few things, but this is a favourite." He grimaces. "I hate to admit it, but I actually miss breadish. You know, the texture. Not the ingredients."

I laugh, because I suspected as much. For me, those few days were enough. I definitely *don't* miss it.

I order the blueberry pancakes, because they're the furthest thing from breadish on the menu. Then Liam asks me about work. Although I took three weeks off after my 'disappearance', and I've been back for some time. "Oh! I meant to say last week, Connor left. Remember, that guy I used to go out with?"

"I remember," Liam says, although his eyebrows are quirked in interest. "He's gone, is he?"

"Sure is." I can't hold back a smile. "Never thought I would've outlasted him, but he's gone to a similar role in a different city, closer to where his new girlfriend lives."

Liam pauses. "New girlfriend? You OK with that?"

"Sure. Why wouldn't I be?" Connor and I broke up *ages* ago, and there've been more important things to think about.

"Well...on the day we came back, he seemed awfully friendly with you. I thought you might've got back together, especially with the improvement in your...health."

"Oh." My eyebrows raise. While Connor was happy I didn't die and had expressed some warm emotions that first day, they hadn't lasted, and I hadn't wanted them to. I'd politely thanked him and sent him on his way, and hadn't thought twice about it. "I didn't realise it looked that way. But no, not at all. I didn't even tell him about the, er, health improvement."

"OK," Liam says mildly, and I wonder if he's pleased, or if I'm misinterpreting his expression.

See, when I had all those medical checkups upon arriving home, they found more than just clean scar tissue in my lungs. They also found that the damage to my reproductive system had almost been entirely healed, and the obvious blocks to fertility were now gone. There were no guarantees I could have kids, but…well, there were no guarantees I couldn't, either. Kris's medic-chamber had worked a miracle. Funny, I hadn't even thought twice about it. I wonder why.

I change the subject. "Anyway, back to my work situation," I say. "You know how when I first got back, everyone was tiptoeing around me? And half of them thought I was an idiot who got lost in the wilderness and hallucinated from dehydration, and the other half thought I was abducted by aliens thanks to those news stories that made it out?"

The powers-that-be had tried to keep us quiet early on, but they hadn't reckoned on the rescue team who'd seen us appear out of nowhere. Someone had given a very detailed (and mostly true) story to the media, which then went viral along with our names. *Seven missing persons cases solved!* And closure for those families who'd lost loved ones.

Along with the remarkable natural disasters at the same time, it was enough to keep our stories in the media for weeks.

"Yeah…" Liam says.

"Well, I figure they still think that. Except now no one talks about it anymore. I'm back to ordinary conversations about the weather and sport and someone's house renovations, and when I'll have that report done. It's so brutally ordinary, and I've stopped questioning it myself. I almost feel…normal again." I shake my head with a half-smile. "But then I was only gone a week. I feel like it'll take years before I can feel truly normal, if I ever can."

Liam raises an eyebrow, and I wait for him to scold me, to point out how long he and the others were away. But instead he says, "Do you want to feel normal?"

It's a good question. "Not if normal means forgetting

everything that happened," I admit. "And I couldn't bear that. It's hard enough not being able to really talk about it except with you and the others. I don't *want* to forget. I feel like it's changed me, and I want to be that different person." Braver, maybe, or able to hold on to hope even when life looks terrible. And nothing here could ever be half as bad as what we've already gone through.

"Well, we all know I'm a lost cause," Liam says with a smile. "I'll never be normal again, especially not with Dom as my best friend. But I want to be normal enough to fit in, to help them fit in." He reaches a hand to the black patch that covers his left eye socket. "Or maybe not that normal."

"Normal's overrated," I say with a laugh. "These days I prefer interesting."

Our food arrives, and we dig in with gusto. After Liam's inhaled his plateful, he asks, "So...you haven't said anything about *the gift*. Does that mean you didn't bring it?"

I jolt upright. "I can't believe I forgot all this time! But of course I brought it! You only texted me about it fifteen times."

I lean down and carefully open the top of the large, square box that's been sitting at our feet all this time. Liam leans over, sees the contents, and smiles. "Perfect."

"I thought so, too."

Liam

We finish our meal and head outside with *the gift* in its box, leaving cash on the table. I still have to force myself to walk away from Demi's pancake scraps – reminding myself that I don't need to clean the food from every last plate.

Someone else cleans the plates, and there's enough food that I could eat non-stop and never run out. Probably best not to do that, though – I'd very quickly grow out of my new clothes.

We make our way down to the deep, slow-flowing river that runs through the town centre. It's quiet here, and very green, and the path that runs alongside it is also a shortcut to our destination.

Jerrold, Bianca, Dominic and Jesse's home is a fifteen-minute walk from the centre of town, as far away from other houses as you can get while still being part of the town. It's a four-bedroom, two-bathroom old place that was helpfully arranged for them by the same people who provided them with ID and came up with our official lie-story, and the same people who got me my own little place on the other side of town.

We had the choice to go anywhere at all, to separate ourselves, but I couldn't bring myself to move too far, or back to a city. I reasoned that the others weren't ready for that. Or maybe I just wasn't ready.

I'm still not.

Bianca runs out the front of the house as we walk up. "Did you get it?" she asks in a hushed, urgent voice.

I hold up the box which Demi passed onto me halfway through the walk. The thing's quite heavy. "Right here."

"Oh. Good. Well, come on in. Kasey brought a cake, and it's good to go when you are."

Kasey being her sister, who when she found out Bianca was alive, flew across the country to be with her. She's visited several times since.

A moment later Dominic's head pops out the front door. His fair hair has grown into a short, slightly curly mop, and he's got actual eyebrows now, but his blue eyes are wide. "Did you get-"

"Yes, yes, we got it!" I'm starting to regret how long Demi and I spent having lunch, even though we're back before the agreed time. Everyone's so *nervous*...

"Good," Dom says with a relieved sigh. "It'll be so important to Jesse."

"Not just Jesse," Demi says teasingly, and Dom rolls his eyes.

"Come on inside."

I lean into Demi. "It's OK. We both know the truth." Dominic's as desperate for the gift as Jesse is. Heck, he's the one who convinced Jesse he 'needed' it.

Inside the house, a string of colourful balloons brightens the plain wooden décor, while a trio of children sit at the table wearing bright party hats. The middle-sized child wears a face-splitting grin that somehow widens as we come in. "LIAM!" Jesse screeches. "IT'S MY BIRTHDAY! WE'RE HAVING A PARTY!"

"I know, I know," I say jovially as I quietly pass the box to Jerrold, who puts it out of sight. "That's why I'm here, and Demi too."

"HI, DEMI!" Jesse shouts. The other two children echo him. One's his cousin – Bianca's sister's son – and the other is a neighbour who's become friendly after several run-ins at the local playground.

"Hi, Jesse," Demi says with a big grin. "Happy birthday."

Of course, it's probably not his real birthday. There was no way to keep track of the date in the Wilds, so when we arrived back here and got a little settled, it made sense to pick the closest probable date for both Jesse and Dominic. It's...fun. Really,

really fun to see this kid get to *enjoy* being a kid for once. Not alone. Safe, healthy.

It feels like a miracle.

We sing 'happy birthday', and Bianca's sister brings out a little chocolate cake topped with candles, and Jesse just about implodes with happiness. Then out come the presents. Jesse loves his baseball cap, his colourful toothbrush and the bright sleeping bag Demi got him.

I think she's got a thing for sleeping bags.

And then we bring down the box. It's the sort with holes in the top, and by now it has a noticeable wet patch in the bottom. Jerrold carefully puts it on the table in front of Jesse, wet patch notwithstanding, and there's an audible whimper.

"Sorry," Dominic says. "I'm just really excited."

Bianca laughs and kisses him on the cheek.

And then Jesse lifts off the lid, and up pops this fluffy, floppy-eared grey creature who's surely baffled to be the centre of so much attention.

"Is it a puppy?" Jesse asks, wide-eyed. He's suddenly quiet. "It looks like a boggart."

"Of course it's a puppy," his grandfather chides him. "Now, are you going to get him out?"

Jesse relaxes, and I see one of the kids mouthing 'boggart' as the puppy comes out of the boxes and starts wriggling madly, licking at any part of Jesse he can reach. And then Dominic's leaning in, and suddenly there's a mad mess of excited children, adults and one little mixed-breed pup who slept for the last hour or two, and has enough energy to handle this lot.

Demi and I watch from a distance.

"Huh," I muse aloud. "I guess it does look a bit like a boggart. Grey, lots of fur. Squashy face."

Bogger, bogger, the littlest child is chanting. Demi grimaces. "Oh dear. I think the puppy's been given a name."

An hour later, the kids are fascinated by some cartoon on TV, the puppy – and Jerrold – are asleep, and Bianca, Kasey and Dominic are having a deep conversation over the remnants of the birthday cake. Demi and I take our pieces out to the bench seat in the backyard.

"Well, the puppy was a hit," Demi says. "It's just a shame he couldn't get a more dignified name."

"Could be worse. Boggy's better than Boggart, Bogey or Bogger, which were the other suggestions. And it'll work well enough with our official lie, when people ask where his name came from. That his colour looks like...a bog."

She raises her eyebrows. "There was a bog in the isolated valley we were trapped in, huh?"

"Sure, why not?" The story we'd been asked to stick to was pretty thin, and left room for all kinds of details. And the colour comparison's a stretch, but it'll do.

We eat our cake, and I'm disappointed to find I don't have room for a second piece. It seems my body's not used to the sudden injection of sugar and fat. Probably a good thing, I decide. Otherwise I'll eat everything in sight and end up the size of a house.

"So," Demi says suddenly. "The friend who dropped you off at the café. Did she get the crazy real story, or the official lie?"

I look up in surprise. "Who, Zara?"

"If Zara's the pretty redhead with the hatchback, sure."

Is Zara pretty? I suppose she is – but everyone seems pretty to me out here. Even people I normally wouldn't look twice at. Their faces are so interesting. Clean clothes, well-fed, smiling. But there's something in Demi's tone that makes me glance at her sidelong.

"She got the crazy truth," I reply, then laugh. "She says she believes me, and she thinks I'm some sort of heroic wildman. A kind of involuntary Tarzan."

Demi laughs too, but it sounds a bit forced. "It's nice that you can spend time with all kinds of people now – not just because you've only got one option." She flicks her shiny, glue-free hair, and I'd bet ten to one that she's annoyed with me. "No one likes to be the last resort."

It takes me a moment to realise what she's talking about. Back through the Gate, we'd talked about being each others' last resort at romance – only choice, barring much-older Jerrold – and she hadn't liked the idea. I suppose I hadn't either, but only is better than nothing. I wonder whether I should let her in on the truth. "I've chatted with a few people," I admit. "Gone out for drinks with two girls, now."

"Really." Demi sounds unimpressed.

"But it's not going to work out with Zara," I add.

"Why's that?"

I sneak a sidelong glance, trying to read her expression. But I've really got no clue. I've never been good at that. "Well, there's that red hair. I never really liked red hair."

She scoffs.

"And the car," I continue dryly. "Makes me think of grandmothers, not dateable girls, huh? And I didn't like how she sneezed. Instead of one big sneeze, it was three little ones. Kinda sad."

Demi gives me a dirty look, as if she's now offended on Zara's behalf, and I can't hold back my laughter. "But even if I was shallow enough to care about any of those things," I continue with a chuckle, "I still wouldn't date my own cousin."

"Oh." I've never seen Demi blush, but are her ears darkening? She punches me lightly in the arm. "You jerk. I really thought you were rating some poor girl like that."

Maybe I would have once, I realise. Back before I went through the Gate, when girls seemed interchangeable. Kind of like, 'I don't care what meal I eat on the menu, just as long as I'm eating something'. So to speak.

"Zara's one of my few family members who lives close enough to drive here," I explain, "and I last saw her when she was a kid. So...nothing going on there."

"Sure," Demi says casually, shrugging. "What about the other girl? You know, you said you've been out a couple of times."

I grin again. "Well, that would be you. I was trying to make myself sound more impressive."

"Your cousin and your fellow Gate survivor," Demi says dryly. "You're really getting out there."

"And proud of it."

Just then there's a burst of movement from the trees outside the property, and a brown-winged bird flaps its way madly into the sky. I'm frozen, tense; and I'm holding my plate like a shield. My heart pounds madly.

A moment later I feel Demi's hand on my arm. "It's OK," she tells me. "There aren't any dangerous animals around here, remember? Nothing worse than rabbits or pigeons."

I nod, waiting for my heartrate to go back to normal. "I know. It'll take a while before my reactions change, though." Even making myself sit outside like this is progress. Mount Freedom does have wild goats, deer and a variety of native frogs that occasionally make it to the edges of town, but there's nothing to be afraid of.

Demi doesn't remove her hand, and I move so that our arms are linked together. It feels nice, and normal. "Do you remember what you said when we were back through the Gate?" I ask casually. "That if I had the option to date all kinds of girls, but still asked you out, then you'd consider it?"

"Yes…"

Oh boy. Either I'm about to ruin our friendship, or I'm about to make exactly the right move. "Well…I now have the option to date all kinds of girls, et cetera. In theory." I'd have to actually find the girls, but…eh. "So…how about it?"

Demi glances up at me sharply, but doesn't move her arm. "Liam, are you asking me out?"

"In my ultra-smooth way, yes," I joke. She doesn't answer, and I ramble on, "See, it turns out I'm the kind of guy who doesn't need to try every dish on the menu before deciding I've got a favourite. So to speak."

"It's because you're so deprived that everything tastes delicious," she shoots back. "So to speak."

"I wouldn't know about that," I tease. But inside, I'm nervous. "So…is that a yes? A no? Demi…would you like to go out for a drink sometime?"

Finally she smiles, and leans in a little closer. "Liam, we've been out for drinks or meals like fifteen times. What's the difference?"

It's a yes. I think it's a yes. I lower my voice. "The difference, as Jesse would say, is kissing. Drinks and kissing."

I get her answer soon enough. We've already had the drinks… here's the kissing.

It's sweet and ordinary, but it's the kind of sweet ordinary I thought I'd never experience again. And that makes it beyond precious.

Finally we lean back, and I'm smiling down at her when I remember something. "Uh oh."

"What is it?"

"I just remembered that I was supposed to ask Zara to drive me back to my house, but I forgot," I say apologetically. "Do you know what this means?"

"Uh...no?"

"Demi," I declare. "Take me home."

She laughs. "With pleasure."

Dear Reader,

So. Another book about a killer virus – sorry! I wrote the earliest version of *Take Me Home* in 2012, well before this latest pandemic hit, but I admit that some details were based on current experiences. Quarantine, general panic and so forth. But the original idea for the novel came from a series of dreams.

I dreamed about running around a giant-sized house, trying to hide from giant-sized aliens who were pursuing me. I dreamed about aliens fighting on a ship with no gravity, and about an Earth-like planet with huge chunks missing, like when a little kid chews on a big apple. And at the end of the dream, the chunks were miraculously refilled. Kind of hard to explain in a vaguely sci-fi novel like this one, but I've done my best.

Part of the reason for the slow publication was that until recently, the story wasn't long enough to become a standard novel. I kept waiting for new ideas to pop up, but in the end I decided it should come out as is. Sturdy, humorous in spite of the subject matter, and with a hopeful ending.

Take Me Home is also my first book that's officially for a general audience, rather than for young or new adults. I've written a dozen novels under the name M. Marinan. Really, the only difference is the age of the characters and (to a point) the topics discussed. So if you enjoyed this one, check out *Tyger: an out-of-this-world tale* or *Breaking the Glass Slipper*. Both have a similar adventure/mystery/drama style, with a very light romance.

And of course, if you enjoyed the book, please leave a rating or a review on Goodreads or your favourite online retailer. It really helps with the book's visibility, and shows other readers what to expect.

Cheers,